Stuck with

my

Ex's Brother

Jax KANE

WHERE DANGER
MEETS DESIRE

Contents

Descent

Ava Green

The world dropped out from under me before I could scream.

It started as a jolt. Then a violent plunge. My stomach slammed into my ribs as the plane bucked again, pitching sideways. Oxygen masks dropped from over head like nooses. A child wailed behind me. Somewhere near the cockpit, metal groaned and the engines howled like wounded animals.

I gripped the armrest with one hand and the strap of my carry-on with the other. Emma's empty chemo bag was still inside it. I promised her I'd be back in twenty-four hours. Just a routine supply check with the new vendor in Seattle. But now emergency lights flickered like dying stars and a suitcase crashed into the aisle. An elderly couple beside me clasped hands, white-knuckled and whispering prayers.

A man stumbled forward, shouting about the radio. No flight attendants in sight. No announcements. No calm voice to cling to.

I tried to breathe. I was a nurse. I'd worked in trauma. I'd seen panic. This wasn't panic. This was something worse. Helplessness. The wing outside my window jerked wildly, shuddering like it was about to shear off.

God. We were going down.

"Hard landing coming. Brace!"

The voice cut through the screaming like a scalpel. Low, firm, no panic in it. Just steel. I turned toward the sound. Across the aisle, a man sat rigid in his seat, blood trickling from his temple, but his eyes were locked on me. Focused. Controlled. Military precision.

"Feet flat. Head down. Arms crossed over your head."

It took a second for my brain to catch up to the command. Then I scrambled to do as he ordered, fumbling with the seatbelt as the cabin tilted again. My knees banged against the seat in front of me, and I hunched forward.

Something about his voice. It hit inside me. Familiar. Not in the way of strangers on a plane, not in the way of random chance.

Where did I know him from?

Another lurch interrupted the thought. The lights blinked out completely. The only illumination was the red exit signs flickering dimly, casting everything in a bloody glow. All around me, people were crying, praying, screaming. The man across the aisle didn't move. Didn't flinch. He gripped the seat in front of him like he'd done this before.

I copied his position, breathing hard, focusing on him, his calm.

The plane tipped nose-down. My stomach floated. Then everything slammed into black.

The crash was chaos and sound and pain.

Metal screamed like a hundred car wrecks as the plane hit something solid. It was not a landing. It was a collision. My body whipped sideways despite the seatbelt, shoulders wrenching. A bottle flew through the cabin, shattering somewhere nearby. The lights were gone. Every sense was saturated with pressure and motion.

The plane lurched again, skidding, scraping. I heard trees snapping. The unmistakable grind of steel on rock. My head slammed into the seat in front of me and stars exploded behind my eyes.

Then, stillness. A horrible, ringing, stomach-twisting stillness.

I breathed in. My ribs hurt. My shoulder throbbed. Something heavy was on my legs. My carry-on bag maybe, or debris. My ears were ringing, but I could make out groans and gasps from the people around me.

I lifted my head, vision swimming. The cabin was crooked, the floor tilting left. Overhead bins were busted open. Someone was sobbing. A baby wailed. The air smelled like smoke, blood, and burning plastic. I choked on it, blinking through the gloom. My fingers trembled as I pushed the bag off my legs. I thought of Emma again: her fragile little smile, the IV line in her arm. I had to get out. I had to help.

A hand grabbed my arm.

I jerked, heart hammering, and came face to face with the man from earlier. His temple was streaked with blood, but his eyes were clear. Alert.

"You're awake," he said. His voice was even, if not really kind. "Can you move?"

I blinked at him, trying to place where I'd seen that face before. Strong jaw, short-cropped dark hair, military bearing.

"What ... happened?" My voice was raw, barely there.

"Plane's down," he replied. "No fire yet, but it won't stay quiet forever. People are hurt. You're the only medical personnel onboard, right?"

I tried to answer, but my throat closed. My hands were shaking.

"My sister," I croaked. "My bag ... my phone ..."

"Focus," he snapped. Then, a breath softer, "Look at me."

I did. His expression was hard, but his tone shifted slightly. "You're a nurse, right?"

I nodded.

"People *need* you."

That sliced through the fog. I sucked in a breath and forced my limbs to move. My legs protested, but I rose to my feet. Pain radiated from my left hip where the seatbelt had crossed it.

The man steadied me. "You good?"

"No," I said truthfully. "But I can work."

He nodded once, already turning to check the next row.

That voice. That face. Wait—Gavin?

As I limped into the tilted aisle, pain slicing up my leg, realization crashed into me harder than the plane had. Gavin Henderson. My ex-husband's older brother. I'd only met him once, at the wedding. He'd flown in late, stayed quiet, barely said ten words to me. Back then, I remembered thinking he looked like he could level a man with a single look. Cold. Guarded. Not someone you'd want to cross. Now he's barking commands like a battlefield commander. Calm. Effective. Covered in blood that might not all be his.

I hesitated, old memories rushing back, of a failed marriage, of my sister's first diagnosis. Everything that had broken me. Did he know? Did he come on this flight because of me? Nah. But there was no time to dwell. Someone was crying out. I shoved the thoughts down and slid into triage mode. I crouched beside a woman clutching her abdomen, checked her pulse, lifted her shirt, bruised but not bleeding. Could be internal injuries. I talked to her gently, calm and clear, my voice steady despite the adrenaline roaring through me. I knew there was little I could do here other than immediate first aid.

I caught Gavin's eye as he dragged luggage off another passenger. For a second, something passed between us. Recognition. And regret. I looked away. Later. I could fall apart later. Aisle by aisle, we moved through the carnage. I crawled over a fractured tray table and found a middle-aged man with a gash across his forehead. I pressed fingers to his neck. Nothing. My stomach knotted. I pulled my hand back. Moved on.

Farther down, I found the copilot, his leg was bent at an impossible angle, lips pale. He was semi-conscious, muttering. I grabbed gauze from an emergency kit wedged beneath a seat and pressed it to a wound on his shoulder, whispering nonsense reassurance as I worked.

Gavin appeared beside me with a coat. "We need to keep his spine stable. Roll him onto this."

We worked in sync, saying little, each action purposeful. I was surprised at how seamlessly he stepped into triage, like he'd done this before. Had he? Possibly.

A child's wail pierced the air. I glanced over to see a young mother curled around her toddler, both of them sobbing but unhurt. I nodded toward them. "You okay?"

She nodded frantically; face covered in tears. "Maybe ... I think so."

I wanted to tell her I wasn't, not even close, but I didn't. I moved on.

Gavin began tagging the injured with strips of duct tape, marking them with Xs and short notes. It was quick, efficient. My brain latched on to the logic. Still, it was not enough. There was never enough of me to go around.

Halfway down the cabin, I stumbled over a body slumped in the aisle. He was in some uniform. Dark blue. Tactical boots. A shoulder holster barely visible under his jacket. U.S. Marshal badge. I reached out to check for vitals. He seized my wrist. I gasped. His eyes fluttered open. Blood bubbled from his mouth.

"Lev..." he rasped and mumbled something about a password or code.

"What? Slow down." I leaned closer, heart hammering.

"Not... accident..."

I froze.

"What are you saying?"

"He did this... not alone..." The words slipped out like sand through his lips. Then his hand went slack.

I sat back on my heels, bile rising. I wanted to scream. But something stopped me. The force from his gaze. The fear. The warning.

A shadow fell across me. Gavin crouched beside me, eyes on the Marshal's body.

"He said this wasn't an accident," I whispered.

Gavin's jaw tightened. "Damn it."

He didn't look surprised. More like confirmation of something he already suspected.

I stared at him. "What do you know?"

Before he could answer, a groan echoed from the rear of the cabin. Low. Wet. Wrong. We both turned toward the sound. Something was moving. Something that maybe shouldn't be moving. And suddenly, I understood the Marshal's fear.

Something worse survived the crash.

The sound sharpened. A scrape of metal, the crunch of boots on debris.

From the shadows at the rear of the plane, a man pushed himself upright. His shirt was soaked with blood. His face was pale, a nasty cut above his brow, one eye already swollen. But what snagged my attention were the handcuffs.

Or rather, just the one still dangling from his left wrist.

He stretched, cracked his neck, then grinned at us.

"What luck," he said. His voice was smooth, heavily accented. Russian, maybe. "A soldier and a healer. This day just got interesting."

I took a step back. Gavin stepped forward, coming between the man and me, blocking me with his body.

The man didn't flinch. He sauntered forward, as calm as if he were stepping into a dinner party. He glanced down and spotted the Marshal's body. Crouched. Picked up the gun where it had slid near him. Stood. The gun looked very small in his hand. Very deadly.

"Welcome to my escape," he said, like he was announcing the start of a magic show.

He leveled the weapon at us. And smiled.

Gavin tensed, calculating. I barely breathed.

The man winked. "Let's make things interesting, da?"

The safety clicked turned off. And the real nightmare began.

Everything in my body screamed to run, but my feet wouldn't budge. And where?

Gavin's arms extended slightly, shielding me, but I could tell he was gauging angles, distances, threats. His breathing slowed, controlled. Intentional. Like he was about to pounce.

The man, Lev, he has to be Lev, rolled his shoulders as if he were limbering up for a fight.

"How many alive?" he asked, glancing around. His eyes glinted red in the emergency lighting, like some devil or vampire.

I said nothing. Gavin didn't either.

Lev sighed, almost theatrically. "No manners. Americans."

Then he pointed the gun at the ceiling and fired twice.

The sound was deafening. A child shrieked. People screamed. I flinched so hard my knees nearly buckled.

"Now," he said, still calm. "Bring me anything useful. Food. Bandages. Weapons. Oh, and no tricks. I hate tricks."

He gestured with the gun, signaling Gavin to move. Gavin didn't move.

Lev tilted his head. "Do you want to die now, or later?"

Still, Gavin didn't budge. But I saw it. His fingers twitched. His stance shifted ever so slightly. He was readying himself. He was going to try something. I wanted to scream 'no'. There was already enough death. Because if he missed...We all died.

Lev looked around Gavin, eyes scanning the cabin, like he was savoring the fear bleeding off everyone. He tapped the gun barrel on an overhead bin in some horrible hollow cadence that set my teeth on edge. But the gun was still leveled at Gavin.

"You know what else I hate?" he mused. "Doctors. Always judging. Always thinking they know best. You are a nurse, da?" He glanced at me. "You will be useful."

I stayed silent, heart pounding so hard it hurt.

He pointed the gun at a sobbing teenage boy. "Unless you want him to bleed next, you will move."

Gavin's fingers flexed at his sides.

"Don't," I whispered.

Lev heard it. He grinned wider. "Ah. So, you two are friends. How touching."

He backed up a step, gun still aimed, watching Gavin like a predator sizing up a rival alpha or dinner.

"Come," he said, curling his finger at me. "Help me next. Show me you are useful because if you are not...."

I wanted to fight. I wanted to scream. But survival demanded something else. So, I nodded.

Gavin's jaw flexed. He didn't like it. But he stepped aside, just barely. And I moved forward, knowing one thing for sure. This was not a crash. It was a setup. And we were trapped with a killer.

First Responder

Gavin Henderson

The moment the plane hit dirt, my body moved before my brain caught up. Years of training snapped into place like a reflex. Blood trickled from a gash above my right eyebrow, but I barely felt it. Smoke stung my eyes, the tang of scorched metal already burning in my throat. Screams erupted behind me, panicked, high-pitched, chaotic. But inside, I was ice.

Don't freeze. Don't think. Just move.

My seatbelt clicked loose with a practiced tug. The woman across from me stirred, her hands trembling as she struggled with hers. She wasn't crying. That was good. I reached over and unlatched it for her.

"You okay?" I asked, voice low but firm.

She blinked at me, dazed, but nodded. "I think so. I'm Ava."

I scanned her: no visible injuries, just superficial cuts and bruises. Sharp eyes. Steady breath. Still in shock, but holding together.

"You a nurse?" I asked as a glimmer of memory surfaced.

She hesitated, then nodded again. "Yeah."

"Good." I stood and braced myself against the seatback to stand since the fuselage was tilted at an angle.

Around us, chaos reigned. A man cried for help near the wing. A child wailed from the back of the plane. Smoke drifted through the cracked air vents. Panels hung loose above the aisle like broken ribs. The floor was slick with something dark—oil, maybe blood. Luggage littered the walkway. People were dazed, some bleeding, most frozen in fear and shock.

I raised my voice without shouting. "If you can walk, help someone. If you can't, stay where you are. Do not open any exits unless I say so."

A younger man clawed at the emergency door near the rear.

"Stop!" I barked, pointing. "You trigger that wrong, you'll light us all up."

The guy froze.

I pushed forward, shoving open an overhead bin and fishing out a first-aid kit. I sliced open a seat cushion for splints, ripping the stuffing free. My mind ran emergency triage: fire risk, secondary injuries, structural damage, possibility of hostiles. A flight attendant was slumped over two rows ahead—unconscious. Maybe worse.

I turned back to Ava. "Can you help me sort the injured?"

Her jaw clenched. She squared her shoulders. "I'm with you."

That was when I noticed the empty holster on the downed US Marshal sprawled across the aisle and felt my gut sink like a stone.

"He said it wasn't an accident." Ava said to further my suspicions.

I knelt beside the body of the Marshal, one hand checking for a carotid pulse, the other already gripping a compress from the med kit. Blood seeped from the man's stomach in a steady, dark rhythm—too much, too fast.

"Marshal," I said firmly, needing confirmation. "Stay with me."

The man's eyes fluttered open. Red-rimmed, unfocused. His lips moved again, dry and cracked.

"Lev..." he rasped.

I froze.

"What did you say?"

The Marshal coughed, crimson flecks speckling his chin. "Lev... Rostova."

My spine locked straight. I hadn't heard that name in four years. Not since a cartel raid in a warehouse outside El Paso. It had been my last op before burning out of that world. Lev Rostova. One of the most sadistic lieutenants in a Mexican drug syndicate. I had testified at his sentencing. The bastard was supposed to be behind bars for life.

"No," I muttered. "No way."

The Marshal's bloodied fingers gripped my sleeve with surprising strength. "Crash... not mechanical. They took us down. Targeted."

Ava crouched nearby, her face pale beneath a smear of something dark. She met my gaze, and I saw the realization settle behind her eyes. She'd heard the name. Probably recognized it from some news story. She understood.

The Marshal gasped again. "He's... on board..."

My hand slipped. My chest stilled. I sat back, blood singing in my ears. If Lev Rostova was on my plane, then everything had just shifted from rescue to survival.

I looked at Ava. "You saw him? A guy they would have loaded on in shackles?"

Her mouth parted. "The prisoner... yeah. He was in the back."

"Stay close," I said. "We're not dealing with an accident. We're dealing with an ambush."

I stood, eyes scanning for movement, for weapons, for leverage. The cabin was a broken cage. And somewhere in it, a monster could be waking up. A sharp thud echoed from the rear of the cabin: metal scraping against metal. I pivoted, blood roaring in my ears.

Through the broken shadows and hanging wires, a figure emerged. He walked with a limp, his shirt soaked in red from a wound across his ribs. Steel cuffs still dangled from his one wrist, one hand bloodied but functional. He moved like a predator who'd just scented weakness. Then he smiled.

"Ah, Mr. Henderson," the man said smoothly. "We meet again."

I slid in front of Ava without thinking, placing my body between her and the approaching threat. Lev Rostova. Even through the grime and blood, I recognized the bone-white teeth, the glint in his eye like someone starting his own chess match. Nothing about him said desperation. He looked like a man in control.

"I should've guessed you were on this transport," Lev continued. "You have the stink of law enforcement on you, even when you try to hide it behind civilian clothes."

Ava's voice came low and confused. "You know each other?"

"Stay behind me," I ordered, never taking my eyes off Lev.

Lev's gaze flicked to her, curious. "She's even prettier than the wedding photos."

My jaw locked. "You remember my brother?"

"Vividly," Lev said, with a chuckle that had no warmth. "He cried when I dislocated his knee. What was his name again? Colson? Carter? Yes. Carter. The one who pretended so hard to be brave."

"Shut. Up."

"Oh, come now, Gavin. We shared such an intimate little skirmish, you and I. You really shouldn't hold a grudge. I survived. You survived. Water under the proverbial bridge."

Ava didn't move. She stood frozen beside me, eyes flicking from Lev to me, probably trying to piece it all together. I could almost feel her pulse even without touching her—rapid, uncertain, but steady.

I kept my voice low and lethal. "You should've stayed buried."

Lev smiled wider. "I would have missed this chance to finish what we started."

Lev crouched beside the dead Marshal, expression casual as if he were tying his shoes. He had found the Marshal's missing pistol and stood, cradling the weapon with a reverence that turned my stomach.

"I really did try to be a model prisoner," Lev mused. "But extradition? That was a step too far. No one drags Lev Rostova across a border without blood."

I shifted slightly, calculating angles. He was close—seven, maybe eight feet—but Ava in the line of fire. One wrong move and she'd be the one catching a bullet.

Lev noticed. His eyes twinkled with amusement.

"You're injured," I said, trying to buy time. "You're bleeding like a stuck pig."

"And yet," Lev replied, lifting the gun, "I am still the most dangerous man on this plane."

He fired two through the roof and leveled the weapon at Ava. "Your nurse. Bring her here or that boy behind you bleeds more than me."

Ava didn't wait for permission. She stepped forward with trembling hands, her face pale but set. I reached for her arm, whispering, "You don't have to—"

"Yes, I do," she snapped, louder than necessary.

Lev chuckled. "Fiery. I am liking her already."

She knelt beside him, grabbing the med kit with movements that were jerky but controlled. I could tell she was thinking through every step. I could see the nurse surface, the one who had snapped into gear minutes ago. But this was different. She was forcing herself to work. This was theater.

Lev kept the pistol trained lazily on her while she cleaned the wound across his ribs. "Make it quick," he said. "My men will be here soon, and I'd hate to bleed out before they arrive. Very poor form. You'll fix me, sestrichka," he murmured. "And I won't kill anyone... Yet."

Ava worked with clinical precision, but I could see the storm behind her eyes. Her fingers moved steadily, cleaning and dressing Lev's wound, but every motion was just slightly off rhythm. There was a calculated hesitation, some purposeful distraction. She was working slowly, maybe buying me time.

Lev, still watching her like a cat tracking prey, spoke casually. "Your brother was small. Not in size, you understand. In spirit. So desperate to matter. So eager to impress the great Gavin Henderson."

My jaw ticked but I didn't take the bait. Ava glanced up, her eyes flicking to the floor, then to me, then back to Lev. I wished I had the time and space to ask her about what happened between her and my brother.

"Do you know what his last words were?" Lev mused. "He begged me. Pathetic."

My fists clenched so tight my fingernails bit into my palms. I took a step forward, but Ava moved first.

"You're not as stupid as you look," Lev murmured to her.

My rage sharpened, but I stayed still. Not yet. I stepped closer, fists at my sides, breathing hard. The air inside the plane felt tighter, thicker. Like it was pressing in.

"You don't get to talk about my brother," I said. My voice was quiet and lethal.

Lev's mouth curled into a smirk. "You should thank me, Gavin. It gave your career a little boost, didn't it? Made you a hero."

"You tortured him."

"I used him," Lev corrected. "There's a difference. He was useful... until he broke."

My vision pulsed red at the edges. I could almost see it: Carter's bruised face, that final face call before the mission, the ghost in his voice when he said, *Don't worry, big bro. I got this one.*

He didn't get it. He never came back.

"I should kill you right now."

Lev's eyes narrowed, daring me. "You won't. You're too professional."

Ava's voice cut through the heat like ice. "Gavin."

I looked down. She shook her head once, firm. Not now. I stepped back, barely. But Lev caught it, that moment of restraint, and grinned like a devil. Lev shifted his weight, wincing as the wound in his side tugged. Ava had taped it with gauze and improvised butterfly bandages, but I could tell she hadn't done him any favors.

Still, Lev smiled. "You know what I like most about snow? It hides bodies."

A chill ran down my spine.

Lev gestured toward the broken windows. "My men are punctual. Sunset at the latest. Maybe sooner if they don't get lost in the trees."

Ava looked at him, stunned. "You planned the crash?"

"Of course. You think your government could move me quietly? I arranged a... change in itinerary. A more scenic route."

I exchanged a glance with her. Dread coiled in my gut. If we were off our designated flight path, no one would find us soon. Simply surviving the cold and whatever injuries had been sustained would be problematic.

Lev looked pleased with himself. "They'll kill everyone who's still breathing. Witnesses are a loose end I do not need."

"We can't stay," I muttered. It was no longer about the cold, about injuries. Now we had incoming armed hostiles.

Ava swallowed. "We?"

Her eyes searched mine, uncertainty, fear, and something else. Trust? She nodded. I turned toward the aisle, muscles tense.

More than a handful of passengers still huddled behind torn seats, heads low, eyes wide. No one moved. The air had gone still, charged, like the moment before lightning strikes. They'd all heard our exchange. They knew the stakes had risen.

We'd survived a plane crash. Now we had to survive Lev.

Hostile Takeover

Ava Green

"**Y**ou are wasting time. I bleed more every minute you hesitate."

Lev's voice was lazy and amused, but the muzzle of the pistol pressed against my head wasn't. I knelt beside him, my knees screaming protests against the warped metal floor, fingers shaking as I fumbled with gauze from the kit. The stink of blood and burned plastic filled my lungs. My heart pounded so loud I could barely hear.

Focus. Be the nurse. Stay alive.

He grinned down at me like we were old friends sharing a joke. His shirt was soaked with blood from the jagged slice along his ribs. The last thing I wanted was to touch him. But here I was. Doing it. Pretending it was a just some regular guy and not some maniac threatening to kill us all.

Behind me, Gavin was completely still. I glanced up. His eyes were locked on me. No panic. No fear. Just... watching. Waiting. I recognized something in that stare: control. Trust. A silent question.

Can you do this?

I breathed once. Nodded.

Lev shifted, gun tilting toward Gavin for just a second. "Don't worry, I'm keeping score. You've got quite the bodyguard look going, friend. But you know what they say. Even the best can bleed."

I swallowed hard and lifted Lev's arm. "I need to check for other wounds."

"Don't get shy now," he murmured. "I won't bite. Unless you stop being useful."

My fingers were steadier than I expected as I probed. I was not even sure what I was looking for. I had stopped the worst of the bleeding. This was now theater. He didn't really want my help now—only control. Every second was a countdown. And I was the only one close enough to change the ending.

Because I'd be damned if I'd survive a plane crash only to have his men come in to kill me. Not. Happening.

I moved slower than necessary. Not too slow to arouse suspicion. Just enough to stretch time like a thread pulled as taut as my nerves. Lev didn't seem to notice. He watched my fingers as if they were performing for him.

Every nerve in my body felt electric. If I moved wrong, if I flinched, if I breathed the wrong way, he'd shoot. But that was not what scared me most. What scared me was the silence. The kind of awful hush that falls right before the world exploded. The whole plane was watching our little drama and I knew their lives were on the line, too.

"Careful," Lev murmured. "Would hate for you to make a mistake and bleed me dry."

"I'm doing my best," I said, keeping my voice steady.

Gavin broke the silence. "You're bleeding all over the carpet. Someone's going to charge you for that."

Lev chuckled, amused. "Always with the jokes. I missed you, Henderson. You and your pretty mouth."

He looked away from me, just for a breath. I let the suture kit fall onto the floor amidst the debris there. Lev's head snapped back. The pistol lifted.

"Try that again," he said coldly, "and I'll put one in your leg. You do not need legs to do stitches, da?"

I froze, lips pressed tight. Gavin's stance shifted—subtle, predatory. I saw it. He was preparing to strike. One wrong breath and everything would explode.

"I'm sorry," I whispered—to Lev, to no one, to everyone.

I didn't know who I was apologizing to. My voice was barely audible, lost beneath the groaning tick of the cooling metal and shallow breathing. Lev didn't notice. But Gavin did. I risked a glance. Just a flick of my eyes—up, then back down. A nod so small it barely existed.

Gavin gave no reaction. No sign that he saw it. But I was sure he did. My pulse raced as I bent closer to Lev's wound. One hand pushed his skin, the other pressed gently against the soaked bandage. I kept my touch light. Too light. Just enough to make him curious.

"Don't go delicate on me now," Lev muttered.

I shifted my weight forward, keeping my tone smooth. "Sorry. Just checking the depth."

My other hand curled into a fist. Lev didn't flinch. He didn't expect sharp pain. Until I drove my knuckles into the wound. He screamed. It was raw and guttural—a wounded animal's cry—and in that split-second of agony, Gavin moved.

The space between them collapsed. The second Lev screamed, Gavin's boot slammed into his arm. A shot went wild before the pistol flew sideways, smacking into the overhead bin and clattering to the floor. Gavin followed, tackling Lev so hard the wreck groaned under the impact.

I scrambled back on hands and knees, my heart jackhammering in my chest. The force of their crash sent medical supplies scattering like dice. The bandage roll hit my shin. A tray table clanked beside me.

Lev snarled and lashed out with his elbow, catching Gavin in the jaw. Blood sprayed across the shattered window in an arc. It didn't stop Gavin. He drove his shoulder into Lev's gut, trying to pin him, but Lev was fast—terrifyingly fast. He had some type of training and it showed in every movement. He fought dirty, jabbing at Gavin's throat, knifing his ribs with the scalpel from the med kit, twisting like a serpent trying to crush the life out of him.

Screams erupted around us. One woman grabbed her child and ducked behind a row of seats. Another man looked ready to help but stopped, uncertain of what to do.

My gaze locked on the chaos. My hand darted out, found the broken edge of a tray table. I grabbed it—heavy, sharp, jagged—and swung with everything I had.

Lev saw it coming. He twisted. My makeshift weapon slammed against the wall by a window instead of his head. It jarred free of my hands. He kicked out, hitting my chin, and the tray clattered away. I went down hard into the aisle hitting the gun. It spun across the metal floor, sliding to a stop right beside my boot.

Everything froze.

Gavin was pinned. Lev's arm was crushing his windpipe.

I looked down.

Gunmetal glinted beside my foot.

Time froze.

I stared at the pistol like it was a live wire. Everything around me—the shouting, the gasps, the groan of the wrecked fuselage—faded into muffled noise. All I saw was the gun. All I heard was my own ragged breathing.

I had never even held a loaded weapon. My training was all needles and scalpels and compression dressings. Not this. Not life or death in the curve of my finger.

Gavin was losing the fight. He was flat on his back now, Lev's forearm pressing down against his throat. His lips were tinged blue. He clawed at Lev's shoulder, struggling, slipping. His legs kicked once—twice—then slowed. The madman was winning.

"Gavin," I breathed. The panic nearly paralyzed me.

Behind me, someone cried out. A passenger, maybe but I couldn't understand the words. The others were still frozen in place, too afraid to intervene.

My hand moved on its own. Down. Grasping the pistol.

It was heavier than I expected.

Gavin's eyes met mine, bloodshot, desperate, but clear. There was no plea in them. No fear. Just a command.

Do it.

My hands trembled. Sweat slicked my grip. I lifted the gun with both hands, elbows locked. Just like Gavin showed me that one time, years ago, during that stupid Sierra Bravo safety seminar I half-slept through.

"Always keep your stance wide," he'd said with a smirk. "And don't flinch when you squeeze."

I had never thought I'd need it.

I was wrong.

My finger curled over the trigger.

"Back the hell off him."

The words burst from my throat before I knew I was saying them.

Lev didn't move at first. His arm was still pressed across Gavin's throat, but his eyes locked onto mine, curious.

The gun wavered in my grip for half a second, then steadied. I planted my feet wide like Gavin taught me. Elbows bent. Both hands on the weapon. Not a nurse anymore. Something else. Something fiercer.

"I said, let him go."

Lev lifted his free hand slowly, theatrically, as if applauding me with invisible claps. "You don't even know how to take the safety off."

I flicked it. The click was loud in the frozen air.

He blinked.

"Try me," I growled.

Gavin took that moment to twist, bucking his hips and rolling. Lev lost his balance. His arm slipped. Gavin shoved him off, gasping as air rushed back into his lungs. He scrambled back on elbows, sucking in a ragged breath but careful not to block my sight line.

I didn't lower the gun.

"Cuff yourself," I said, voice firmer now. "Now."

Lev sat up, bleeding from the mouth and smiling like I just sang him a love song. "You're shaking, sestrichka."

"I'll shoot if you move slower," I said, a lot more bravely than I felt.

He didn't. He lifted his hands and reached for the loose cuff dangling from his wrist. Snapped the one back into place. Gavin tossed him a cable tie from a pocket. Lev threaded it around his other wrist with exaggerated patience. The moment it cinched tight, Gavin stepped forward and grabbed the gun from my hands—gently. I let him. But my eyes didn't leave Lev's face.

"You okay?" Gavin asked.

"Ask me after I stop shaking."

Gavin dropped into a crouch beside me, chest still heaving. His jaw was already swelling, his lip split wide open. Blood seeped down his chin and through his shirt.

"Nice timing," he muttered.

I let out a shaky laugh that was halfway to a sob. "Yeah, well... next time, maybe don't let a psycho get on top of you."

The wreck was silent again, no movement, no talking. Just shallow breathing and the metallic creak of cold wind through torn fuselage. Around us, passengers peeked out from behind seats, wide-eyed and pale, trying to process what just happened.

My hands wouldn't stop trembling. Now that the danger had passed, or at least changed shape, my body was catching up. Muscles twitched. Knees threatened to collapse. My stomach flipped as the weight of it hit me all at once.

I almost killed a man.

I almost didn't.

"You did good," Gavin said, voice low, so it was just for me.

"I could have shot you."

"But you didn't."

I looked down at my hands. Blood smeared across my palms. My fingers twitched.

"You saved my life," he said.

I swallowed hard. "I didn't have a choice."

Gavin's gaze was steady. "That's where you're wrong."

A beat of silence passed between us.

Aftermath

Gavin Henderson

"We've got ten minutes—maybe less—before company shows up."

I shoved Lev into one of the twisted aisle seats, forcing the bastard's shoulder down until he slumped. The Russian didn't resist but he was still smiling. He was bruised, bleeding, and bound, but not broken. The cable tie bit into his wrists. Salvaged headset cords wrapped around his ankles, lashed to the base of the seat frame. I gave them one last yank.

"Comfortable?" I asked, deadpan.

Lev hummed tunelessly under his breath. "Your nurse has good aim," he said with a bloody grin. "And surprisingly good instincts. You should marry her."

I didn't answer, just turned to face my rescuer.

Ava was leaned back against a seat, ash smeared across her cheek, blood drying on her neck. Her hands were still trembling, but her eyes met mine steadily. I crossed to her.

"Nice work," I said.

She let out a breath. "Tell my adrenaline that."

The wreck had quieted. No screams now, no chaos—just a few gasps, a crying child, and the muffled thump of wind gusts pressing against the hull. I scanned the scene. Seven civilians, all upright. One unconscious co-pilot. And no radio. No backup and nobody coming for some time.

I did a quick mental inventory. Passengers: rattled. Weapon: recovered. Immediate threat: bound. Ava: stable, for now. Next threat: inbound of unknown number. We had a sliver of time. Not enough.

Ava was already moving.

I watched her crouch beside a middle-aged man cradling a broken arm against his chest. She tore open a gauze pack with her teeth and began splinting him with quick, confident movements, barely flinching as he winced. Her voice was soft but firm, calming. She didn't even hesitate when the man threw up beside her boots.

A young mother sobbed near the front, rocking a wide-eyed toddler in her lap. Ava slid beside her, brushing the child's hair back and murmuring something I couldn't hear. The woman started to breathe easier. The kid stopped crying.

I moved through the wreckage, checking passengers, yanking seat cushions free to insulate open windows, dragging a blanket over the unconscious co-pilot. My hand throbbed, bruised or maybe worse, but I ignored it. Lev's knife to my chest was going to cause some problems but it wasn't slowing me down. Yet. When I turned again, Ava was kneeling beside the co-pilot too. We'd converged at the same body without meaning to.

"You're bleeding," she said without looking up.

"So are you," I replied.

She arched an eyebrow at me as she cut open the pilot's jacket. "How bad?"

"I've had worse."

She didn't roll her eyes, but it was close. "You really need a new slogan."

We worked in silence, shoulder to shoulder. I wrapped a thermal sheet around the pilot while she adjusted an oxygen mask. Our hands brushed. Just for a second. But the jolt that passed through me was enough to make me look at her closely.

"We are gonna need to move soon," I said, softly, so as not to broadcast it to everyone.

"You mean run?" she asked.

I didn't answer. We both knew.

Ava stood too fast.

Her balance slipped as the plane shifted slightly beneath her, metal groaning in the cold. I was already there, catching her with one hand at the small of her back. My fingers splayed across the ridge of her spine, firm and warm. She froze. So, did I. The contact was meant to steady her. That was all. But it didn't feel like *all*. It felt like a match struck in dry air.

"You're bleeding," I said again, softer this time.

She looked up at me, brow lifted, mouth twitching in something between defiance and disbelief. "So are you."

We were too close. The sounds of the wreck faded behind us, muted moans, rustling fabric, wind hissing through broken panels. Everything else went quiet. I didn't move. Neither did she. Her eyes were the color of storm-tossed water. Not gentle. Not afraid. But searching.

"I'm fine," she said again, voice a little thinner this time.

"You're not."

My hand lingered, just a beat too long. And then I pulled it back like I'd touched flame.

"We need to finish checking for supplies," I said, stepping away before I did something stupid.

Ava didn't reply. But when I turned, I felt her watching me. And I didn't hate it.

Eight survivors. That's all we had. I stood near the front of the wreckage, my voice even as I laid it out for everyone there: no radio, no reinforcements, no guarantees. Outside a winter storm was growing stronger, and worse, Lev's people were closing in.

The businessman with the broken arm shook his head violently. "I'm not going anywhere. We are probably in the Rockies, the national park. It's federal property. Someone will come."

I didn't waste energy arguing. The question was who would come first.

The elderly couple behind him huddled together beneath a blanket, whispering. The woman looked up, eyes full of quiet terror. "We can't walk in the snow. Not far. We'll die."

A young mother held her toddler so tight the child whimpered. "I can't," she whispered. "I just can't..."

Ava stepped forward, gentler than I could've managed. "I know it is scary. But once Lev's men find the plane, they won't care who's armed or who's hurt. We need to move before they get here."

But no one moved. Paralyzed by fear. I felt it settle in my gut like lead. I didn't blame them. I couldn't stay. There was a small chance to get far enough down the mountain to find cell phone reception to call for help and that it would come soon enough to make a difference. Honestly, I would not put any money on that but staying? There was no chance of survival in that scenario. We had crashed right between the proverbial rock and hard place. Our only shot was getting out of here.

"If you do stay," I said, "block the doors. Hide in the bathroom if you have to. Do not open for anyone unless you hear my voice or someone say Sierra Bravo. That's the outfit I work for and who I will call."

Ava looked at me. There was a silent question in her eyes: *You're still going?*

I met her gaze. "With or without anyone else."

I really wanted her to go because to stay felt like a death sentence, but I wouldn't ask. I knew she felt an obligation to help these injured and scared people. I couldn't force her to choose. She didn't smile. But she nodded.

I started preparing to leave. I rummaged through the overhead compartments like a man finding a way to defuse a nuclear bomb. Every second and every choice mattered. I pulled out thermal blankets, crumpled but usable. A cracked emergency flare. A survival vest stuffed with hand warmers and a half-eaten protein bar. Better than nothing. Everything from the flight attendant's area. Anything remotely usable, I took because I didn't think anyone here would be needing them and we were heading out onto an unforgiving mountain into a snowstorm. We couldn't get to the baggage department. Whatever we salvaged here would be all we had.

Behind me, Ava didn't ask questions but started her own scavenger hunt. She gathered things I might have left, tucked it into a repurposed duffel bag, grabbed medical supplies from the kit. Our rhythm was wordless, almost practiced. Like we were a team. We were simply guided by gut-level survival instincts.

"Once we're out," I said, "we follow the slope northeast. If we can get elevation, we might catch a signal. Maybe even a drone pass."

"Big ifs," she said, panting slightly from moving debris.

I gave her a grim smile. "Big world."

She didn't laugh, not really. Just a half-sputtered breath. "You really think help's out there?"

"I think it's better than waiting for the devil's fan club to kick in the door."

She turned to me, brushing her hair from her face. "You're not very reassuring, you know that?"

"I'm not here to reassure you. I'm here to get you out alive."

Ava stared at me for a moment. Then she nodded once, sharp and sure.

"Then let's go."

We didn't have everything we were sure to need. Not even close. But we had everything we could get our hands on. Probably more than we could comfortably carry.

"Tick, tock," Lev said with a chuckle.

I was tightening the straps on the backpack I'd found when the sound came.

A muffled thud. Distant, but close enough to register as wrong. Not wind. Not shifting debris. Something heavier. Then another. Closer.

Ava froze mid-step. Her hand clutched the back of a seat as she turned toward me, eyes wide. I crossed the plane in three strides, ducking low to peer through the shattered window frame. Headlights. Low to the ground. Moving fast. More than one. I swore under my breath. Snowmobiles. That thud had been one probably going over a mogul. Ava stepped in beside me, gaze locked on the same terrifying truth outside.

"They're coming," she said.

"No," Lev crooned behind us, voice warm with satisfaction. "They have arrived."

I turned slowly. Lev sat right where we'd left him, cuffed, tied, bleeding, and smug as hell.

"I told you, Mr. Henderson. My men are very punctual."

Ava backed up, one hand instinctively brushing my arm. I didn't wait. I grabbed her wrist and yanked her down into a crouch, shoving us both behind a half-collapsed row of seats.

"They saw us," I muttered. "They'll circle."

Ava's voice was low. "Then what do we do?"

"We run."

Lev's laughter echoed beside us like a dirty secret. I disarmed the rear door, but it wouldn't budge against the gathered snow.

The first shot cracked the air like thunder.

I shoved Ava flat before the echo finished. The bullet punched through the tail window behind us, glass shattering in a violent burst of noise and cold. Screams followed. One man dove to the floor. Someone cried out for help. Another shot. Closer this time. The round slammed into a metal support beam, ricocheting with a screech. Sparks flew. The cabin lit up with panic.

I didn't think. I reacted.

I wrapped my arms around Ava and threw her beneath the row of seats, landing hard on top of her. She gasped, her breath forced from her lungs.

"Stay down," I growled.

She didn't argue.

Another shot ripped through the fuselage, splintering part of the emergency exit. Then, silence. The kind that carried weight. The kind that meant someone was repositioning, not retreating. My pulse thundered in my ears. I twisted to glance back toward Lev. The bastard was still tied to the seat, still smiling like this was entertainment.

"They're getting closer," I whispered.

Ava nodded against my shoulder. "So, we're really doing this."

I looked into her eyes, just for a second.

"We don't have a choice."

Outside, boots crunched against snow.

I pressed a hand against the floor, coiled and ready.

"Time to go," I said.

And when we moved, it would be fast.

And final.

No Way Out

Ava Green

Gunfire. Glass. Screaming.

The next shot tore through the ceiling, sending insulation raining down like ash. I flinched under Gavin's weight, my ears ringing. A round snapped past, punching into the far wall and spraying splinters of plastic over the aisle.

A woman screamed behind us. I twisted, heart jackhammering, and saw her. It was the woman with the toddler, now crouched low, shielding the child with her whole body. One of the elderly passengers sat in stunned silence, rocking slightly, sobbing without sound.

"Stay down! Stay quiet!" Gavin barked, already low, crawling toward the shattered window. His voice was steel and certainty.

I pushed myself up, glass crunching beneath my knees. My palms were sticky. Blood? I didn't know whose. Maybe mine. Probably everyone's. I crawled to the nearest row, where a woman clutched her bleeding shoulder and stared at me with wide, unfocused eyes.

"I'm a nurse," I said automatically, as if the words meant anything now.

The woman didn't respond. I tore gauze from the kit, pressing it into the wound.

"You're going to be okay," I whispered automatically. I doubted she believed it any more than I did.

The air inside the wreck was brittle with fear. Shadows danced across the seats as the snowstorm outside refracted the light from the vehicles. Somewhere deeper in the wreckage, a man coughed, wet, rattling. My mind was spinning. I should stay. I had to stay. That was what nurses did. I'd sworn an oath on leaving nursing school. The old do no harm yadda yadda similar to what doctors swore

But what good would it do anyone to stay here and die?

I crawled over broken seat frames and scattered supplies, toward the co-pilot slumped near the front bulkhead. The blanket Gavin had wrapped around him earlier had slipped. Blood soaked through his shirt in deep maroon patches, darker now. His breathing was shallow, rattling. Wrong.

I knelt beside him. "Hey," I said softly, my hands already checking his pulse, searching his face.

His eyelids fluttered. "Don't... let them... get me..."

His voice was barely a whisper. Each word cost him something.

"I'm here," I said, blinking hard. "You're okay. Just stay with me."

He coughed, wet and weak. Blood bubbled at the corner of his mouth. "I can't... move... they'll kill us..."

"You're not alone," I whispered, though I wasn't sure if he could even hear me anymore.

His hand found mine. It was cold, slick with sweat and blood. His fingers barely curled around mine, more reflex than grip.

"Make it out," he breathed. "Just make it..."

"I'll send help," I promised, even as my chest cracked with guilt. "I'm sorry."

My heart clutched as I heard footsteps crunching the snow, outside. Gavin knelt beside me. His face was pale, eyes hard. "Ava. It's time."

I looked down at the co-pilot. I had no doubt he was dying. His lips had stopped moving.

My eyes burned with unshed tears. "I know."

I squeezed the co-pilot's hand one last time, then let go. There really was nothing more I could for him or for any of them really. Something inside me cracked but I didn't have time to mourn it. The best I could do was try to get help, try to survive this, to send that bastard Lev to some hellish prison.

I rose.

Gavin was already moving, checking the pack, counting ammo, looking outside. I just stood there, frozen, my gaze sweeping over the faces still scattered in the wreckage. A man with a broken arm. A woman with a baby. An elderly couple barely speaking, just holding hands like the grip itself could shield them. These weren't strangers anymore. They were mine. My patients. My responsibility. And I was leaving them. But I would never forget them.

My stomach twisted as I bent to grab the first aid kit. My fingers closed around the handle but my feet didn't move. What kind of nurse ran? A flash behind my eyelids, Emma, pale but smiling in a hospital corridor, one hand dragging a chemo IV pole like it was a fashion accessory.

"Just promise me you'll keep living," Emma had said, grinning through cracked lips. "Even when you feel like quitting."

I squeezed my eyes shut. "I'm trying," I whispered.

The wreckage creaked. A distant voice rose outside the fuselage, amplified by a bullhorn, guttural and loud. Russian accent.

"You have ten seconds to come out," the voice barked, "or we come in."

I jerked toward Gavin.

His eyes were hard, face set in firm lines. "Now."

I clutched the first aid kit to my chest. My pulse screamed behind my ribs. But my voice was steady.

"Let's go."

I didn't look back. Because if I did, I wouldn't be able to leave at all.

"We need to move. Now," Gavin said to the rest, his voice like a steel wire pulled tight.

But the businessman with the splinted arm shook his head, eyes wild. "No. I'm not going anywhere. I'll negotiate. They'll listen."

"With bullets?" Gavin snapped.

"I know people—"

"You think they care who you know?" Gavin turned toward the others. "We stay, we die. It's that simple."

The mother clutched her toddler closer, rocking him like it would stop the panic. Her face crumpled, and she turned to me, more tears waterfalling down her soot-stained cheeks. "Please... please take him. He's light. You can—"

"No," I choked, throat closing. "I can't. He'll die out there in the cold."

The woman pushed the child forward. "Then take me, too!"

"We can't," Gavin said sharply. "We take him, we slow down. If we slow down, we get caught."

The cabin cracked open again. Arguments. Pleading. A man cursed. Someone shouted for the rest to stay calm. Chaos bloomed like a fire catching dry leaves.

I wanted to scream. My hands trembled as the little boy stared up at me, wide-eyed and silent. I bent, kissed his forehead. My lips were shaking.

"Be brave for your mama, okay?" I whispered.

He nodded once, too young to understand what those words costed me. I was either going to throw up or stay or scream. This was impossible.

Gavin touched my arm, gentle this time. Not dragging. Just waiting. Together, we moved to the emergency hatch. I gripped the metal frame, took one last breath, then slipped into the cold.

The raging snow swallowed me whole.

I dropped from the emergency hatch into a drift nearly to my knees. It gave me a second to catch my breath, to recover from that last heart-breaking wrench of leaving them. The cold hit like a slap, sharp and immediate, but it was the silence that unnerved me most. The wreck behind us groaned like something alive, and beyond it... nothing.

Gavin landed beside me, already moving. A pack strapped tight to his back, pistol drawn low in one hand. His movements were smooth and skilled. Controlled chaos.

I stumbled after him, boots crunching through the soft layer and on through a crusted top layer of snow. My breath came hard, fogging the air. My thighs burned with every step. The first aid kit slapped against my side with every jolt.

A knife was taped to my thigh. Gavin had handed it to me seconds before we dropped, no explanation needed. I hadn't even asked where he found it or if it was sharp. The fuselage loomed behind us, shielding us from their line of sight, for now. Snowflakes drifted lazily in the air, beautiful and mocking. This place was still. Untouched. Like the world hadn't just fallen apart.

Then the gunfire started again.

I turned, stumbling. A scream echoed from the wreckage. Glass shattered. Then another shot, closer. My legs froze.

"I have to go back—" I gasped.

Gavin caught my wrist mid-turn. "No."

"But they—"

"They made their choice," he said, eyes blazing. "You go back now, we all die. We survive. That's the job now. It's how we honor them."

I clenched my jaw, breath hitching as sobs clawed at my throat as their faces marched across my eyes. I didn't let the tears win or I'd fall down and never get up. I nodded once. I would honor them. I would survive. For them. For Emma.

And we ran.

The forest wrapped around us like a trap, tall pines lined with frost, snow-laced branches arching overhead. It should've been beautiful. Should've felt safe. But every root hid a fall. Every gust of wind sounded like footsteps.

Gavin took point, his body slicing through the knee-deep snow like a snowplow with a gun. I followed, stumbling but pushing forward. My legs ached. My shoulder throbbed from the pack's weight. My chest was a fist of guilt. Behind us, the wreckage was out of sight. But not out of mind.

Smoke trailed into the sky, a dark thread against the pale storm. Then, clearer, sharper, a scream. Just one. It ended fast. I stumbled to a stop, bent double as my breath sawed in and out of my lungs. The scream echoed in my chest, rattling loose everything I'd tried to stuff down.

"We left them," I gasped. "I left them."

Snow clung to my lashes. My lips trembled. I wasn't crying, not exactly but it felt worse than tears.

Gavin dropped beside me, steadying my shoulder with a gloved hand. "If you'd stayed, you'd be dead."

I shook my head, lips moving with no sound.

"You want to help them?" he said. "Then stay alive. That's how we win."

It was the most he'd said since we hit the snow. This time it landed like a sledgehammer. I nodded, jaw tight, and forced my legs back into motion. Froze the spiraling thoughts. Step. Breathe. Repeat.

We ducked behind a fallen tree, its roots torn up by wind or age. Either way, it made decent cover from the cold wind. Gavin dropped to one knee, pulled out a battered GPS unit from his jacket, and stared at the screen like he could will it into life. No signal. Just static and frustration.

I wiped snow off my cheeks, my breath coming in harsh pulls. "I'm not your responsibility."

Gavin didn't look up. "Didn't say you were."

"Then why are you helping me?"

He glanced at me then, something raw in his expression. "Because I know what it's like to lose people."

A beat passed. Then another.

I didn't want to ask, but it came out anyway. "Your brother?"

He nodded once. "Carter was always chasing a big score. Never knew how to slow down and live."

I swallowed. Carter had been my ex-husband. My voice was quiet. "You blame me?"

"I did." His eyes met mine, hard, unblinking. "For a long time." I let that settle. Didn't flinch.

"But it wasn't you," he added, softer now. "And I came to realize that. Doesn't make losing him easier."

The silence between us felt charged. Not heavy. Not awkward. Just true.

Snap. Not snow. Not wind. A twig. Behind us. We both froze.

Gavin held up a hand, fingers spread wide. I dropped lower behind the tree, heart racing. My fingers tightened around the first aid kit. I guess it was the only thing I had I could swing at somebody. Gavin reached for his sidearm. And the woods went still. No bird or animal noise

"They're tracking us." Gavin barely whispered.

I didn't so much as breathe. Couldn't.

Somewhere in the trees behind them, a branch snapped again. It was heavier this time. Then a voice, low and sharp, barked something in Russian. Another responded. Closer. A beam of light sliced through the darkness. It scanned the trees, bobbing fast. Too fast.

Gavin didn't wait. He grabbed my hand, the gesture sudden and firm. "Go. Now."

We ran.

Branches clawed at my face, icy needles scratching skin. My breath came in gasps. The snow was deeper here, uneven and treacherous. My boots slid, caught, dragged. Behind us, more voices. Louder now. Angry.

A shot rang out.

I flinched, ducking instinctively as the bullet zipped past, striking bark with a *crack*. Another followed. Closer.

Gavin yanked me sideways, behind a snowbank. We tumbled down together, landing hard, limbs tangled. Snow exploded around us, muffling the next round of gunfire. He rolled, covering me with his body again. His chest heaved. My heart thundered.

"Keep low," he said, breath hot against my ear.

I nodded, trying not to sob or make any sound.

Another shout. A flashlight beam swept just past us, missing by inches.

"We keep moving," Gavin whispered. "We don't stop. No matter what."

His hand found mine again, tight, grounding.

We lay there in the cold, under the shadow of pine and fear, surrounded by the hiss of snowfall and the chaos we barely escaped.

I closed my eyes for a breath. Then I opened them. And ran.

Signals

Ava Green

I followed Gavin out of the hunter's blind into the white world. The radio signal seemed like a beacon of hope to me. If it didn't give away our position to the men following us.

"You think your company is out here?" My voice was hoarse.

"Yeah," Gavin muttered. He was crouched near the edge of the blind, one hand adjusting the dented antenna, the other rotating the radio unit like it was a safe he could crack. "Signal's weak. Could've bounced off the ridge. Might be a search channel. Might be someone else."

"But it's something." I leaned forward, ignoring the throb of protest in my muscles. "We're not just screaming into the void anymore."

He didn't smile. He never did when it was news wrapped in maybe. But his eyes flickered toward me. I saw hope, barely banked.

"It's enough to keep moving," he said. "Before someone else finds us first."

A gust of wind sliced through the mouth of the shelter flapping the tarp. I shivered, but Gavin was already back in motion, tucking the radio carefully into a side pocket like it was a relic of the gods. I exhaled slowly, forcing my hands to stop trembling. The signal was real. Not a hallucination. Not a desperate dream. Somewhere out there, someone was transmitting. Someone could be listening. And by those broken branches someone else could be hunting.

I pulled on my gloves and staggered to my feet, swaying just a little before the pain settled into its usual dull roar. Gavin glanced back once. Didn't comment. He knew I'd keep up. Because at this point, it was about survival. Stopping wasn't optional. Not for either of us.

The smoke from the crash site was long gone, swallowed by the ridge. But it lingered in my lungs, in the raw sting behind my eyes. I saw ghosts now. Not just from the plane but from the ER. A dozen faces I couldn't save over the years.

The college freshman with the ruptured aneurysm. The father of three crushed in a rollover. A child, blue-lipped and silent after a seizure that wouldn't stop. Names I never learned. Lives I couldn't fix. They all blurred together, trailing me like smoke.

"I'm supposed to be strong," I whispered. "Not crumble every time I lose someone."

Gavin didn't say anything. He just stood, gaze fixed on the snow like he was guarding me from memory itself.

"I can't save everyone," I said. "I know that. But it doesn't make it easier."

"You don't want it to be easy." His voice was quiet. Not a challenge. Not even comfort. Just a truth laid bare. "If you didn't feel it, Ava..." He finally looked at me. "You wouldn't be worth saving."

That hit me harder than I wanted to admit. My eyes snapped to his, but there was no sarcasm there. No stoic mask. Just him. Raw. Real.

"I didn't think you noticed," I said, meaning more than I wanted to.

"I notice everything," he said. "Especially about you."

It was too much. I looked away, blinking hard to push back the tears. But then he added, softer, "And I'd still pull you out of that wreck. Every time."

Silence dropped between us, heavy as a weighted blanket. I stared at my boots. He watched the trees. Neither of us knew what to do with the thing he just said aloud.

But something in me shifted. A hairline fracture giving way. Not a break. Just... an opening. Because maybe I wasn't alone out here. Not really.

Gavin pulled the pistol from beneath his jacket. Metal glinted dully in the half-light.

"How many?" I asked.

He slid the clip free, checked the chamber. "Two. That's it."

My stomach flipped. I hated guns, always had. I had seen the carnage they caused too often in the ER. But I hated feeling defenseless up here even more.

He placed one round back into the chamber with a smooth, practiced motion. The other he tucked into the webbing on his vest. Everything about the way he moved was quiet, calm, precise. Not scared. Not freaking at the lack of bullets. Prepared.

"We're not going to die out here," I said, my voice firmer than I felt.

He didn't answer right away. Just clicked the gun back together, slow and measured. Like the weight of our survival lived in the click.

Finally, he said, "We'll do what we have to."

It was not exactly reassurance.

"You ever run out before?" I asked.

He lifted his eyes to mine. "I don't."

It should sound arrogant. Cocky. The way some guys would have said "I never miss" right before they did. But with him, it just sounded like fact. Like gravity. I tried to picture what that kind of certainty felt like. What it meant to carry death in your hands and not flinch. To walk toward danger instead of away from it. To protect someone, not because you were told to, but because you decided they mattered.

He pocketed the gun aside and stared at me.

"You okay?" he asked but not like he was expecting a yes.

I nodded anyway. "Ask me again when we're warm and fed."

His mouth twitched. That almost-smile I was starting to chase.

"I'll hold you to that."

I think he meant it.

And weirdly, so did I. Thinking of an *after* where he would be asking me things.

The world outside the blind was pale and brutal. A flat gray sky stretched overhead. The clouds were thick and low enough to press on your thoughts. Snow blanketed everything in silence, but every footstep seemed to crunch as loud as a gunshot.

I followed Gavin's lead. Always Gavin first. He tested each patch of ground before he committed his weight, scanning constantly, weapon tucked close. My legs ached. My arm burned. But I kept moving.

He didn't say much now, just gestured when I needed to duck under branches or skirt a patch of ice. His hand touched mine briefly as I stepped over a frozen log, steadying me. We didn't talk about it. We didn't talk about anything. The silence between us was louder than words.

Every tree felt like it had the potential to hide something. Every gust of wind sounded like a warning. My fingers curled tight around the knife he gave me, small, utilitarian, deadly. I was not a fighter, but I was not defenseless either. Not anymore.

"You still think we should be heading uphill?" I asked, my breath fogging between us.

"It's the only shot we've got," Gavin replied, eyes flicking upward toward the ridge. "If we can get line-of-sight, Bravo might pick us up on drone coverage."

"And if they don't?"

"Then we go further."

I nodded. Not because I agreed. But because there was no alternative and Gavin knew that. We hiked in silence for another stretch. My boots slipped once. He caught my elbow, didn't let go right away.

"Sorry," I muttered, hating to be weak.

"Don't be." He said it with such finality it shut me up.

Above us, a crow cawed. Sharp. Close. We both stopped. Frozen.

Just a bird. Just wind. But Gavin turned slowly in a circle, scanning the tree line like he was memorizing exits we didn't have. I tried not to feel exposed. But I did.

Still, when he turned back toward the ridge and said, "Come on," I followed.

Because moving was better than waiting. And because I trusted him. Even when everything inside me said he might not have any better idea of where we were headed than I did. But at least he had some. I had none.

We hiked in a zigzag pattern now to get up the hill. We were angling for higher ground, taking cover where we could. Trying not to slide back down the mountain or off the steep cliff face. My arm throbbed in time with my pulse, but I didn't let it slow me down. Couldn't. No choice really. Gavin kept glancing over his shoulder. At first, I thought he was checking for danger. Then I realized, he was checking on me.

"Seriously," I said after the third time, "why do you keep looking at me like that?"

He paused mid-step, boot crunching in a drift. "Like what?"

"Like I'm going to disappear."

His jaw shifted, muscles ticking like there was a whole war happening behind his eyes. "Habit."

"That a military thing?"

He shook his head. "It's a loss thing."

The silence stretched between us, brittle and cold. Then he said, "I lost track of someone once. Thought they were right behind me. They weren't."

I swallowed the lump rising in my throat. "I'm not your brother."

"I know," he said, looking at me full on. "You're not."

He said it like it meant more than the words. Like maybe I'd already started to carve out my own place in his head, in his chest. Somewhere he didn't expect me to be.

I didn't know what to do with that. I didn't know what to do with the flutter in my stomach at the idea either. So, I kept walking. But I let my hand brush his arm this time. A silent acknowledgment. I was still here. I wasn't going anywhere. He didn't flinch.

We kept climbing. Every branch snagged like claws. Every patch of snow was a trap. But Gavin kept pacing himself to me, not ahead of me. Protecting. Not leading.

At one point, I stumbled. Not enough to fall, just enough to feel the weight of it. He steadied me, yet again.

"You good?" he murmured.

"No worse than five minutes ago."

He gave me a sideways glance. "You're something else, Green."

"You say that like it's bad."

"I didn't say that."

I almost smiled. But the mountain didn't allow for softness right now. I was almost afraid my face would crack it was so cold. So, I buried it. But my chest still warmed like maybe something real just passed between us.

Crack.

I gasped. The sound sliced through the quiet like a whip. Not a tree branch. Not a falling rock. Something sharper. More deliberate. Gavin dropped instantly into a crouch, hand up in warning. I froze mid-step, heart stalling. Another shot, muffled by snow but unmistakable.

"Gunfire," he confirmed, voice low, taut as a bowstring. "Close."

My skin went cold in a way that had nothing to do with the wind. "How close?"

"Too," he murmured, sweeping the slope below us with his eyes. "They're not spraying. Controlled shots. Someone's tracking."

Us. They're tracking us. What were they shooting?

A new voice filtered through the trees. It was male, loud, and unmistakably accented. Russian. A clipped command, followed by another voice barking back. I didn't understand the words, but the name was clear.

"The nurse," Gavin muttered. His expression turned to stone.

"Me?" I breathed, almost choking.

He nodded. "They're not after us. They're after you."

A lead weight dropped into my gut. "Why? I'm just a nurse. I didn't see anything. I don't know—" I stopped. "The marshal."

Gavin's gaze narrowed. "Lev. The man you treated. The one I fought."

I nodded. "The marshal was mumbling about something. Something he wanted me to know but it was incoherent."

Gavin's knuckles whitened around his grip on the pistol. "If they think you know something..."

"I don't." I insisted.

"They don't care."

The woods went deathly still for a beat. Then: another gunshot. Closer.

Gavin pulled me behind a thick cluster of pine, shielding me with his body. "We have to move. Now."

"I thought you said uphill—"

"We stay with the plan. But fast."

I nodded, knees trembling. But I pushed off with him anyway. Every step felt like an explosion waiting to happen. I kept expecting a bullet to punch into my back, a shout to ring out behind us. The skin on my back felt like it was climbing up into my hair.

We kept moving. One breath. One step. One heartbeat at a time.

I think I finally understood what Gavin meant back on the plane. *Disappear or die.*

I slipped and went down on one knee. His fingers clamped around my elbow as he pulled me quickly to my feet. Not gentle, not cruel, just necessary. I staggered for a second, my injured arm screaming, my legs sluggish from cold and fear. But I moved. Because he was right.

Behind us, voices rose. They sounded angry and urgent. The crunch of snow, the snap of tree limbs. They were not being quiet anymore. They didn't care if we knew.

"They're close," I panted.

"Left," Gavin growled. "Hard left. It's a steeper climb with less cover. They won't expect it."

I glanced toward the slope. It was damn near vertical, studded with slick rocks and frozen brambles.

"You sure?" I asked, breath clouding, thinking he had lost his mind.

"No."

His eyes locked with mine, feral and fierce.

I nodded. "Great. Sure. Good reasoning."

We scrambled. Snow swallowed my boots as I fought for footing, grabbing at roots and jagged stone. Gavin was always just ahead, clearing a path, offering a hand, yanking me upward when I slipped. Twice,

I went down hard. My knee slammed into a rock, my arm took the brunt of a branch. Pain sparked behind my eyes, white and hot.

"Keep going!" he barked.

"I'm trying!" I snarled back.

We crested a narrow ledge, both gasping. The ridge was close. Maybe another hundred feet. Might as well be an eternity. I risked a glance behind us and lost my breath. A dark figure breached the tree line below. He raised a gun. Another followed.

"Gavin!" I cried, pointing.

He spun, leveled his weapon.

But then—

A shout from below. "I see them!"

The bullet whistled past my ear. I ducked instinctively, heart leaping into my throat. Gavin fired once, controlled, deliberate. One of the shadows stumbled.

"We have to split apart," he said. "I'll draw them off—"

"No." My voice surprised us both. Steady. Absolute.

"We stay together," I said. "Or nothing."

Gavin stared for a beat, then gave the faintest nod.

The voices rose again. Another shot echoed through the trees.

We ran.

On the Run

Gavin Henderson

"**W**e disappear, or we die."

I didn't slow. Not when my boots slipped on the ice-slicked slope. Not when branches slapped across my chest and face. And definitely not when a gunshot echoed behind us. It was dull and distant through the trees, but too damn close.

I kept Ava in my peripheral vision. She was close, fast, breathing hard but still upright. She wasn't just keeping up. She was matching me stride for stride, her jaw tight with determination, her eyes sharp despite the exhaustion pulling at both of us.

Snow crunched underfoot, louder than I liked but it was the obvious trail that bothered me more. Though I had no time to do anything about that now. They were too close on our tails. My breath came in harsh bursts, misting into the cold air like steam from an overworked engine. My lungs already burned. My legs ached.

We hadn't stopped since the fuselage.

Every instinct screamed to keep moving.

The wreck was long gone now, swallowed by the pines and distance. Faint cracks of gunfire echoed far behind, fading but not gone. I didn't trust it. Silence was a trick. False calm before the next ambush.

"We're heading uphill," I said over my shoulder. "Better elevation, better chance of a signal."

Ava didn't argue. Just nodded once and kept moving. She was tougher than I expected. And she'd already looked tough.

I pulled us into a shallow dip between trees, just long enough to reassess. I shrugged off my pack, dropped to one knee, and unzipped it fast. Fingers flying.

Thermal blanket. Two energy bars. Flare gun. Knife. Half a topographic map from a state park miles to the west. Compass. One emergency parka still vacuum-sealed. Not enough but better than nothing.

Ava stood behind me, arms wrapped tightly around her middle. Her lips were pale. She was shaking. I ripped open the parka pack and turned to her.

"Put this on."

"I'm fine," she muttered, chin lifting.

"You're freezing."

"And you're bleeding."

That made me pause. My arm, the one Lev had caught during the fight, was soaked down to the elbow. I'd barely noticed. Adrenaline had done its job. We stared at each other, two forces digging in. She didn't move. Neither did I. Finally, I stepped forward and threw the coat around her shoulders myself. She didn't stop me, but she didn't help, either. Stubborn to the bone. Our eyes locked. Guess we'd call that fight a draw.

I turned away and scanned the sky through the tree canopy. No bars on the phone. Not even one. Still no radio signal. The sitch was about as bad as it could get. We were out in freezing weather with no shelter.

We couldn't build shelter and start a fire with trouble close behind and looking for any sign of where we were. I had no idea of Ava's physical abilities. She might collapse on me, physically or mentally. She didn't have my training in how to survive in this kind of environment or under this level of stress. But I wouldn't leave her behind. I wouldn't have left any of them, if they had agreed to come. It wasn't in my nature.

"Keep moving," I said quietly. "We'll stay warm and keep ahead."

Ava pulled the coat tighter around herself but didn't answer. We walked. After another hundred yards, I stopped abruptly.

Ava nearly bumped into me. "What is it?"

I crouched and pulled out a fallen pine branch to sweep over our trail, slow, deliberate strokes. The snow wasn't deep, but our bootprints were obvious. Too obvious.

"You really know what you're doing," she said behind me, voice low.

"SERE school," I replied, standing. "Survival, evasion, resistance, escape. Military training for when everything goes to hell."

"Well," she muttered, "seems we crashed in the right department for that training."

I gave her a quick look. Her lips were blue, but her sarcasm was alive and well.

She pointed at the branch. "What else did they teach you?"

"How to disappear. How to endure. How to stay alive."

She looked carefully at me. Not just with fear or gratitude. There was something else simmering under her expression. Something thoughtful. Maybe even respect.

Then she added, "Bet they didn't mention babysitting your brother's ex."

That stopped me for a breath.

I turned to face her fully, snow falling between us like static on a blank screen. "Not exactly."

But I didn't say it with annoyance. Not this time. And I wouldn't term this babysitting. She was holding her own. Hell, she'd saved me on that plane.

She didn't say the next thing. But I saw it in her eyes. There was more here. More than adrenaline. More than shared survival. It just wasn't the time to unpack it.

I turned and kept walking.

We found a moment of stillness beneath a fallen log and boulder outcropping, moss-covered and half-frozen. I was weighing the rest break against losing the heat we generated by keeping moving. At the point, it was a toss up. I scanned the woods with military precision, every branch a potential threat, every gust of wind another layer of white noise that could cover pursuit. Ava slumped against the stone, unzipping her coat halfway. Her breath came fast and shallow.

I pulled out a dented canteen and passed it to her. "Small sips."

Her hands trembled as she took it. The metal clinked softly against her teeth.

"You're allowed to be scared," I said after a beat. Quiet. Matter-of-fact.

"I'm not scared," she said automatically.

I raised an eyebrow. "Lying doesn't help out here."

That hit harder than I expected. She barked out a laugh, sharp and cracked.

"I left people back there. I told them to wait. Promised them help. And then I ran." Her voice broke on the last word.

I didn't rush in with comfort. Didn't try to offer what I didn't have. I'd left too. And I knew exactly what she felt because I had the echoes of it in my head, but it had become a battlefield decision. I'd made it knowing full well the consequences. Instead, I crouched beside her and met her eyes. Steady. Clear.

"You ran because you had to," I said. "You ran because you're not done yet."

She blinked at me. "What does that even mean?"

"It means if you die out here, those people died for nothing. But if you make it out, someone remembers. Someone tells the story. Someone sends help. And someone tracks down Lev and takes him out for what he did."

Ava stared at me, silent tears slipping down her cheeks. She didn't nod. Didn't argue. But she stood up on her own. That was enough.

The terrain changed fast. What had been a forest path turned into a steep incline slicked with packed snow and hidden roots. Each step felt like a test. One misstep and we'd be tumbling. I moved with practiced confidence, my boots cutting a sure path through the slope. Ava followed, slipping more than once, but catching herself with grim determination.

"Watch that branch," I warned, reaching out just in time to steady her. My hand gripped her elbow, firm and warm even through the layers of clothing. She didn't pull away. Not this time. But I could tell she was struggling.

"We need shelter soon," I muttered, eyes scanning the canopy. "Storm's building."

She glanced up. The sky had gone from steel gray to bruised charcoal. Wind whistled through the pines in growing gusts.

"Can you smell weather? More SERE training?" she asked, half-joking, breathless.

"I can feel it in my knees," I said without missing a beat.

She laughed, really laughed. Not bitter or broken, but bright, a flare of warmth in the cold. I glanced at her. That smile was trouble.

Trouble I didn't need. Trouble I could feel myself already sinking into. Still... I smiled back. Just a little. Dangerous, that smile. Because it didn't feel like relief. It felt like something beginning.

Ava stumbled again, and this time I caught her by the waist, steadying her as we reached a patch of exposed stone.

"Careful," I said low, voice closer to gravel than words.

She didn't reply. Just looked up at me as the wind howled.

We moved on.

I spotted it just past a downed tree, a collapsed wooden lean-to, half-buried in snow. The tarp still clung to the top beams, tattered but intact. Not perfect. But better than dying.

"This'll do," I muttered, brushing snow away from the entrance. I waved her in. "You first."

Ava arched a brow. "You're the one with the hypothermia knees."

"And you're the one shaking."

We both hesitated. Then she crawled in. The space was barely big enough for one. Shoulder to shoulder, thigh to thigh, pressed so close every breath mingled. I stretched the tarp tighter across the entrance, blocking some of the wind. Inside, it was still freezing. But less deadly.

"Cozy," she said wryly, curling into the thermal blanket I'd pulled from the pack.

"You want cozy, I'll build a log cabin next time," I grunted.

Silence fell, tense and charged.

Our boots bumped. Ava's leg pressed against me. Neither of us moved. She looked at me, her face half-shadowed. Her lips slightly parted. "You okay?"

"Been through worse," I said. "But not with company this... sarcastic."

She snorted softly. "That your polite way of saying I'm a pain in the ass."

"I didn't think I was polite."

Another quiet moment. Then her hand brushed mine beneath the blanket. Not intentional. Not entirely accidental either.

"I?" she said softly.

I looked at her.

"This isn't how I imagined dying. In the woods with a stranger."

"I'm not a stranger."

"No," she said, voice just above a whisper. "Not anymore."

Ava shifted beside me, her cheek grazing my collarbone. Every movement felt deliberate, even if it wasn't. Her breath brushed my neck, soft and warm.

"You smell like pine," she murmured, "and sweat... and bad ideas."

I gave a low chuckle. "You smell like blood and sarcasm."

She laughed, then winced. "Right. Bruised ribs. Forgot."

Her hand moved beneath the blanket, fingertips brushing my side. I stiffened, half from the pain, half from the contact.

"Let me check it," she said, not quite asking.

"You're not exactly gentle. Just ask Lev." I replied, but I didn't stop her.

Her fingers probed gently along my ribs, more nurse than flirt, but I still felt every inch like being touching by a live wire.

"You'll have a hell of a bruise," she whispered.

"I've had worse."

A pause. Her fingers lingered. Not at all medical now.

"That thing you said earlier," she said quietly, "about not being done."

"Yeah?" I said gruffly.

"Thanks for not letting me give up."

I turned slightly. The movement closed the last inch between us. My nose brushed her hairline. Her breath hitched.

"I didn't do it for thanks," I said.

"I didn't think you did."

She looked up, and our eyes locked in the dim lean-to. No humor now. No teasing. Just raw, unsaid things humming in the space between us. My hand found her hip under the blanket, the contact light but definitely not accidental.

"I should back off," I murmured very conscious of the woman so close.

"You should," she breathed. "But you won't."

A second passed. Maybe two.

Then she looked away. "Tomorrow we'll pretend this didn't happen."

"Sure," I said, voice rough, pausing a beat. "Tomorrow."

A sharp chirp cut through the wind.

I froze. Not the forest. Not a bird. Electronic.

I twisted, reaching behind us into the dark corner of the lean-to. My fingers dug through my pack until they hit hard plastic. The emergency radio. I yanked it out. It was old, battered, barely held together with duct tape and stubborn hope. The LED blinked red. Battery low. But alive. Static crackled. Then—

"...Bravo...niner...—opy?"

Ava shot upright. "Did you hear that?"

"Yeah." I tapped the side, adjusted the antenna, angled it toward the open slit in the tarp. "It's weak."

"Was that... Sierra Bravo?" she asked, scooting closer. Her knee pressed against me.

"Could be." I held my breath, twisting the dial with the delicacy of a bomb tech. More static. A garbled string of syllables. Then silence. "Come on," I muttered. "Say it again. Lock on."

Nothing.

I set the radio on my thigh, shielding it from the wind, hands cupped around it like a prayer. My pulse thundered louder than the static.

Ava's voice was soft. "Do you think they're looking for us?"

I didn't answer right away. Didn't want to lie. Didn't want to kill the hope on her face. But they would know I hadn't landed in Seattle. There was a slight possibility a search had been mounted though it seemed too rapid.

"I think someone's out there," I said at last. "And I think they don't know where to look."

"Then we make them see us," she said.

I glanced at her, shivering, scraped, but still fierce as hell.

"We will," I promised.

Outside, the wind howled louder, whirling snow like ghosts past the shelter. Inside, the red light blinked, faint, but steady. Still alive. Still fighting. Just like us.

The Cold and the Chase

Ava Green

I couldn't feel my damn fingers. I woke to the sound of my own teeth chattering.

Everything hurt, my arm, my legs, my pride, but it was the burning throb in my left arm that yanked me from half-sleep. I was curled against Gavin like a space heater, tucked into the crook of his body inside the lean-to, but the warmth didn't reach my fingertips.

I flexed my hand. Nothing. Then pins and needles. Then hot, searing pain. Shit. I gritted my teeth and tried to ignore it. There wasn't anything I could really do other than keep moving my hands.

Pulling my sleeve back carefully, I squinted in the faint morning light filtering through the tarp's frayed edge. The cut on my arm was uglier than I'd thought, raw, swollen, ringed in crusted blood and bruising. It had started to leak again. Fantastic.

I shifted, trying not to wake Gavin, but of course he stirred. Of course he noticed. Of course he saw me cradling my arm, and instantly keyed into threat mode.

"Let me see it," he said, already sitting up, reaching into the pack.

"I'm fine," I lied, again. It was practically my mantra at that point.

He gave me that look, the one that said I wasn't fooling him, not for a second. "You said that yesterday. While actively bleeding."

"I've got a brand," I quipped. "Bleeding With Confidence."

He didn't smile. Just peeled back the rest of my sleeve like it was fragile silk, not stiff cotton soaked with dried blood. His touch was gentler than I expected. Reverent, almost.

"You should've said something sooner," he muttered.

"And miss all this cozy winter bonding?"

He huffed out air that was almost a laugh, but it disappeared in the cold before it could become one. Gavin opened the med pouch with practiced fingers and pulled out antiseptic wipes, gauze, and surgical tape. He didn't say anything about the frostbitten pink of my fingertips or the way I was trying not to breathe too hard.

"This might sting," he warned, tearing open the wipe.

"It already does," I said, bracing my hand against my knee. "Do your worst, Marine."

He didn't smile. Just set his jaw and got to work.

The antiseptic was fire. My back arched, and I bit the inside of my cheek hard enough to taste blood. I would not cry out. Not here, not now, not in front of him.

"You're allowed to scream," he said without looking up. "You're not a machine."

"I scream inwardly," I managed. "Keeps the drama to a minimum."

That earned a chuckle. Low and rough, like a stone rolling over gravel. Unexpected and deeply unfair. It made something flutter in my chest that had nothing to do with pain.

When he glanced up, his eyes met mine, steely blue with flecks of gold, sharp and burning even in the weak daylight. For a moment, everything paused. The cold faded. The pain dulled. It was just him, me, and the snow-silent woods beyond that flimsy shelter. Then he went back to work, wrapping the wound with efficiency and care. His fingers were callused but precise.

"Nice hands," I said through clenched teeth. "You moonlight as a masseuse?"

"Try not to associate compliments with blood," he muttered. But the edge of his mouth tilted.

It was gone in a flash, but I saw it. That twitch of a smile. Like a spark buried under ice. And God help me, I wanted to chase it. I wanted to see it flare into a full fire.

Every step was stiff and brought out pain in places I didn't know could hurt. But so did standing still.

We packed up in silence. My arm was wrapped tight, but the pulsing ache hadn't dulled. I tucked it close to my body and pretended it didn't exist. Figured ranting and raving about it wouldn't make it hurt any less.

Gavin shouldered his pack like it weighed nothing, didn't pull at the cut on his ribs. He scanned the tree line before nodding once. "Northwest. Uphill. Slow and steady."

"Great," I muttered. "Exactly what I was on my to-do list today. Climb Everest in a snowstorm with an infected arm."

He glanced back. "That sarcasm means you're still functional."

"Barely."

The lean-to disappeared behind us as we pushed into shin-deep snow. Every step ground fire through my thighs and radiated through my ribs. The world became nothing but white blur and pain.

"Pace yourself," he said, eyes scanning the ridgeline. "We don't need fast. We need invisible."

"You're not exactly subtle," I muttered, watching him move.

Gavin didn't respond. He just pulled a pine bough from a nearby tree and started dragging it behind him, erasing our footprints. Military precision. Every step was deliberate. Every glance was calibrated for threat. I kept watching his squared shoulders, the way his body moved like it had been carved for endurance. My legs were trembling, and he hadn't even broken stride.

"How are you still upright?" I asked, breathless.

He didn't look back. "You're upright. That's the only thing that matters."

I wanted to snap at him, to yell that this wasn't normal, that we shouldn't have to be this strong. But my voice caught in my throat because I knew bottom line that there could be human wolves at our backs. So, instead, I pushed forward, following the faint tracks he didn't let last more than a few seconds. Snow packed my boots. Cold bit my fingers. But Gavin kept walking. And so did I.

"You always this bossy?" stopping to catch my breath.

"Only when death's involved." He replied looking back analytically over our trail.

We slogged through the trees. The silence seemed to grow louder with each crunch of snow beneath our boots. My lungs burned. My shoulder was on fire. My lips felt like cracked ice. My stomach was so empty it was gnawing my spine. I needed to say something—anything—or I'd shatter from the inside out.

"So," I began, breath misting as I panted, "what's the weirdest thing you've eaten in a survival situation?"

Gavin didn't even pause. "Cactus rat. Tasted like if regret were chewy."

I snorted. "Tell me you didn't cook it in your boot."

"Didn't have a pot. Had to improvise."

"Please tell me that's a joke."

He gave a long, deadpan stare. "Wish I was kidding."

"Gross."

A silence stretched. Not hostile, just space.

Then I offered, "We used to place bets in the ER. Like, would the cafeteria serve something edible today, or would it be 'meatloaf surprise' again."

He lifted a brow. "What was the surprise?"

"No meat."

That earned the smallest chuckle. "Sounds like my last deployment. MREs for two weeks solid. You haven't lived until you've tried swallowing those."

It was easy for a minute. Easier than I expected. We walked side by side. Close, but not touching. Snow drifted gently through the branches like confetti in an almost silent display. It wasn't windy. That was a relief.

"You know," I said slowly, "I hated you at the wedding."

"Back at you," he replied. "I had to wear a tux for that disaster because you wanted it formal."

"I remember. You looked like someone handed a grenade to a grizzly."

He actually smirked. "It was a rental. Didn't survive."

"And then you ghosted."

Gavin's face hardened just a fraction. "Didn't seem like I was wanted."

The air between us sharpened. I didn't have an answer for that. Not yet. So, we kept walking. But something had changed. Then I didn't so much fall. I folded. There was a difference. Gavin saw it before I felt it. My vision tilted, then jerked sideways. My legs simply collapsed under me. My knees crashed into the snow, and suddenly I was on the ground. Pain spiked through my arm like a live wire.

"Shit—" I hissed, clutching my side as my shoulder screamed in protest but refusing to cry out.

Gavin was there in an instant. "Ava—"

"I'm fine," I lied, breath catching.

"Stop saying that," he snapped, kneeling beside me, voice low and rough.

His hand curled around my uninjured arm, steadying me as I tried to sit upright. "You're allowed to need help. Especially from me."

"Why?" The word slipped out before I could stop it. "Because you feel responsible?"

He didn't flinch. Didn't let go. Just looked at me with something fierce simmering behind those storm-colored eyes.

"No," he said, voice quieter. "Because I want you alive."

It punched the air out of my lungs more than the fall did. I blinked, hard, because I would not cry. Not here. Not like this. But my throat burned, and my eyes stung and it wasn't just from the cold.

"I didn't ask for this," I whispered, swallowing back those threatening tears.

"I know."

We stayed like that for a breath too long. He was kneeling in front of me like a warrior ready to catch the pieces, and me barely holding them together.

Finally, I drew in a shaky breath. "Okay. Help me up, super soldier."

His hand was solid, strong, and warm through the chill as he pulled me to my feet. And this time, I didn't pretend I didn't need it.

To add to our adventure, the wind picked up, blowing snow like icy spears at us. We spotted a dent in the rock face just as the wind clawed through the trees with another icy howl. Half-covered in snow, Gavin was already moving toward it, scanning the tree line behind us.

"It's barely a cave," I muttered.

"It's more than we had five seconds ago." He brushed snow aside, revealing a narrow hollow. It was maybe four feet high, six across. It was cramped, dark, but blessedly windproof.

I ducked inside first, brushing pine needles off the stone floor. Gavin followed, tossing the thermal blanket across the floor like the thinnest makeshift mattress. He pulled off his pack and shrugged out of his coat, his movements slow and tight.

"Sit," he said, not looking at me.

I hesitated.

He turned and arched a brow. "Now."

God, he was bossy. But I sat. Because I was cold. Because I was tired. Because, fine, he wasn't wrong. I was at the end of my endurance and about ready to fall down if I didn't voluntarily sit. The blanket crackled under us as I eased down beside him. We both groaned, muscles aching from hours of trekking through snow and ice. Our shoulders touched. Then our thighs. There was no avoiding it in here. Slowly, a thrum of shared heat through too many layers rose. I rested my head back against the rock. The cave wall was freezing. Gavin's arm wasn't.

"Tomorrow," he said, voice low and steady, like he was already plotting twelve ways out of this. "We'll aim for the ridge. It's a long shot, but it might get us a signal."

"Copy that," I said, closing my eyes, saying something I'd heard on some tv show.

A moment passed.

"I'll follow your lead," I added.

There was a long pause before he answered, almost too soft to hear. "You already are."

The wind moaned outside, battering the cave like a living thing. Inside, he managed to spark a tiny fire. It was just twigs and dry pinecones in a shallow pit Gavin had dug out with his knife. It threw soft light across the cave walls, painting shadows over stone and skin. I stared at the flames. My chest ached as I fought back exhaustion and loss and feeling we were pointlessly trekking towards nothing.

"I didn't leave your brother because of cheating by either of us," I said suddenly to keep my brain from spinning out of control. My voice sounded foreign in the hush. "He never hurt me. He just... never really saw me."

Gavin shifted beside me but didn't speak. Just waited.

"He said I was the safe choice. The one who'd never leave. Dependable." I snorted. "So, I left. Proved him wrong."

Silence stretched.

"You deserved better," he said at last.

"So did your brother," I whispered.

He flinched. I felt it in the way his body tensed beside mine. But he didn't argue.

"Yeah," he said finally. Quiet. Rough.

I turned to him. His profile glowed amber in the firelight. That hard jaw, those unreadable eyes. He met my eyes and something unspoken seemed to jump the space between us.

His voice dropped. "So do you."

It wasn't a compliment. It was a truth. Something broke loose in my chest.

I reached for his hand because I needed to. He let me. Our fingers intertwined like it was the most natural thing in the world. The fire crackled. His thumb brushed my knuckle, once, twice. Slow. Gentle. I should've pulled away. I didn't. A flicker of orange licked the edge of the cave wall. Gavin's head snapped toward it. I sat up straighter, pulse spiking.

"What the hell—" he muttered, already moving toward the entrance.

I crawled after him, ignoring the sharp stab of pain in my arm. Cold air knifed in as he parted the pine boughs shielding the opening. We peered out together.

And I gasped.

Down in the valley, where we could see the plane wreckage, crumpled and broken, flames were rising. Big ones. Orange and red and wrong against the soft twilight blue. It was burning.

"They're torching it," Gavin said, voice flat. "Covering tracks. No survivors. No evidence."

Smoke rolled upward in thick coils, blotting out the sky.

"But the people..." My words died. I saw it clearly now. Glass twinkled in the light. The fuselage cracked in half. That tail section where the mother and child had huddled. In a blaze. Gone. My stomach turned.

"We should've stayed," I whispered. "I could've done something."

Gavin grabbed my wrist tightly, not rough, not painful, just grounding. "You'd be dead. We both would."

I wanted to scream. To cry. To throw something into our fire just to watch it shatter. Instead, I sat there, shaking as the wind whipped ash-scented snow into the sky.

"I'm sorry," I breathed into the universe.

"So am I," he said, and for the first time, his voice sounded like it might break.

We watched the plane burn in silence. The sky grew darker. The fire below raged higher. The light painted his jaw. A promise crawled through me: we would not be erased. We were the last witnesses now. We would be the ones to survive and remember.

Into the Wild

Gavin Henderson

I woke before the sun rose, like always. It was a habit I'd never shaken. It was either military conditioning or something deeper, more primal. The moment consciousness returned, I scanned: surroundings, threats, Ava.

She was curled beside me, wound tight like a question mark, breath fogging faintly in the cold. Her lashes fluttered. Her lips had a blue tinge. That wasn't good.

I checked the bandage on her arm. The gauze was dry, but her skin was pale beneath it. Her pulse was steady but thready. She needed food. Warmth. Rest. Three things I couldn't give her out here. My gut knotted.

I unzipped my pack in silence, careful not to wake her. Melted snow in a plastic bottle went next to an energy bar I'd split in half. I chewed on part of it and studied the tattered map under weak morning light. The nearest town was hours away, days, maybe. But if we reached the ridge before sunset, there was a chance for a signal. A drone sweep. A miracle.

The thermal blanket rustled behind me as Ava stirred, groaning softly. "Morning already?"

"Time to move," I said, not turning. "We'll only get colder."

She shifted, sat up with a wince, and muttered something that sounded like a curse. I handed her the water. She sipped it without complaint.

"Appetite?"

She grimaced. "Do sarcasm and spite count as calories?"

"Barely." I tossed her the other half of the bar.

She took it, eyes scanning my face. "You didn't sleep."

I shrugged. "Don't need much."

A beat passed. Then, softly: "Thanks for keeping me warm."

I glanced at her. "Thanks for not stabbing me in my sleep."

That earned the faintest smile. It's what I was going for. It was enough.

The climb wasn't optional. Neither was the pain of moving stiff muscles and going out into the cold again. We broke camp just after first light. The trees groaned around us under a crust of snow, branches heavy with frost. I led us toward the eastern slope. Uphill, always uphill. My boots punched through knee-high drifts. The air bit harder the higher we climbed as we left deeper tree cover.

Ava trailed me in silence for the first half-hour. She was limping, but she didn't complain. That was one of the things I'd noticed about her. She talked when she was afraid, but she shut up when she was hurting. She stumbled over a hidden root. I caught her elbow before she faceplanted, steadying her.

"I've got it," she muttered, pulling away. Her breath hitched.

"Not the point," I grumbled, watching the way she favored her injured arm. "You shouldn't have to."

"Oh, I'm sorry, were you expecting a dainty woodland nymph?" she bit out. "You think I'm weak?"

"I think you're bleeding," I shot back.

She stopped dead on the incline, eyes blazing. "I can take care of myself."

I stepped toward her, close enough that our breaths mingled in the freezing air. "That what you were doing as the plane went down?"

Her jaw tightened. "That's low."

"So is your energy level." I dropped my voice. "We're in survival mode, Ava. It's not about pride. It's about staying upright."

Our stares locked. Her fire met my ice. Something between us crackled, familiar, dangerous. I wasn't exactly sure who was bending but I feared it was me.

She exhaled hard and shoved past me. "Just point the damn way."

I let her lead for a few paces. Watching. Admiring. Cursing myself. Because that spark in her glare? It was the same one I'd been trying not to get addicted to. I shouldered my pack and followed.

The storm raged on, its fury unrelenting as snow swirled in a chaotic dance around us. Ava and I had been on the run for what felt like an eternity, our breaths visible in the frigid air, each one a testament to our shared determination to survive. My SERE training had kept us one step ahead of our pursuers, but the mountain was unforgiving, and the storm was a relentless adversary.

We moved with purpose, our footsteps crunching through the snow, the only sound breaking the silence of the wilderness. Ava's tall frame was hunched against the wind, her medium-length hair tucked beneath a woolen hat, but I could still see the determination in her eyes. She was stubborn, decisive, and a force to be reckoned with, qualities I'd grown to admire as we navigated this hellish landscape together.

By midafternoon, the cold turned brutal. The wind cut sideways through the trees, dragging sharp snowflakes like razors. Ava's cheeks were raw, her lips cracked, and I was starting to worry about frostbite for both of us. We needed shelter. Fast. I scanned the terrain and spotted a shadowed shape ahead, half-buried under a drift.

"Over there," I shouted, my voice barely carrying over the howl of the wind. I pointed to the dark shape, its outline barely discernible against the white expanse. It was an abandoned hunting blind, its tarp flapping wildly in the gusts. We didn't have a choice; the storm was worsening, and we needed shelter.

Ava nodded, her face tight with urgency, and we scrambled toward it, our hands numb, our bodies exhausted. The blind was little more than a makeshift structure, but it was enough. We dug through the snow to uncover the entrance, the cold biting at our fingers as we worked. Finally, we slid under the tarp, the wind's roar muffled to a distant hum. The space was cramped, the air thick with the scent of damp wood and earth. We sat facing each other, our breaths coming in ragged gasps, our bodies trembling from the cold.

"We need to warm up," Ava said, her voice steady despite the tremor in her hands. She was right. Hypothermia was a real threat, and we couldn't afford to let it take hold.

I nodded, my mind racing. The only way to generate heat was through body contact. I reached out, hesitating for a moment before placing my hand on her shoulder.

"We need to spoon," I said, my voice low. "It's the only way."

Ava's eyes met mine, and for a moment, I saw a flicker of something I couldn't name, vulnerability, perhaps, or something deeper. She nodded, and we shifted positions, her back against my chest. I wrapped my arms around her, pulling her close, our bodies pressed together in a desperate bid for warmth. The contact was electric, her heat seeping into me, my breath ghosting across the back of her neck. I could feel her tension, her muscles rigid against mine, but slowly, she relaxed, her body molding to mine.

The storm raged on outside, but in that small, confined space, the world seemed to shrink to just the two of us. I could feel her heartbeat, steady and strong, against my chest, and I found myself marveling at her resilience. Ava was a mystery, a woman who kept her cards close, but in that moment, I felt a connection I couldn't ignore. My hand rested on her waist, my fingers brushing against the waistband of her pants. It was a small touch, but it felt significant, a bridge between us in the darkness.

And then, she pressed back into me, her movement deliberate, her body seeking mine. My heart skipped a beat, and I felt a surge of desire I hadn't expected. Slowly, cautiously, I slid my fingertips under her waistband, my breath catching in my throat. I waited for her to pull away, to protest, but instead, she held my hand there, her grip firm, her silence speaking volumes. It wasn't just about warmth anymore; it was about something more, something unspoken but deeply felt.

I closed my eyes, my mind racing as I grappled with the intensity of the moment. The storm, the danger, our pursuers, it all faded into the background. There was only Ava, her body pressed against mine, her hand holding mine in place. I could feel her breath quicken, her tension giving way to something softer, more yielding. My fingers traced the curve of her waist, my touch gentle, exploratory. She shivered, but it wasn't from the cold.

"Gavin," she whispered, her voice barely audible over the storm. My name on her lips sent a jolt through me, and I tightened my hold on her, my other hand moving to her hip, pulling her closer still. The tarp above us rustled in the wind, but inside, it was as if we were in our own world, insulated from the chaos outside. I leaned down, my lips brushing against her ear, my breath warm against her skin.

"Ava," I murmured, my voice rough with emotion. "Are you sure?"

She nodded, her hand tightening on mine, her body pressing back into mine with a hunger that mirrored my own. I didn't need her to say it; her actions spoke louder than words. My fingers moved lower, my touch deliberate now, my intentions clear. She gasped softly, her head tilting back against my shoulder, her body arching into mine.

The cold was forgotten. The danger faded like a distant memory. There was only the heat between us, the urgency of our desire, the raw, unspoken connection that had been building since we first set foot on this mountain. My hand moved beneath her clothing, my fingers tracing the curve of her hip, the incredible softness of her skin. She moaned softly, her body trembling, her breath coming in short, ragged gasps. I shifted, my other hand moving to her breast, my touch gentle but firm. She arched into me, her head falling back against my shoulder, her body surrendering to the moment. The storm raged on, but inside the blind, it was as if time had stopped. There was only Ava and me, our bodies pressed together, our desires intertwining in the darkness.

"Gavin," she sighed again, her voice thick with need.

I kissed her neck. My lips trailed down her skin. My hands moved with an urgency I couldn't deny and didn't want to. She was responsive, her body moving with mine, her hands gripping my arms as if to anchor herself to me. The tarp above us seemed to shrink, the space between us disappearing as we lost ourselves in each other. We were all over each other, touching, trying to stay under the blanket even while pulling down pants.

"This is worse than my first time in the back of a Chevy." Ava giggled.

I had to laugh because she was right. We couldn't really strip. The space under the tarp was too small and it was just too cold but we both knew what went where. And we fit together like our bodies had been made for each other. We found each other in the ancient rhythm as our desires built ever higher. Her hands clutched my back, as she held me to her. Her body tightened around me like a vice.

"Gavin," she panted, her voice a plea. "Don't stop."

I smiled and the expression felt both foreign and exhilarating.

"I won't," I replied, my voice hoarse with need. I quickened my pace. Our bodies moved faster, harder, the tension building until it was almost unbearable.

And then, with a cry that seemed to tear from her throat, Ava shattered, her body convulsing around me as she came. Her release triggered my own. My guttural cries mingled with hers. It was over. We lay tangled together, our breaths coming in sync, our bodies glistening with sweat despite the cold. The storm still raged outside, but inside, there was only stillness, only the sound of our hearts beating in unison. Ava turned in my arms. Her eyes met mine but her expression was unreadable. I brushed a strand of hair from her face, my touch gentle, my heart full.

"Thank you," she whispered, her voice soft, her hand resting on my cheek.

I smiled, a warmth spreading through me that had nothing to do with the physical.

"For everything," she added, her eyes holding mine. Her two words spoke volumes.

I pulled her close, holding her tightly, our bodies still pressed together, our hearts still beating as one. In that moment, there was only Ava and me. Our connection was forged in the fire of survival in an unbreakable bond. And as the snow continued to fall outside, I knew that no matter what came next, we would face it together.

Ava's breathing slowed, but she didn't pull away. Her fingers traced an idle circle on my forearm. Barely there. Just enough to make my chest ache.

"We have to get dressed." I said, hating to ruin the close moment but we couldn't afford to lose heat.

"So tender." She said but she smiled and sorted out her pants.

"You're quiet," she said eventually, voice soft. "Too quiet."

"Thinking."

"About?"

I exhaled through my nose. "Rescue. Exit routes. You, bleeding to death because you won't let me help you."

She let out a soft laugh. "Nice dodge."

I went still. Then, because she earned it, I gave her a sliver of truth.

"I joined the military to escape."

"From what?" she asked gently.

"Everything."

There was a long pause. No pity in it. Just space. Space I didn't realize I needed.

"My old man was a mean drunk. My mom tried to love him sober. That didn't work out."

Ava shifted, didn't interrupt.

"My brother—the one you were with—he was the golden child. Always good, always clean. I left. He stayed. And when he needed me... I wasn't there."

I stared at the worn tarp roof like it might give me some kind of forgiveness.

"I got the call six years too late. Mom overdosed."

Ava's hand found mine under the thermal blanket. Warm. Solid. Present.

"I'm sorry," she said.

I shrugged like it didn't cut anymore. It still did.

"She didn't deserve that ending," I muttered. "And Carter sure as hell didn't deserve to have a ghost for a brother."

"You didn't desert him."

"I didn't help him either."

Her thumb brushed a line along my knuckle. "You carry too much."

"Better me than anyone else."

She didn't argue. Just whispered, "You deserved better, too."

That—somehow—landed hard. And I didn't know what to do with it.

Ava shifted, just a little, her head resting against my shoulder like she was testing the waters. I didn't move. Not because I didn't want to but because if I did, I might pull her all the way in. I didn't know what that meant. What any of this meant. Not yet. Not here.

Her hand found mine beneath the blanket. Small fingers, ice-cold but steady. She didn't grip, just laid it there like a question. My heart stuttered.

"You're not as much of a hardass as you pretend," she said, voice a warm breath against my neck.

"Don't spread that around," I muttered.

She chuckled, the sound soft and scratchy from cold and exhaustion. I felt the curve of her cheek against my chest. Every nerve ending hummed with the sensation that this was somehow right, good. Even though I didn't deserve either.

"You ever think about what happens after this?" she asked.

I swallowed. "Survival comes first."

"That wasn't an answer."

"Wasn't meant to be."

She didn't press. Just breathed. But the silence felt heavier now. Full of maybes I didn't have names for. I thought about her hair brushing my chin. Her breath warming my collarbone. The strength in her, wrapped in sharp edges and dry wit. The way she kept getting up, kept going, even when everything hurt. I thought about how easy it would be to let myself want her. But easy never lasted.

So, I said nothing. Because if I said one thing, I might not stop. And right now, my job was to keep her alive. Not fall for her while I was doing it.

I felt it before I heard it, that low, irregular buzz of dying tech. The radio.

I shifted just enough to reach into the pack, careful not to jostle Ava too much. She stirred anyway, lifting her head as I pulled the device into the sliver of light leaking through a tear in the blind. It was still there. Faint red light blinked like a pulse on the edge of death.

"Please," I muttered. "Just give me something."

I twisted the dial slowly, pressing the speaker to my ear. For a second, one perfect, impossible second, a voice.

"...Bravo...hold...repeat..." Then static. Then silence.

Ava sat bolt upright beside me. "Was that—was that real?"

"Could've been interference," I said, voice clipped. "Could've been anything."

"But it wasn't nothing." Her eyes were wide, alive with something I hadn't seen in her since the crash. Hope. "They have to be nearby."

"Or someone else is," I cautioned. I was already running scenarios: how far the signal could travel, if it was local or long-range, if they were calling out to us or to someone else.

She grabbed my wrist. "We're not alone."

Her voice wasn't panicked. It was not even afraid. It was certain. And I believed her. Not because the radio confirmed it. But because I'd been feeling it too. A prickle at the base of my neck. A tightening in my gut that said the woods weren't as empty as they pretended to be. I just hoped that sensation wasn't from Lev's followers.

I tucked the radio back into the pack, zipped it half-closed for speed.

"We move at dawn," I said. "But we sleep light."

Ava nodded. "We don't stop now."

No. We didn't. Not with something out there. Waiting. Watching. Listening.

Snap.

Not a bird. Not snow. Wood under weight.

Ava stiffened beside me. I already had my gun out, safety off. I lifted a hand. *Wait.* Another crack. Closer this time.

She shook her head and mouthed, *"Not the wind."*

I nodded. Definitely not.

I shoved the pack into her hands and pressed her gently down behind me next to the crumpled wall of the hunting blind. She hunkered into the shadows without a sound. She was getting good at that.

Another sound. Breath? A footfall? It was muffled, padded like boots in snow, but the cadence was unmistakable.

Someone was moving through the trees.

Tracking us.

I rose slowly to a crouch, back pressed to the blind's support beam, every nerve firing like a tripwire. My heart thudded in rhythm with the wind. I didn't even blink.

The radio flickered again.

"...copy...hostiles in—"

Dead.

"Shit," I hissed afraid the sound had carried. Afraid we'd lost our only source of communication.

Ava's hand found mine in the dark. Tight. Grounding.

She leaned in close, breath brushing my cheek. "We have to run."

"No." I shook my head. "Too exposed."

"Then what?"

I scanned the trees. Too late for backtracking. We were on a slope, and above us the ridge rose steep and jagged. Below? Open. Exposed.

Unless—

"There." I pointed toward a narrow game trail veering down into the ravine. Steep, slick, maybe a hundred-foot drop on one side, but tree cover. Shadows. A chance.

"We slide," I whispered. "We don't fall."

She didn't question it.

We moved.

Just as another step broke behind us, closer than it should be. A shape emerged in the gloom. Masked. Armed.

I yanked Ava with me, and we plunged into the dark.

Feet skidding. Snow flying. Branches clawing.

No turning back.

No one there to save us if we fell.

Just the wild and whatever came next.

Survival Lessons

Gavin Henderson

I led us uphill, carving a trail through the snow crust as fast as I could move. The trees thinned the higher we went, but every gust of wind felt like a whisper from the danger below. The voices from earlier were gone. But that didn't mean we were safe. They had spotted us. They knew exactly where we were. And they were close.

Behind me, Ava's boots crunched against the icy path, her breathing a little too quick, a little too loud. I paused behind a large boulder half-buried in the drift and signaled a stop with one raised hand. She didn't complain, just leaned into the rock and exhaled, her breath fogging in the frigid air. I turned and studied her for a beat. She was winded but alert. Her sharp green eyes locked on me, waiting.

"Check your six," I murmured.

She glanced behind her, then lifted an eyebrow. "Clear. Unless a squirrel wants to mug me."

I didn't smile, but I was tempted. She had spunk even now. Reaching into my coat, I pulled out the laminated fragment of a topo map and the old compass I salvaged from the co-pilot's vest. I knelt, spreading the paper over my knee while Ava moved beside me, curious.

"You want to survive out here, you've got to start paying attention to terrain," I said, tracing a gloved finger over a faint line. "See this ridgeline? That's our best chance for drone contact. We'll have open sky and a high elevation."

She leaned closer. "What's that squiggle?"

"Elevation markers."

She snorted. "Looks like a drunk earthworm."

"Then let the worm guide you," I deadpanned. "Slope angle matters. Shade, wind direction. Shelter options. You read the land like you'd read vitals."

She tilted her head. "So, this is your survival TED Talk?"

I glanced at her. "You want to live, sunshine, shut up and learn."

That earned me a grin, quick, bright, defiant. A flash of warmth in this frozen hellscape. And just like that, I felt too much all at once. She was more than a mission. And I was one wrong look away from forgetting why that was dangerous, maybe fatal.

We pushed forward, hugging the slope. The snow was packed tighter along what used to be a game trail, barely visible beneath a layer of frost. A few broken branches and a faint indentation in the powder were all I needed to identify it. A shortcut northeast, if it held.

"Deer used to run this," I said, motioning to the faint track. "Cuts our climb by at least an hour."

Ava nodded and followed, boots crunching noisily. She was trying, really trying, but every third step she slipped. Her footing was off. Too much heel, not enough flat.

I slowed and glanced back. "Stop."

She did, stiffening. "What?"

"Come here."

She raised an eyebrow but stepped closer. I moved behind her, keeping it clinical in my head, but the second I was near, her heat slammed into me. I reached around her hips, adjusting the angle of her stance, then slid my palms over her waist to shift her balance forward.

"Distribute your weight evenly. Walk flat-footed. Quiet. Controlled." My voice was steady. My pulse sure wasn't.

She stiffened when my fingers grazed the hem of her jacket. Then, just for a second, she relaxed into it. Into me.

"Better?" I asked, voice low near her ear.

She didn't answer at first. Her breath hitched. Then: "I was doing fine."

"You were loud enough to wake a bear from its winter sleep."

"Maybe I wanted its warm den."

That pulled a short, surprised laugh from my chest. It was dangerous, this banter. Too much fire under too much pressure. I stepped back. Fast. Before I forgot why I couldn't touch her again. That there were men with guns too close on our tails. Before I decided I really wanted to. I pulled the compass from my jacket and flipped it open, the needle quivering as it steadied north.

"Your turn," I said, holding it out.

Ava blinked at me like I'd handed her a live grenade. "You want me to lead?"

"You've been paying attention. Let's see if it stuck."

She hesitated, looking down at the compass like it was going to bite her. "What if I get us lost? What if I walk us right into a ravine?"

"Then I'll haunt you," I deadpanned.

That earned a short laugh, sharp and surprised. The kind that slipped past defenses before she could stop it. She snatched the compass from my palm.

"Fine. But if I die, I'm blaming you."

"Fair."

She studied the terrain, then pointed northeast toward a gentler incline that hugged the tree line. "That way?"

"Looks solid."

We started moving, her in front, checking her footing with a new caution. The wind was at our backs now, pushing us forward like even nature wanted us off this mountain. Not as much as I did. I hung back just a step, watching her. Not for protection this time. For admiration. Her stubbornness. Her sharp eyes. The way she didn't whine when her injury flared. She was all steel beneath the softness.

"You're good at this," I said without thinking.

She glanced back, surprised. "Yeah?"

"You read the slope. Chose cover. You're learning fast."

She grinned, quick and sly. "I had a good teacher."

I didn't smile, but something inside me shifted, warmed me. Because it meant something. Because she meant something. We had become a team out here and I didn't want that to end.

We stopped at a break in the trees. The sun had dipped behind the ridgeline, casting the forest in that cold, gray hush that came before full dark. Ava pulled out the canteen and took a sip before handing it to me.

"You didn't say how he died," she said suddenly.

I paused, cap halfway twisted. "Who?"

"Your brother."

I lowered the bottle. The cold didn't bother me much. Her question did.

"He got caught up in something he didn't understand," I said. "Trusted the wrong people."

Ava sat down on a snow-covered rock, quiet. Waiting.

I forced the words out. "He was idealistic. Always thought he could fix things. Make things right. Lev saw that. Used him."

"Used him how?"

I shook my head. "Doesn't matter. What matters is I wasn't there. I should've seen it coming. I didn't."

Silence again. Then she whispered, "I'm sorry I left him."

I looked carefully at her.

"You're not responsible for what he became," I said, voice low. "He made his choices. But... I appreciate you saying that."

She nodded, eyes glossy but clear. "He wasn't always cruel. There were times when—before the addiction, before everything—I thought I saw something decent in him."

"You probably did since you did marry him," I said. "Doesn't mean you owed him your life."

Her gaze lifted to mine. There was something raw in it. Real. For a second, everything else faded, the mountain, the cold, the men hunting us. And I was just a man, sitting in the snow with a woman who saw right through me.

We'd barely gone fifty yards from our last stop when I heard it, Ava's sharp yelp and the thud of her body hitting the snow.

I spun around. "Ava!"

She was sitting on her ass in a patch of slick, packed ice, her leg twisted awkwardly under her.

"I'm fine," she said quickly, wincing as she tried to untangle herself. "Just... hate this stupid mountain."

I was already beside her, crouching. "Let me see."

She waved me off but then huffed, defeated. "It's not broken. Just bruised. Like the rest of me."

I offered a hand. She took it with a grunt, and I hauled her upright. Her hand lingered in mine. Neither of us let go right away.

"Sure you're okay?" I asked again, quieter now.

"No. I'm tired. I'm freezing. I'm packing guilt like it's my carry-on bag. And I really do hate this mountain." She said it like a confession and a dare at once.

I actually laughed. "Sounds like you're human."

She narrowed her eyes. "I was hoping for superhuman by now."

"Not yet," I said. "But you're getting there."

She stepped closer, her fingers still caught in mine. "You say that like you mean it."

"I do."

She looked down at our joined hands, then back at me. "Thanks."

I nodded, reluctant to break the moment but knowing we had to keep moving. We started walking again, side by side. No more distance than necessary. But every inch closer than before.

We reached a rise. It was just a bare crest of jagged rock and wind-scoured ice that opened to a narrow plateau. One wrong move and we would be silhouetted against the snow like easy targets.

I raised a fist, signaling stop, and gestured to a fallen tree partially buried beneath frost. Shelter. Temporary, but it'd have to do. It was getting too dark to continue. We slipped, we could end up halfway down the mountain, in a ravine or off a cliff. Ava didn't argue this time. She sunk down onto the trunk like her bones had given out, arms wrapped tight around herself. I crouched a few feet away, scanning the ridgeline, but I felt her watching me.

"Why are you doing this?" she said.

My eyes flicked to hers in confusion. "What?"

"Risking your life. For me." Her voice was low, almost a whisper. "I'm your ex-brother's mistake."

I stiffened. The words were unexpected.

"You're not his anything," I said. "You're you."

She huffed a bitter laugh. "I'm baggage, Gavin. Trauma wrapped in sarcasm."

I shook my head. "No. You're brave. Smart. Stubborn as hell. And I'm not letting you die out here. They'll have to kill me to get to you."

She looked stunned, like she didn't know what to do with that.

"So, you're my bodyguard now?" she said, a ghost of a smile teasing the edge of her cracked lips.

"Damn right."

We stared at each other, breath fogging the air between us. The cold bit, but it was nothing compared to the heat building behind my ribs. I didn't move. Neither did she. But something between us shifted. A weight neither of us could carry alone started to feel just a little bit lighter.

I built a fire in the lee of the rock, just big enough to take the edge off. Low flame, zero smoke, camouflaged with care. My gloves were off, fingers stiff and cracked, but I didn't care. Ava sat close, her shoulder brushed mine, that too-small blanket wrapped around both of us like a fragile truce. She peeled the wrapper off the remaining protein bar and tore it in half before handing me a piece like we were splitting a meal at a five-star bistro.

"Dinner, monsieur," she murmured.

I grunted. "Better not be our last supper."

She leaned her head lightly on my shoulder. Didn't ask. Just did it. My body went taut, tense in the worst and best ways. I let her stay there. I didn't trust myself to find any words. Her fingers found mine beneath the edge of the blanket. Just a graze at first, then a light, deliberate pressure.

"You ever think about after?" she asked.

I glanced down. Her lashes were lowered, breath slow. She wasn't teasing. Not posturing. This was real.

"After?" I echoed.

"After this. The running. The blood. The fear." Her voice was soft. "I don't know. Maybe I want more than just surviving."

My throat worked once before I could speak. "Yeah?"

She nodded, the movement brushing her hair against my neck. I wanted to pull her in. I wanted to taste what this fight had cost us. I wanted to clutch this moment forever. But I didn't. Instead, I let my hand close around hers. Strong. Steady. We sat like that. Quiet. Still. Trying not to want too much, too fast. But every glance, every breath between us, was a promise waiting to ignite.

Ava stiffened beside me. I heard it, too.

A faint hum. At first it blended in and out with the wind, but then it sharpened. It was higher pitched, mechanical. Not a bird. Not a snow squall.

I stood slowly, brushing snow from my legs, head tilting to catch the sound. It was getting closer. The question was: friend or foe?

"A drone?" Ava whispered, rising beside me.

"Maybe." I scanned the tree line; eyes narrowed against the white glare. "Or something worse."

She followed my gaze, shielding her eyes. "Could be Sierra Bravo."

"Could be Lev's people."

My fingers tightened around the flare gun. The red casing was cold, but familiar. It was a signal, a beacon, and a gamble.

"If it's friendly, they'll see this," I muttered, checking the barrel. "If not... well, they already know we're up here."

She didn't argue. Just watched me, lips slightly parted, every muscle tense.

The hum grew louder. Now it echoed off the rock around us. I lifted the flare gun vertical over my head. My finger hovered on the trigger.

Ava whispered, "Gavin—are you sure?"

"No," I said honestly.

And fired.

The flare arced up. The red fire cutting through the gray twilight sky like blood against ice. We both watched it rise... and waited.

Hope in the Hum

Ava Green

The hum pierced the stillness like a blade through cloth.

I jerked my head up, heart already racing. The clouds above were thick with snow flurries, sky the color of wet cement, but there. A flicker. A glint of silver cut through the gray, hovering low, too steady to be a cloud in the wind.

"There!" I gasped, pointing.

The drone shifted instantly, banking hard like it saw the firework and decided we were worth the detour.

"Oh my God..." I breathed, knees going loose. "It's coming."

"Yeah," Gavin muttered, already scanning the horizon. "It saw us."

My pulse jackhammered. "So... what now?"

His tone was grim. "Now we find out if it's bringing help or death."

The drone dipped lower, slicing the air with a mechanical whir that made my skin crawl.

"It's bigger than I expected," I said, breath hitching.

Gavin's eyes narrowed. "Military-grade. No Bravo ID tag. No green stripe, no corporate colors."

My stomach turned. "That's... bad, right?"

He didn't answer with words. Just grabbed my arm, already moving.

"We move. Now!"

I stumbled after him, heart thudding in my ears. My legs felt like wood, my boots dragging through the snow like I'd forgotten how to run.

"Gavin—" I tried, but the panic was rising fast and hot in my chest. I couldn't breathe. I couldn't—

"Look at me." He spun, gripping both my shoulders hard. "Breathe. In. Out."

I locked onto his eyes. Steel and storm. Grounding. Real.

"In," he said again, slower. "Out. You've done harder things than this."

Had I? I couldn't remember. Right now, all I felt was the weight of cold and fear and every death I'd ever witnessed flashing behind my eyes.

"Come on, Ava," he said, tugging me along. "Don't let that drone write our ending."

So, I forced myself forward. One foot. Then the other. The way he taught me.

Because whatever was in the sky, it was not here to help. It was hunting. We ran.

Branches slashed at my arms, snow blasted against my cheeks, and my boots kept sliding off roots and rocks I couldn't see. I tripped. Slammed into the base of a tree. The bark scraped my palms through the gloves. My lungs seized like they'd turned to stone. I couldn't breathe. Not just winded—*couldn't*. Everything caved in.

The crash. The bodies. That mother with the baby. The radio. The drone. The explosion. It crashed down like a wave of ice water and grief, and I couldn't stop it.

"I can't—I can't—" I gasped, shaking, trying to crawl to my knees.

Gavin was there in a heartbeat. Dropping down, shielding me with his body, his chest rising and falling fast.

"You're okay," he said, gripping my shoulders, trying to catch my eyes. "Ava. Listen. You're having a panic attack. Not dying. Not alone."

His voice was low but firm. A tether in the storm.

"I—I left them—" My voice was a sob. "That drone, what if it's *them*? What if it's not? I told them to wait, Gavin. I left them to die—"

He cupped my face, both hands strong and gentle all at once. "You did everything you could. You stayed alive. That matters."

"But I—"

"You are *here*." He leaned closer, forehead almost touching mine. "*You are alive. You are not alone.*"

The sob that tore from me didn't feel human. It was pain made into sound. I curled into him, fists clenching his jacket like it was the only thing keeping me tethered to the earth. And maybe it was. I was still trembling, cheek pressed to Gavin's chest, breath catching on every inhale. He didn't move. Didn't speak. Just held me like the storm outside couldn't touch us as long as he stayed between me and the world.

I whispered, "Make it stop."

His hands shifted, one cradling the back of my head, the other smoothing along my spine like he could rub the fear right out of me.

"I don't know what to do with you," he murmured, voice rough against my temple.

"Then don't think," I said.

My fingers fisted in his jacket. I lifted my face. And then his mouth was on mine. It was not soft. Not careful. It was raw, messy, searing. It was a kiss lit by desperation and something else we'd been burying since the crash. Survival turned into fire. I pressed into him, gripping the collar of his coat like I might fall backward into hell without it. His hand slid to my waist, anchoring me. My lips parted on a gasp, and his answer was a groan deep in his throat that made my toes curl inside soaked boots. We were still on the frozen ground. Still hunted. Still bleeding. But none of that mattered.

For one blistering moment, it was just breath and mouth and heat. Snowflakes melted where they landed on our skin. I'm not sure where my heartbeat ended and his began. When we finally broke apart, we were both panting like we had run a mile. I stared at him. He stared back. And I knew this changed everything. Gavin pulled back first, eyes scanning mine like he was trying to take the kiss back and hold onto it at the same time.

"That shouldn't have happened," he said, breath ragged.

I pressed my fingers to my still tingling lips. "Then why did it feel so right?"

He didn't answer right away. Just stared at the sky above the trees like it might have the answer he didn't want to give. His jaw worked silently, clenched tight enough to crack a rock.

"Because we're both running," he finally said. "And this is the first thing that's made sense since the crash."

I wanted to say something clever. Something cool and detached. But I couldn't. All I could think about was how he kissed me like I was the only person alive and how I kissed him like he was the only one who could bring me back to life.

"It wasn't just adrenaline," I said softly.

His eyes snapped to mine. And I saw it. It was everything he was trying not to feel. Hunger. Guilt. Longing so sharp, it could slice through the snow into the bedrock. He didn't speak. Didn't need to.

Then we heard it: the buzzing. It was back. I jerked my head up as the sound swelled overhead. Closer now. It somehow sounded angrier.

Gavin's head tilted toward the tree line. His whole body shifted, from man to protector in a single breath.

"We have to move," he said, voice suddenly clipped and controlled again.

The fire between us was buried, completely gone. But the echo of it still burned in my chest.

We ducked beneath a rocky outcropping, the overhang just deep enough to press our backs against frozen stone. Gavin crouched beside me, watching the sky through the crisscross of skeletal branches.

The drone whirred above us, slower now. Circling.

"It's scanning," he muttered. "Thermal. Maybe facial."

I swallowed hard. "That mean it can see us?"

"Not if we stay low and cold. But it's looking." His tone was clinical, almost bored.

I recognized the voice. It was the one he used when he was scared and trying not to show it. I pulled my coat tighter, curling in on myself, heart hammering like a drum inside a coffin. The drone shifted again, sweeping back over our position. I could feel it. A presence in the air. Like a predator tasting the wind.

"This isn't rescue, is it?" I whispered, already knowing the answer.

Gavin didn't say anything at first. Then: "No. It's confirmation."

I turned toward him. "Of what?"

"That we're still alive." He glanced at me, face grim. "And worth chasing."

A fresh chill crawled down my spine, colder than the snow at my back. I thought of the fire at the crash site, the smoke curling into heaven like a funeral pyre. Erased evidence. Erased people. And now a drone, scanning for survivors not to save but to eliminate.

"We should run," I said.

Gavin shook his head. "We run too soon, it sees movement. We hold. Then we vanish."

His arm pressed against mine. Steady. Warm. I closed my eyes and pretended, just for a second, that this was just another hike. That we were just another couple caught in a snowstorm. The drone shifted again, louder now. Closer.

Tick-tick-tick.

Like a clock winding down.

We laid side-by-side in the shallow dip beneath the overhang, buried under snow-dusted brush Gavin arranged like a makeshift ghillie net. The drone's buzzing had faded to a low murmur in the distance, but neither of us dared move. Snow blanketed the forest like a muted scream. Everything was still, too still. Not even the forest breathed.

I stared up at the stone ledge above us, my breath finally evening out. Every inch of me ached from fear and cold. But my heart... that was the part that wouldn't shut up.

"I kissed you," I whispered, voice so low I was not sure he heard me.

But he did. His head turned slightly, breath visible between us.

"And I'm not sorry."

A pause. Then a slow blink. "That's a first," he said, a dry rasp of humor threading through the tension.

I smiled. Barely. "What, me not apologizing?"

He didn't answer. Not right away. Then: "Neither am I."

His hand shifted under the blanket, knuckles brushing mine, just a graze. But it felt like a fuse being lit. One I was not sure either of us was ready to follow to the end. At least, not here. Not now with death circling overhead.

"We don't get to fall apart right now," he said quietly. "We survive first. Everything else... later."

Later. I wanted to believe there would be a later. The tension in his voice, the ache behind his eyes, they said everything I couldn't. He wanted it too. Wanted *me*. But he was holding the line. For both of us.

"Then let's live long enough for 'later,'" I whispered, threading my pinky through his.

He squeezed once. It was a promise.

A new sound cut through the stillness. Not the drone's buzz. Something higher-pitched. Mechanical. Whining.

Gavin sat up fast. "That's not right."

I followed his gaze skyward. The drone, now hovering lower, adjusted its angle. Something small detached from its undercarriage. It spun, blinking red as it dropped, a deadly firefly.

"Is that—"

"Grenade!" he shouted, lunging for me.

He tackled me just as the device hit the snow twenty feet away.

BOOM.

The forest convulsed. Snow exploded in a blinding wave, a white wall of sound and fury. A tree trunk cracked like a rifle shot. Branches snapped like brittle bones. My ears rung. Heat seared across my scalp. Something sliced past my shoulder, too close.

I hit the ground hard. Pain bloomed everywhere. I couldn't tell if I was bleeding or just stunned. Gavin shielded me as debris rained down, needles, wood, ice. Smoke and snow clouded the air.

"Ava!" he yelled, his voice a distant thunder in my damaged ears. "Can you move?"

I blinked up at him. His face was ash-smeared. Snow clung to his jaw. Blood trickled down from his temple. But he was alive. Alive and braced over me like a human shield.

I nodded, coughing. "Yeah."

Another buzz, closer now. The drone wasn't done.

Gavin grabbed my wrist. "RUN!"

He yanked me upright and we staggered through the drifts, slipping, scrambling, half-blind from smoke and panic. My lungs burned. The world tilted.

But I ran.

Because he said to. Because the sky was dropping death. Because if we stopped now, we didn't get our later.

We disappeared into the trees, shadows swallowed by dropping death.

Tag, You're It

Gavin Henderson

The explosion ripped through the silence like a goddamn thunderclap. Snow blasted into the air, bark sprayed like shrapnel, and the heat bit across my cheek even through the bitter cold.

I didn't think. I moved. We were in a combat zone now.

The boom rung in my ears like a tuning fork jammed in my skull. Ava groaned beneath me, and for one terrifying second, I thought she was hurt, really hurt. I shifted off her just enough to check her face. Her eyes were open, unfocused but blinking.

"You good?" I yelled over the ringing.

"I think so," she gasped, blinking hard. "That was not Sierra Bravo."

"No shit." I helped her upright, keeping low. My hands did a fast sweep. No blood. No obvious trauma. She was lucky.

We were not going to stay lucky.

Smoke lingered like fog. A nearby tree leaned at a crooked angle, blackened and cracked at the trunk. Flames bloomed. The impact radius was close but not direct. That drone had a payload and dropped it like a message.

I slung my arm around Ava's waist to keep her moving, biting back the pain thudding through my shoulder. My body was screaming in protest, but pain was not the problem. Hesitation was. They had too close of a fix on our position. And one grenade could mean another.

"We've gotta move," I said, eyes darting upward.

The drone hummed somewhere above the treetops, circling like a vulture. I ejected the empty shell from the flare gun and shoved it back in my pack. Useless now. I drew my sidearm, cold steel, reassuring weight, and checked the chamber. One bullet loaded. One in my pocket.

"Two shots," I muttered. "Better make 'em count."

I spotted the bastard just beyond the break in the trees. It was a sleek black drone, military-grade, not some backwoods rigged-up toy. It was not firing again. Not yet. But it was not retreating either.

"It's hovering," Ava said behind me, voice tight. "Why isn't it attacking?"

"They don't need to," I growled.

It was watching. Steady. Calculating. A green pulse blinked from the undercarriage, steady, like a heartbeat. Or a beacon.

Ava shifted beside me and muttered something creative under her breath.

I raised my weapon instinctively but held fire. No point. The drone was out of reach, and the bullet was too valuable to waste.

"They tagged us," I realized aloud. "That blinking? Transponder. Passive tracking. We're lit up like a goddamn signal fire."

Her jaw clenched. "So, we're... what? Prey?"

I nodded shortly.

A beat of silence. Then she said: "How do we lose it?"

"We run."

"Of course we do," she muttered, exhaling hard as I grabbed her hand and tugged her back into the brush.

The drone didn't follow, but it didn't need to. It already did its job. The hunt was officially on.

We crashed through underbrush like animals, feral, hunted, and too cold to care about anything but momentum. Every step jarred my spine. My ribs screamed. The ice underfoot was a damn trap. The trees were too thin for cover. But we kept going.

Behind us, the drone's hum faded. The tag had done its work. They didn't need eyes now. Just the signal.

"Watch your footing!" I barked, hauling Ava up the side of a boulder slick with frost.

She scrambled after me, nearly slipping again.

"You okay?" I asked, not letting her answer with silence.

"I'm gonna murder that drone with a butter knife," she panted.

I huffed, almost a laugh, almost. "Good. Hate keeps you warm."

"So does adrenaline."

"Then let's keep yours pumping."

Crunching foot falls echoed behind us. It was faint, distant, but wrong. They were closing in.

"Left," I said, yanking her into a gully covered in wind-fallen branches. She stumbled once, but I steadied her.

The wind howled through the trees like it was warning us. Maybe it was.

"Do not stop," I growled. "If we stop, we die."

She didn't argue but maybe she lacked the breath to do it. She ran. And I followed. We reached a break in the trees, and the ground just dropped away. A ravine. It was steep, narrow, slick with ice and shadow. I recognized this path. Trained on it during recon runs back when we used this part of the Rockies for SERE exercises. We called it the "Devil's Gullet."

"This is the fastest way to lose a tail," I told her. "But it's rough."

Ava peered down and visibly paled. "What does that mean in non-Gavin-speak?"

I glanced back. No visual yet, but the drone's tag would keep them on our scent.

"It means don't fall."

I went first, bracing my feet, using elbows and knees like a mountain goat. The terrain wasn't forgiving: scree, ice crust, branches that whipped your face if you were dumb enough to let your guard down.

I paused three feet down and held up a hand. "Your turn."

She lowered herself onto the slope, shaky but game. Her boots skidded, and I lunged, grabbed her by the waist just before she lost control and started sliding. Our eyes locked. Her breathing was ragged. So was mine.

"Told you," I murmured.

"You're enjoying this," she fired back, sharp and breathless.

"You'd know if I was enjoying myself."

The look she gave me, wary, wide-eyed, a flash of heat under all that fear, hit me unawares. I released her and kept moving. Because one more second of that and I'd forget the mission and the men after us entirely. We wedged ourselves into a cleft between two slabs of stone, the overhang above just wide enough to block the drone's overhead view. For now.

Ava collapsed beside me, gasping, her bad arm clutched against her side. Her jacket had darkened again. She was bleeding through the bandage. Damn it.

I knelt beside her. "Let me see."

"No time," she croaked. "They're still coming."

"I don't care about the mission," I said. "I care about you."

Her eyes snapped to mine, pupils wide with shock and something deeper. Something raw.

"Say that again," she whispered.

"You heard me."

"Yeah." Her voice cracked. "I really did. And I'm holding you to it."

I reached out, touched her neck, felt her pulse fluttering like a trapped bird. Not just adrenaline, fear, exhaustion, maybe... me.

"I need you to hang on, okay?" I murmured. "You're strong. You've made it this far. Don't check out on me now."

"I'm not," she said. "I just... I didn't expect to care this much."

The drone buzzed faintly above. Distant. Circling.

She leaned into me, just a fraction. But it was enough to shift gravity. I didn't say anything else. I just stayed close. Because if I lost her now, I'd lose more than the op.

We made it to the ridge, barely. I drug us up the final slope, heart pounding, snow caked to my boots, Ava listing against me. The trees thinned out, and for a moment, there was only open air and a drop-off steep enough to give vertigo. Below us: miles of unbroken forest. Too much ground. Not enough cover. A goddamn shooting gallery.

I pulled off my pack and yanked out the radio. I extended the bent antenna as best as I could. The tracker lit up with one red blip, maybe two. Nothing moving.

Ava sat beside me, hugging her knees. "Tell me that thing works."

"If Sierra Bravo's in range, they'll pick us up," I muttered, twisting the dial. A burst of static. Then silence.

"What's our range?"

I glanced at the cracked screen. "Optimistically? A couple miles. Maybe less."

She didn't flinch. "And realistically?"

"We're shouting into empty air."

I jammed the antenna higher, angled it towards the western horizon, then hit the transmit. "Sierra Bravo, this is Henderson. Code Whiskey-Six. Two survivors, requesting immediate exfil. Hostile pursuit. How copy?"

Nothing.

I tried again. Same dead static.

Ava's hand slipped into mine. "And if they don't answer?"

"Then I get you out anyway." I squeezed back. "The old-fashioned way."

Her eyes shone, not with fear, but with faith. In me. I didn't deserve it, but I held onto it like it was oxygen.

She nodded. "I believe you."

I didn't say thank you. I couldn't. Because the lump in my throat made speech impossible.

Ava's head jerked up, eyes wide. Then I heard it too. Voices. Low, deliberate, foreign. Russian. Another thread of English, barked like a command.

"Shit," I growled, crouching instinctively. "They flanked us."

"How many?" she whispered.

"Too many."

I scanned the tree line. Movement. Shadows peeling from the snow-crusted pines. They were smart, spaced out, using the terrain. Classic pincer tactic. Which meant we had maybe thirty seconds before we were boxed in.

I shoved Ava behind the largest granite outcrop I could find. "You stay here. Low and quiet."

"What are you going to do?" she asked, eyes narrowing.

"Not get us killed."

I pulled my sidearm. One round chambered. One in my pocket. A really bad hand.

She crouched beside me, pale but steady. "Just tell me what to do."

"Don't move unless I say so. You're not trained, and I don't want to lose you to friendly fire."

"That's comforting."

"Distract them if it comes to it. With anything. That mouth of yours? Weapons-grade."

Despite everything, her lips twitched. "You're flirting now?"

"Now? Always." I scanned the ridge again. "But right now, I'd really like it if you didn't die."

"Copy that."

The brush rustled, closer this time. I raised the gun, steadied my breath, and prayed I didn't have to use it. It would pinpoint our location and use half our bullets in one go. The whine returned, high above, cutting through the tree-filtered light like a scalpel.

Ava tensed beside me. "Drone's back."

I tracked it through the canopy. It was lower now. Closer. But different this time.

Then it spoke.

"Zdravstvuy, sestrichka," crackled a thickly accented voice. "I see you."

The blood in my veins turned to ice.

Ava went still. "Lev," she whispered, and the word was more breath than sound.

The drone swooped over the clearing, pivoting midair like a hawk. Its undercarriage flashed. A red light blinked.

"You run well," the voice continued, tone almost amused. "But not well enough. My men are eager to greet you. Again."

A chill lashed up my spine. I raised the gun on instinct, sight trained on the machine. But it veered just out of range, taunting me.

"You should not have left," the voice hummed. "I was not finished with you."

Ava shuddered. I wrapped my free arm around her shoulders, steadying her even as fury clawed at my throat.

"Come on," I murmured. "We need to disappear."

Her voice cracked. "How?"

"Smoke and shadow."

I tucked the gun close, already planning our exit path.

The drone looped overhead again. Watching. Waiting. Marking us for the monster coming next.

Beneath the Stars

Ava Green

We stumbled into a shallow alcove tucked between boulders and a gnarled pine, the roots twisted like frozen fingers trying to hold the world together. Snow clung to the ledge above us, and the wind howled low. It was too soft to cover our tracks, too loud to count as silence. Gavin swept the area with the sidearm before lowering it and nodding me forward. His jaw was clenched so tight I thought it might snap.

I dropped to my knees, breath rattling. The pain in my arm was a steady burn now, no longer sharp, just relentless. My legs trembled from exertion, from adrenaline. From fear. But I was still upright. Mostly.

"No one's shooting," I managed to say, half to myself.

Gavin crouched beside me and cleared a space in the shallow depression, scraping away snow to reveal dry pine needles and brittle twigs. "That'll change," he said. "But not this minute."

He knelt, glancing at the tree line again. "This is as safe as it's going to get tonight."

I nodded, arms wrapped around my knees. The stars glittered like tiny glass shards on a dark highway overhead, distant and cold. "Then let's make it count."

He looked at me, a flicker of something in his eyes I couldn't name. Or maybe I just didn't want to name it yet. Not when everything still hurt this much. Not when the world still wanted us dead. But tonight, there was no screaming. No gunfire. Just frost, breath, stars. A pause. And him.

Gavin got a fire going with the kind of focus that said he'd built a thousand of them and broken more than that. The flame flickered to life in a whisper, small and steady, tucked behind a natural wall of stone and root. He used pine needles, strips of bark, a handful of twigs. Efficient. Controlled. Just like him.

Warmth seeped toward me in slow waves. I edged closer, holding my frozen hands near it, watching them tremble. Not from the cold anymore. He shrugged off his outer jacket and without a word draped it around my shoulders. It smelled like pine, gunpowder, and something deeper, salt and smoke and man. Him.

"You're shivering," he said, settling beside me on the pine needles, close but not touching.

"I'm always shivering around you," I murmured, half-smiling.

That got his attention. He turned toward me fully, gaze sweeping my face like he's trying to read between the lines. Trying to decide if I meant it. If he wanted to mean it back.

"Don't say things like that unless you mean them," he finally said quietly, the words low and rough.

I met his gaze. "Who says I don't?"

His jaw flexed. His hand twitched at his side like he was fighting the urge to reach for something. Maybe me. But he didn't look away. Neither did I but I broke first. I stared into the fire hoping it might have answers. The flames licked upward, orange tongues against a black sky, and I wondered how something so small could fight off so much dark.

"My whole life," I said slowly, "I've been surviving. For Emma. For... everyone but me."

Gavin didn't interrupt. He just watched, letting me get it out. Letting me decide if I was brave enough to go further.

"I always told myself I didn't need anything. Helped my mom get through dad's death. Helped raise Emma and kept her from self-destructing. Got through school. Jumped into a bad marriage and then gave up on love. Concentrated on work. Didn't need love or help. Just get through, right?" I shook my head, blinking hard. "Then you showed up. With your gravel voice and stupidly broad shoulders and... walls around your heart like barbed wire."

That earned a faint huff from him. It wasn't quite a laugh.

"And now I feel things I shouldn't," I admitted. My voice dropped. "Like I want to live for me. With you."

His throat worked like he's trying to swallow something sharp. "You don't mean that."

I turned to face him, eyes burning. "I do. And I think you do too."

Gavin looked like I reached inside him and ripped something loose. But he didn't run. Didn't deflect with a joke or a grumble or a tactical plan. He just... stayed. And in the silence between us, the truth hung there. Thick. Raw. Waiting.

He leaned in slowly, like I'm a wire he's afraid to trip. His breath brushed my cheek, warm despite the freezing air. Our knees touched. Then our thighs. A live current zinged through me. His hand came up to my jaw, callused, steady, rough in a way that made me shiver for a new reason.

"I can't do this halfway, Ava," he murmured. "I don't know how."

"Then don't," I whispered. "Do it all the way."

His lips grazed mine. Barely there. Testing. Tasting. Then he kissed me like he meant it. It was not slow. It was not polite. It was hunger. Pent-up need and the emotions we'd been denying since that crash split our worlds open.

I grabbed his shirt and tugged him closer until there was no space left. His other hand fisted in my hair. The world narrowed to breath and skin and fire. All the reasons we shouldn't do this fell away, stripped by heat and heartbeat and want.

Snowflakes melted against my neck. My pulse roared louder than the wind.

And Gavin Henderson kissed me like I was the last real thing on Earth.

It started with a kiss. But it didn't stop there. That first time might have been an accident, but this was a deliberate choice. Clothes fell away—not tossed, but peeled—slow, reverent, aching with the weight of what this meant. Every touch was a confession. Every breath, a surrender. My wounded arm was forgotten as I traced the planes of his chest, the scars, the heat beneath his skin.

He worshiped me like I was the miracle, and he was the sinner. Like he didn't deserve this, but he was not strong enough to resist. I gave him everything. Not just my body. My trust. My fear. My hunger.

His mouth found my throat. My pulse. My hip. He said nothing, but the way he moved, careful, patient, then desperate, told me more than words ever could. It was not perfect. It was real. Urgent. Messy. Breathless. I felt safe in a way I hadn't in years.

His hard body merging with my softness. I melted under him, arcing into his demanding thrusts as his heated passion rose higher than the pines around us.

"Don't stop." I begged, hoping this sensation was sending me somewhere I had read about.

"Never." Gavin breathed latching onto my lips, his tongue invading my mouth.

I had to lean away to gasp for air as my body exploded. I clutched his back riding waves of shuddering euphoria hardly realizing that he was climaxing as well,

"Oh God." I cried, feeling tears, "Oh Gavin. That's never happened."

"I'm sorry." He said raising up on his forearms to look into my face and comb back my hair.

"I'm not!" I said grinning. "I meant that it hadn't happened before. And I'm blaming you."

"I can handle it." he said smiling and laid down beside me.

We laid tangled in his coat and the last glow of the fire, his arms around me, his hand tracing slow circles on my spine. I pressed my ear to his chest and heard the steady beat of something new. Us.

I traced a long scar over Gavin's ribs with one fingertip, slow and wondering. The fire had gone to embers, but his body was a furnace beside me, steady, grounded. I'd never known stillness like this. Not in the chaos of the hospital. Not in the storm of the last few days. Only now, in the wreckage of everything, did I feel whole.

"How long have you been this broken?" I asked, my voice barely more than a whisper against his skin.

His breath caught, but he didn't flinch. "Since the war. Since my brother died. Since I stopped believing I could be anything but a weapon."

I rested my hand flat against his chest, feeling the beat beneath my palm. "You're more than that."

He turned toward me, eyes shadowed but unguarded. "You make me want to be."

I shifted closer, my forehead pressing to his. "Good. Because I'm not done with you yet."

He didn't answer. He just pulled me tighter, and we laid there like that, two broken people trying to remember what it meant to feel whole.

The silence shattered with a faint *beep*. Just once. Then again.

Gavin tensed beside me, reaching across the alcove like a soldier snapped to life. He grabbed his satchel, unzipped it fast and careful.

"What is it?" I asked, sitting up, heart rising from the ashes.

He pulled out the compact radio unit, eyes flicking over the tiny screen. "The tracker. It just pinged."

Adrenaline flooded my veins like a second heartbeat. "Bravo?"

"Maybe," he muttered, turning the dial. "Or someone piggyback-ing the signal. But we're in range of something."

The static crackled. Then—words.

"...rescue...coordinates...hold..."

It was barely audible, broken by static and distance, but it was there.

I scrambled for my clothes, heart in my throat. My fingers fumbled the buttons of my jacket. "Is it real?"

Gavin was already halfway dressed, jaw clenched as he scanned the tree line. "We're about to find out."

Gavin was still fiddling with the frequency when a soft glow cut through the trees.

Then another. Moving. Closer.

I froze. "Those aren't drone lights."

"No." He was already grabbed the gun, voice low and hard. "Those are boots on the ground."

"Bravo?" I whispered, hope sparking but already dying.

A shout echoed through the dark, harsh, guttural. Russian.

"Shit," Gavin breathed, spinning to me.

The stars vanished behind his shoulders as he pulled me close, lips brushing my ear.

"Time to run. Again."

Hunted

Gavin Henderson

The warmth of her skin still clung to my fingertips. The scent of pine smoke and her hair lingered in the space between my ribs. But it all shattered with the sharp *crack* of brush snapping just beyond the tree line.

I was on my feet before thought caught up, shoving gear into my pack, sliding my pistol into the coat, eyes scanning the trees with cold calculation. Ava was already yanking on her boots, hair wild, mouth parted as she listened to the growing murmur of voices threading through the snow-heavy woods.

"We have to move. Now," I said, not quite a whisper but too low to echo.

Her gaze met mine. Wide, alert, no hesitation. "We should've had longer."

I swallowed the ache that crawled up my throat. I grabbed her hand and led the way, boots crunching through snow crust, heart thundering against bruised ribs. Every tree seemed to hide a threat. Every shadow might bleed gunfire. I angled us northeast, deeper into terrain I had once trained on. It was a warren of gullies and switchbacks perfect for losing a tail. Behind us, voices sharpened. Grit in my gut. Love behind my ribs. And danger coming fast.

Branches whipped across my arms as I pushed through a pine thicket. Ava was right behind me, her breath short, sharp. I should be focused on escape, on our perimeter, on the half-dozen ways this could go sideways. But all I could think about was her. Bare skin against mine, the soft way she'd whispered my name, the heat of her mouth beneath the stars. The way she'd looked at me like I wasn't just a weapon. Like I was a man. I should've stopped it. Should've never started it.

"I should never have let you..." I started as guilt scraped my throat raw.

"Don't." Her voice sliced through the branches like a blade. "I can feel the guilt radiating off you like a goddamn space heater."

I half-turned but kept moving. "You were vulnerable."

"So were you."

"Exactly."

She stopped. Grabbed my arm, forced me to face her. Her cheeks were flushed with more than the cold. It was fury. "What we did wasn't weakness, Gavin. That wasn't some tactical mistake. That was two people grabbing something real before it gets blown away."

My jaw tightened. I didn't respond but I didn't pull away either. Didn't move a muscle as her hand lingered on my sleeve. She saw it. Felt it. Because she was saying what I wanted to believe. And then she let go.

"Come on," she muttered, pushing past me.

I followed, pulse hammering. Regret wasn't going to keep her alive. But neither was denying what was already inside me.

The terrain shifted. Snow gave way to packed ice and fractured rock as I led us down a narrow pass carved into the mountainside. The walls pressed in, jagged and close, towering above like a jaw about to snap shut. Sunlight didn't reach this far down. Just shadows. Deep ones.

Ava stumbled behind me, her boots crunching on gravel and frost. "Where the hell are we?"

"Ravine," I muttered. "Natural cover. Hard to spot from above."

"Unless you're already down here."

"Exactly."

I crouched, fingers brushing the ground. Two sets of boot prints, fresh, heavy, wrong. Not ours. I straightened slowly, every muscle tightening. "We're being herded."

Ava stiffened. "Does that mean what I think it does?"

I scanned the ridgeline, eyes narrowing. "It means they're flanking us. Closing the exits. Driving us into a trap."

Ava swallowed hard. "And where's the trap?"

I met her eyes. Grim. Certain. "Someplace we die."

She didn't flinch. Just reached out and grabbed my hand, fingers lacing with mine like a lifeline.

"We're not dying today," she said firmly.

"No," I agreed. "We're not."

But the air felt heavier. The ravine colder. And somewhere in the stillness, something shifted. A breath seemingly held by the mountain itself.

We pressed forward through brittle underbrush and narrow switchbacks. I led with long, deliberate strides, until my steps hitched. Just once. But Ava caught it. I tried to shake it off, adjusting my grip on the sidearm and scanning for cover. Every breath scraped like glass in my lungs. The seeping warmth beneath my coat told me the wound had opened again, too much movement, not enough healing time.

"Stop," Ava said behind me.

"I'm fine."

She sped up until she was in front of me, blocking the narrow path. "You're bleeding again."

"It's nothing," I growled, already trying to edge past.

She didn't move. "Everything with you is 'nothing' until you pass out on me. Sit."

"Ava—"

She shoved me, lightly, but firm enough that I sat back against a snow-dusted boulder. "Sixty seconds. Give me that much or I'll scream and let the bastards find us."

I had to give her a grudging smirk, but I didn't argue. I watched as she tore a strip from her shirt, already frayed and bloodstained, and crouched in front of me.

"You should save that," I said quietly.

"For what? A fashion emergency?"

She peeled back the fabric at my waist and pressed the makeshift bandage to the wound. Her fingers were like ice but surprisingly gentle. Strong.

"That's what I'm here for," she murmured. "Not just heat-of-the-moment sex. Not just a target to guard."

My gaze dropped to her hands, then lifted to her face. I didn't know what to say. But something cracked inside me.

"I don't want to lose you," I said, the words barely audible.

Ava met my eyes, steady and unflinching. "Then don't."

And for the first time, I let myself believe that might be possible. We moved again, one step ahead of death.

The climb steepened. Slick ice was layered over snow, turning the hill into a vertical death trap. I let Ava lead now; so, I could watch her footing, my body coiled tight in case she fell. Every few yards, I glanced behind us, scanning for movement. Every shadow could hold a rifle.

Every gust of wind sounded like a breath. I was running out of time. Out of ammo. Out of options.

Ava slipped. I lunged forward, catching her under the arms before she could slide down the slope. Our bodies pressed tight against the incline, breath tangled, hearts racing.

"You're the worst patient I've ever had," she huffed, clinging to my forearm.

I smirked, voice low. "And you're the most stubborn civilian I've ever tried to protect."

Our noses were inches apart. Her lashes sparkled with frost. Her lips were cracked but curved. For one breathless second, the world went still. No guns. No drones. No death. Just this. Our shared heart-beat. But then—

Snap.

A twig. Sharp. Close. Too damn close.

I shoved her upward, urgency surging. "Go," I growled. "Now."

And the crystalline moment, fragile, beautiful, was gone.

We found a tiny sanctuary just before dusk, a narrow fissure in the rock wall, half-hidden by snow and gnarled roots. I brushed the entrance clear with a gloved hand.

"In," I said, "Quiet."

Ava ducked in first, grunting as she scraped her knee against jagged stone. I squeezed in behind her, sealing the opening with a low-hanging branch. Inside, the world was muffled. Cold. Still. I knew this cave. Used it once, years ago, on recon training. Back then, it felt like a tomb. It still did. Cramped and damp, barely wide enough to lay flat. But it would do.

Ava collapsed onto the rocky floor, her body shivering uncontrollably. "Well," she whispered, voice shaky, "this is cozy."

I dropped my pack, peeled off my outer layer, and draped it over her. Then I went to work, no fire, just insulation. I pulled emergency foil from the med kit, created a blanket out of spare clothes, and stacked our packs as a barricade against the entrance.

Ava leaned her head against my shoulder. "Do you think they know we're close?"

I didn't answer at first. Just listened. The wind moaned beyond the rock. And then, faint but unmistakable, *crunch*. Footsteps on snow. Not far. And then a sweep of light, flashlight beams, cut across the far ridge beyond the mouth of the cave.

I whispered, "I don't think. I know."

Too close.

We sat in silence. Ava's body pressed against mine. Her breathing slow now, the kind that comes with trust or exhaustion. I didn't move. I didn't dare. One hand rested lightly on the pistol at my side. The other was wrapped around her shoulders, holding her like she was something I was afraid to lose. Because she was. Not a mission. Not an assignment. Not just some innocent civilian caught in the crossfire. She was *mine*. The sudden thought lodged in my chest like a bullet.

It'd been years since I let myself want anything. Really *want*. Not just survival. Not just a job. But *her*. Every sharp, stubborn, brilliant part of her. The way she challenged me. The way she touched me like I was not dangerous. The way she *saw* me long before I saw myself.

"I don't deserve this," I breathed out, so quiet it felt like confession.

Ava stirred against me. "Then earn it," she murmured. Her words landed soft, but they landed deep.

I went still. Maybe... just maybe... I could convince myself I could. *Crunch.*

The unmistakable sound of boots in snow snapped my body into motion. I tightened my grip around Ava and covered her mouth gently, eyes scanning the narrow cave opening. Flashlights bobbed outside, bright beams slicing through the dark like searchlights.

"They're here," I whispered, barely audible over the rising wind.

Ava's eyes widened. She nodded, silent.

Muffled voices drifted in, Russian and English mixed. Calm. Confident. Predatory. They were too damn close. I pulled her deeper into the stone crevice, careful not to make even a breath of sound. I crouched, body between her and the entrance, pistol raised. One bullet in the chamber. One in my pocket. That's it.

Ava leaned in, whispering in my ear so faintly I could barely catch it. "Do we fight?"

I shook my head. "We wait. If they don't see us, we live."

She nodded but I could feel her trembling against me.

Then a voice called out. It was clear, accented, and far too familiar. "Ava..."

It echoed through the trees like a taunt.

"I know you're near," Lev's voice purred. "Let's talk."

My heart pounded like a drum in my chest. Ava went rigid beside me.

The flashlight beam swept just feet from the cave mouth. I didn't move. Didn't breathe. Neither did she. But Lev's voice kept coming.

"I am not angry," he said, like it was a joke. "You've led me on quite the chase. But we both know how this ends."

The light paused. Then moved on. I exhaled, just a sliver. We hadn't been seen. Not yet. But we were surrounded. And Lev never bluffed.

Heat in the Shadows

Ava Green

"Don't move," Gavin whispered. "He's right outside."

I didn't. My body had forgotten how. The only thing that moved was my heart, thudding so loud in my ears I wondered if it echoed outside the cave. Lev's voice slid through the air like a blade, smooth and cruel.

"You think she loves you, Gavin? She barely knows you."

My fingers twitched, and Gavin's hand found mine in the dark, anchoring me. That touch said everything. *I'm here. I've got you.* I pressed my forehead to his shoulder, eyes squeezed shut, willing the nightmare to pass. We waited, silent and still, while Lev's words twisted through the wind like poison. Then, finally, his voice faded, swallowed by distance and trees.

Gavin exhaled slowly. "They're gone. For now. You're freezing."

"So warm me up."

The tension broke, but the cold rushed in to take its place. My limbs shivered uncontrollably now that adrenaline had abandoned me. My teeth chattered. Gavin didn't hesitate. He pulled me into his lap, wrapping both arms and his outer coat around me.

"We'll have to stay close," he murmured. "Conserve heat."

"You always need an excuse to touch me?"

"I need a hundred excuses," he replied, voice rough. "But I'll take one."

The cave smelled of damp earth and pine, a claustrophobic sanctuary carved into the mountainside. Outside, the wind howled, carrying the distant, menacing murmur of voices. Gavin's hand tightened around mine, his calloused fingers a silent reassurance. We hadn't spoken in normal voices in what felt like hours, our breaths synchronized in the darkness, each sound measured, each movement deliberate. The gangsters were nearby. I could still hear their laughter, their boots crunching against the gravel, their voices a guttural reminder of the danger we were in.

Gavin's thumb brushed the back of my hand, a small gesture that spoke volumes. I turned to him, my eyes adjusting to the dim light filtering through the cave's entrance. His face was a study in tension. His jaw was clenched, his steely blue eyes scanning the shadows as if he could will the threat away. Even in this moment, he was the protector, the soldier, the man who'd vowed to keep me safe. But I saw something else in his gaze, a vulnerability he rarely let surface. It was the same look I'd seen when he'd held me after we'd made love for the first time, when the weight of his past had softened in the curve of my shoulder.

"We should stay quiet," he whispered, his voice rough, almost hoarse. But his hand didn't let go of mine, and I felt the warmth of his touch seep into my bones.

I nodded, my heart pounding against my ribs. The cave was small, barely large enough for the two of us to sit side by side. My clothes were dirty, torn from our frantic climb up the mountain, and my hair fell in unruly waves around my face. Gavin's rugged attire was no better, his dark shirt stained with sweat and blood. We were a mess, two survivors clinging to each other in the face of uncertainty.

But the uncertainty wasn't just about the gangsters. It was about us. About the way Gavin's touch had awakened something in me, something I'd buried under years of sacrifice and duty. About the way he'd looked at me after I'd had my first orgasm with him, his eyes filled with a tenderness that belied his gruff exterior. He'd seen me—truly seen me—and in that moment, I'd seen him too. Not just the ex-soldier, not just the killer he sometimes feared he was, but the man who was risking everything to protect me.

The tension outside grew, the voices louder now, closer. I felt Gavin's body stiffen beside me, his hand tightening on my thigh, a silent command to stay still. My breath caught in my throat as one of the gangsters laughed, the sound echoing through the cave like a taunt. We were trapped, cornered, and yet, in that moment, all I could think about was him.

Gavin's fingers moved, tracing the line of my jaw, his touch feather-light, almost reverent. "Ava," he murmured, his voice a whisper against my ear. "If... if we get out of this, I—"

I pressed my fingers to his lips, silencing him. "Don't," I said, my voice barely audible. "Just... be here with me. *Now.*"

He hesitated, then nodded, his eyes searching mine. Slowly, he leaned in, his lips brushing mine in a kiss that was both tender and desperate. It was a kiss that said everything he couldn't, a kiss that spoke of fear and hope, of the past and the uncertain future. I melted into him, my hands tangling in his hair, my body pressing against his. The world outside faded, the danger momentarily forgotten as we lost ourselves in each other.

His hands moved down my back, his touch firm yet gentle, as if he were memorizing every curve, every line, just in case there were no more moments. I felt his heartbeat against my chest, steady and strong, a reminder that he was here, that we were alive. My fingers traced the scar on his jaw, the one he'd never spoken of, and I saw the flicker of emotion in his eyes, the gratitude, the acceptance.

"You're safe with me," he whispered, his breath warm against my skin. "Always."

I smiled, a small, tremulous smile, and kissed him again, deeper this time, my tongue tangling with his. His hands moved lower, cupping my hips, pulling me closer until I could feel the hardness of his desire pressing against me.

My pulse quickened, my body responding to his with a hunger that surprised even me.

The sounds outside had vanished, as if the world had paused to let us have this moment. Gavin's hands moved to the waistband of my pants, his touch hesitant, as if he were asking permission. I nodded, my eyes locked on his, and he slid them down my legs, baring me to him. My skin flushed with heat, my breath coming in short gasps as he traced the curve of my thigh, his fingers calloused yet gentle.

"Ava," he murmured, his voice thick with desire. "Tell me to stop. Tell me now."

I shook my head, my hands gripping his shoulders. "Don't stop," I whispered. "Never stop."

He kissed me again, his lips moving down my neck, his breath hot against my skin. His hands explored me, his touch both familiar and new, as if he were discovering me for the first time. I arched into him, my body aching with need, my mind a blur of sensation. The cave, the danger, the fear, it all faded as I lost myself in him. And I desperately needed it all gone for at least a little while.

His fingers found me, slipping between my folds, his touch sure and deliberate. I gasped, my head falling back as he teased me, his thumb brushing against me, his fingers sliding inside me. "Gavin," I moaned, my voice a plea, a surrender.

He smiled against my skin, a smile that was both tender and wicked. "Not yet," he whispered, his fingers moving slower now, drawing out the pleasure until I was trembling, on the edge of something I couldn't name.

And then he was above me, his weight pressing me into the cold ground, his lips claiming mine in a kiss that was fierce and hungry. I wrapped my legs around his waist, my hands gripping his shoulders as he positioned himself at my entrance. His eyes met mine, his expression raw, unguarded.

"Ava," he said, his voice a rasp. "Look at me."

I did, my eyes locking on his, and in that moment, I saw everything, the fear, the desire, the love he couldn't yet name. He thrust into me, slow and deep, his eyes never leaving mine. I gasped, my body tightening around him, my nails digging into his neck as he began to move, his rhythm steady, relentless.

The cave was silent now, the only sound our breaths, our whispered moans, the slickness of our bodies moving together. Gavin's hands gripped my hips, his thrusts growing harder, faster, as if he were trying to fuse us together, to make us one. I met him with every movement, my body arching to meet his, my voice a whispered litany of his name.

"Gavin," I cried, my body tightening, my orgasm building like a storm. "Don't stop, don't—"

He silenced me with a kiss, his lips crushing mine as he thrust deeper, harder, his control shattering as he found his own release. I felt him spill into me, his body trembling, his breath ragged against my skin. My orgasm followed, a wave of pleasure that left me gasping, my body shaking, my heart pounding.

For a moment, we laid there, our bodies still joined, our breathing slowly returning to normal. Gavin's hand brushed my hair back, his eyes filled with a tenderness that made my heart ache.

"Ava," he whispered, his voice hoarse. "If we—"

I pressed my fingers to his lips again, silencing him. "Shh," I said, my voice soft. "We're here. Now. That's all that matters. And it's not an if."

He nodded, his eyes searching mine, and for a moment, we just looked at each other, the silence between us speaking volumes. Outside, the voices had gone making the danger momentarily forgotten. But we both knew it was still there, waiting, lurking in the shadows.

Gavin kissed me one last time, his lips brushing mine in a promise I was afraid to claim. And as we lay there, our bodies entwined, the future uncertain, I knew one thing for sure: whatever happened next, we'd face it together.

I traced the lines of a tattoo just above his heart.

"What's this mean?"

"My unit. Marines."

I lifted my head. "All of you?"

He hesitated. "No."

I pressed a kiss to the ink. "Then it's not just a memory. It's a reminder that you did survive. And you'll survive this too."

"Only if you do."

My fingers curled over his.

"We're a team now. You don't have to carry it alone."

He let the words settle. Like maybe, for the first time, he believed them. Gavin dropped his forehead to mine.

"If anything happens to you..."

"You'll keep going. That's what you do."

"But I don't want to keep going without you."

I cupped his face, fingers trembling but sure.

"Then don't let anything happen to me."

It was childish. Impossible. Reckless. But in this moment, we made the stupid promise anyway.

A burst of static cut through the quiet.

Gavin jolted upright, snatching the radio. I rose with him, breath caught, grabbing clothing. A new voice crackled through, low, amused.

"I see you, Henderson. Cute cave. How long do you think it'll last?"

My stomach flipped as I hissed "What the hell?"

Gavin's face tightened. He slammed the radio against the rock wall, splintering it.

"Signal's compromised."

"They're playing with us."

"They're close," I whispered feeling like the walls had eyes.

"And they want us scared."

Gavin scanned the narrow cave, as if pulling up some mental pictures.

"This tunnel connects to an old chute, a mining drop. Steep, about sixty feet."

I swallowed having a bad feeling I knew what he had in mind. "Is it safe?"

He looked me in the eye. "Absolutely not."

I zipped up my coat. "Then let's go. Because if we stay, we're dead."

For the first time since we met, I was sincerely leading him.

And Gavin? He followed.

Fight or Flight

Gavin Henderson

The sharp rattle of shifting gravel jolted me forward around Ava. I pressed her body to the cave wall. Her eyes flew open, breath hitching, but she nodded, silent and alert. A voice echoed through the stone tunnel. Low. Russian. Ahead of us.

I dropped into a crouch, cold sweat beading at my temples. My knife was already in hand. The glow of a flashlight swept across in front of me. One shadow detached from the beam: a scout, moving quietly, disciplined but cocky.

I met him mid-step. The blade slipped beneath the man's chin, clean and fast. The body folded without a sound. I lowered him to the ground as the flashlight rolled away, beam spinning. But just as I turned to grab Ava, a second man rounded the bend.

No time to hide. No time to think. His gun went off.

Pain exploded in my upper arm. A hot, searing line tore across my tricep as the bullet grazed deep enough to bleed but not stop me. I tackled the man, driving him backward against the cave wall with a grunt. Fist met jaw. Bone cracked. Another twist, another knife strike and silence.

But the shot... that one damn loud shot echoed like an announce-ment in the confines of the cave.

I stumbled as Ava rushed to me, hands on my chest, eyes wide with fear and fury. "You're hit—"

"Later," I gritted out. "We've got more coming."

Ava was already pulling me to my feet, blood slick under her palms. The fight had only started.

The moment we cleared the cave to the back near the mining chute, I stumbled. Ava caught me before I hit the rock wall, my slip a jarring reminder that I was not invincible. Blood darkened the side of my shirt, seeping fast from the fresh wound.

"You're bleeding bad," she whispered, breath frosting the damp air.

"Keep going," I gritted out. But my knees buckled again.

"Nope," she said, voice firm. "I've got this."

She dragged me toward the shadows of a low shelf in the cave, scanning for movement. No voices yet. No footsteps. Just the wind howling down the tunnels like a warning. Ava dropped to her knees beside me, ripping the hem of her undershirt and pressing the fabric hard to my wound.

I hissed but didn't stop her.

"This will hurt," she muttered. "But you'll live."

I watched her work with surprising efficiency, hands firm, move-ments precise. "You're calm," I said through gritted teeth.

"I'm focused and it's what I do, you know." She tied the makeshift bandage tight. "I'm banking my panic for later."

She helped me up, slinging my good arm over her shoulders. We moved again, me leaning heavier than I wanted to. The pain was white-hot, my breath ragged. But it was her voice that anchored me. Soft. Determined. Alive.

"You're not the only one who can lead," Ava said, guiding me deeper into the cave's shadows. "So shut up and follow."

For the first time, I did exactly that.

The cave narrowed the deeper we went. The walls pressing in like two clenched fists. My vision swam with every step, the bandage on my side soaked and sticking. My breathing grew shallower, pain curling around my ribs like barbed wire. But I'd be damned if I gave up. Ava led the way, one hand on the wall, the other gripping my shoulder. Her voice was a whisper against the dark.

"There's a fork ahead. Left curves down."

I nodded, but the cave spun. My boot slipped on loose shale, a grunt escaping before I clamped it down. Ava steadied me, her fingers tight around my wrist.

Then, a flash of light. A beam swept through the tunnel behind us, slow and searching.

I froze, pulling Ava tight against the wall. Footsteps crunched on stone. Voices murmured. Russian. Two of them. One paused just feet away, flashlight painting jagged shadows across the rock.

I shifted, silent as death.

He lunged.

My arm locked around the man's throat, dragging him back into the dark before the flashlight could hit Ava's face. The struggle was short, brutal. A gurgle. A thud.

Ava covered her mouth, eyes wide. I swayed. The motion had cost me. My knees nearly went. She caught me again. Held me up.

"I've got you," she whispered.

I wanted to say thank you. Or sorry. Or something. But there was no time, and I didn't have the energy. We moved, deeper into the dark, the echo of that kill clinging to the walls behind us.

Ava tugged me left at a fork in the tunnel, urgency in her stride. "There's a narrow split coming up," she whispered. "It might still be passable."

I nodded, though every step burned. The cave compressed, ceiling dipping lower. The air grew tight with the scent of damp and dust. My shoulder throbbed like a live wire, and the bandage Ava tied felt like it was made of fire and grit. We reached it, an almost invisible fissure in the rock wall. Ava turned sideways and slipped in first, barely fitting through the jagged crack.

"Come on," she urged, her voice bouncing off stone.

I swore under my breath. The gap was tight, too tight for my frame with gear, but we had no choice. There was no turning back. I forced myself sideways, teeth clenched, dragging the pack by one handle. The rough stone scraped my arms, my injured shoulder screaming with every inch. The narrow crawl stole my breath. Claustrophobia clawed at my throat.

There was a shout behind us. Flashlight beams flared down the corridor we had just left.

I gritted my teeth and shoved through the last of the crevice, tumbling out into a small chamber on the other side. Ava helped pull me up as the tunnel narrowed behind us. We didn't stop. We ran, boots echoing off the walls. The tunnel widened, then sloped upward. It was an incline I dimly remembered from before. A minute later, daylight. We burst through a narrow opening in the rock, lungs seizing from the instant bitter cold and adrenaline. Alive. But barely.

The world outside was blinding. Endless white and deathly quiet. A fresh layer of snow muffled everything. No wind. No birds. Just the hush of winter and the hiss of our breath as it fogged the air. Ava took two steps forward and faltered, her boots sinking into the powder.

"It snowed again," she murmured. "Overnight."

"Great," I muttered, staggering to a stop beside her. We would leave a fresh trail for them to follow. My shoulder pulsed in angry waves. Blood was still seeping through the bandage, hot against the cold.

She stepped in front of me. "Let me."

Before I could argue, Ava wrapped my good arm over her shoulders and shifted under my weight. I resisted for half a second, pride prickling but it was either her or land on the ground. Survival won. I leaned in.

Our steps were slow, the snow slick beneath us, but her presence was solid and sure. I watched her from the corner of my eye. The way her jaw was set. The way her breath came fast but steady. The way she didn't flinch at the blood, the cold, or the weight of me.

"I thought you hated the cold," I murmured.

"I hate you bleeding out in caves more."

A flicker of a smile ghosted across my face.

We moved together through the woods, a single shape against the frozen backdrop, half limping, half sliding. It was the first time I'd let someone carry me. And the first time I didn't feel weak doing it. Not with her. Never with her.

The forest swallowed us, tree limbs arching overhead like skeletal arms. Snow clung to the pine needles in delicate crowns. Every step crunched, no matter how carefully we moved. My breathing grew ragged. Ava felt it in the hitch of my shoulder against hers. Still, I didn't ask to stop; so, she did it for me.

"We rest," she said firmly, steering me toward a half-fallen log covered in snow.

She lowered me onto it, kneeling in front of me before I could argue.

"I'm fine," I growled.

"You're bleeding through your second bandage. Sit still or I'll sedate you with a rock."

I huffed. I thought I intended it to be a laugh, but it came out more like a groan.

Ava worked quickly, untying the bloody fabric. "This wound needs more than patches, Gavin. You need real medical care."

I didn't answer. My eyes stayed on her face.

"You're used to being the strong one," she said quietly. "But even soldiers need help."

"I was supposed to protect you."

"You still are," she whispered, pressing a new strip of her shirt over the gash. "But this isn't just your fight. It's ours."

My jaw flexed.

She leaned in. "I'm not leaving you behind."

I met her gaze. It was what I'd been thinking. There was something unsaid in the space between us. Something heavier than fear and warmer than pain. Maybe it was love. Maybe it was too soon. Maybe it was already here. I nodded once, almost imperceptibly. Then I gripped her hand like it was the only thing keeping me alive and sane.

We didn't get much further before I tugged Ava's arm, just enough to stop her.

"What is it?" she whispered, every muscle tensing.

I didn't speak. Just pointed.

Ahead, in the patchy snow between two narrow trees, a line of boot prints cut across our path. Fresh. Deep. Obviously not ours.

Ava stepped closer, heart stuttering. "How recent?"

I crouched with a wince, brushing my fingers over the print. "Last ten minutes, maybe less."

The shape was too crisp. The tread, too sharp. Military grade soles, spread wide in a search formation. We were being tracked.

Ava's breath fogged the air in a short, shallow burst. "They circled."

I nodded grimly. "They're smart, fanning out. Trying to flush us."

Her gaze lifted to meet mine. No panic. Just resolve. "We can out-smart them."

I wished I could believe that.

"Then we need to go dark. No more footprints," I said, scanning the slope. "See that ridge? If we climb, move along the rocks, we'll leave no trail."

"It'll hurt," she said, already slipping my arm over her shoulders.

"You or me?"

We didn't say more. No need. The air was too brittle for hope, too sharp with danger to waste on comfort. Each step forward now was a gamble. Would we slip? Would someone see us before we reached the rocks? Could I make it that far? But neither of us were folding. We were both all in on this. Behind us, the prints stayed like ghosts, silent reminders that time was slipping, that death walked only moments behind. Or ahead. We moved uphill, into the rocks, into the unknown. Together.

We crested the ridge. My breath hitched with every step. My shoulder screamed, but I pushed it down. Couldn't stop. Not now.

Snap.

Not from us.

I spun, dragging Ava behind a boulder just as a voice crackled through the trees.

"—movement on the ridge. Coordinates incoming."

A radio. Too close.

I peered around the edge. Between the trees, maybe fifty yards down, a figure in white camo swept the woods with a rifle and comms headset. Shit.

"They know," I whispered.

Ava's eyes were wide, jaw tight. "What do we do?"

I didn't hesitate. "We run."

"But—your arm—"

"We run," I repeated. "On my mark."

Another voice joined the radio, this one clear, taunting. "Gavin... come out, come out. You're bleeding. You won't get far."

Lev.

I clenched my teeth until my jaw ached. Rage flared, wishing for ammo. Lev was too confident. Too close. Ava reached for me, curling her fingers around mine. Not trembling. Not weak. A partner.

I squeezed back. "Ready?"

"With you, always."

Behind us, boots crunched snow. Three. Maybe four pairs.

"Now," I growled.

We bolted.

Tree limbs whipped past. Snow exploded beneath our boots. My vision blurred from the icy wind, but Ava was solid beside me, my tether, my fire, my future.

Gunfire cracked behind us.

We didn't stop.

We didn't look back.

Because forward was the only way out.

Whiteout Dawn

Ava Green

The wind clawed at my face like it was trying to rip the skin clean off. I couldn't see more than ten feet in front of me, just a blur of white and shadow and swirling fury. But I kept moving. One foot. Then the other.

Gavin stumbled beside me, heavier with each step, and I looped my arm around his waist to keep him upright. Our last sprint had about done him in. He was burning with fever, barely coherent, but every now and then he muttered something under his breath. I caught fragments—"higher ground," "extraction," "don't stop."

So, I didn't.

We were climbing now. Upward, always upward, like he taught me. Elevation gave options. Visibility. A chance to signal Sierra Bravo, if they were still out there listening. The old Ava would've panicked at the thought of being in charge. She would've curled into a ball and waited to be saved. But that girl was gone, buried somewhere under the snow with the rest of my fear.

I tightened my grip on Gavin and kept pushing forward. My thighs burned. My lungs screamed. But I was not stopping. Not until I found somewhere—anywhere—we could catch our breath and regroup.

The storm didn't care that we were broken and bleeding. It raged on, relentless and cold. But I gritted my teeth and screamed into it, "You'll have to do better than that."

And then I kept going. Because I was not letting him die. Not out here. Not today.

The slope evened out for a breath, and I hauled Gavin up the last few steps with everything I had left. My legs felt like water. My fingers were raw from gripping ice-crusted bark and jagged rocks to help pull us forward. But we'd made it, to the top, or something close.

I turned to look. Nothing but blinding white, howling wind, and the endless forest spread below like a sea of frozen ghosts. Visibility was worse than I'd hoped. No sign of movement. No signal bars if I had a phone, which I didn't. Just snow and wind loud enough to smother a scream. There was no way any drone would see us. I doubted Lev's men would either.

Gavin leaned hard into me, his breath ragged in my ear. "High ground... good choice," he mumbled. His eyes barely open but I caught a flicker of approval before they slid closed again.

I pressed my lips to his temple for one second. Just one. Then I squared my shoulders and looked ahead. There was no trail up here. No signs, no markers. Just white and wind and instinct. My body screamed to stop, to rest, to lie down in the drift and disappear. But I couldn't. If I stopped, we both died.

He trusted me to lead. I was not letting him down.

I glanced toward a ridge that looked marginally more sheltered, tucked between two crooked pines and a crag of dark rock. It was risky but everything was risky now.

"Okay," I whispered to myself. "Let's go higher."

I shifted Gavin's weight and moved. Every step punched pain through my spine. But I didn't stop. I spotted it just ahead. It was half-buried in the snow, a massive pine trunk collapsed from some past storm. The roots jutted up like gnarled fingers, forming a windbreak. It was not perfect, but it was enough.

"Here," I said, already pulling Gavin toward it. He stumbled but followed, and together we hunched beneath the fallen tree. The snow here was thinner, the wind dulled by the thick wall of bark and tangled branches. It was not warmth, but it was relief.

He slumped down, breathing in sharp, shallow pulls. I pushed his coat aside and cursed softly under my breath. The bandage was soaked. Blood had seeped through the outer layer again, spreading like ink across gauze and fabric.

"I need to look at it," I whispered, more to myself than him.

He didn't answer. Just closed his eyes.

My hands were clumsy, trembling. I dug into the pack for anything clean. There was nothing left. So, I tore a fresh strip from the bottom of my shirt, teeth chattering. I melted snow in my palm and gently rinsed around the gash. Gavin flinched but didn't complain.

"This is bad," I murmured.

"Could be worse," he rasped. "You could've left me behind."

I shot him a glare. "You're not funny."

He tried for a grin. It failed.

I tightened the wrap as best I could, knotted it off, and rested my forehead against his. "You're going to be okay. You hear me?"

He nodded faintly. I pretended that meant I believed him.

The wind quieted for a breath. A strange, suspended silence descended. Just the crunch of snow settling on branches, and the sound of Gavin's ragged breathing beside me. I turned to check his pulse again, fingers brushing his neck. Steady but weak.

His eyes opened, half-lidded, but focused on me. "You're amazing, you know that?"

I scoffed under my breath. "Tell that to the icicles on my eyelashes."

He lifted a trembling hand, and brushed a few of them away, fingertip light. The touch froze me. Not from cold but from everything I felt. Everything I was afraid to.

I didn't know who leaned in first. Maybe it was mutual. Our foreheads pressed together, slow and deliberate. A grounding point in the chaos.

"You saved me back there," he said, voice raw. "And not just from the gunmen."

I traced my thumb along the cut on his cheek. "You've saved me more times than I can count."

"Doesn't matter. I'd do it again. Every time."

My throat tightened. I kissed his temple, soft, lingering. His skin was chilled, but the contact warmed something deep inside me.

"I'm not letting you go," I whispered.

His hand curled around mine. "Then I'm not going anywhere."

We stayed like that, still and silent beneath the broken tree, as the storm howled on. A thousand things could kill us out here. But in this moment, we were alive. Together. And I was not giving that up.

Snap.

It was faint, almost lost in the howl of the wind, but I heard it. A branch, somewhere behind us. Not the kind that fell on its own. The kind that broke under a boot.

I sat bolt upright, heart punching my ribs.

Gavin shifted beside me. "What is it?"

I raised a hand, shushing him. Every nerve in my body strained toward the noise, but the wind kept shifting, throwing sound in every direction. Another rustle. Closer this time. Or maybe I imagined it. Didn't matter.

"We're not alone," I whispered.

Gavin pushed himself up with a grunt. "You sure?"

"No." I grabbed our pack. "But I'm not waiting to find out."

He tried to stand, nearly fell. I caught him with an arm around his waist and shouldered his weight like it was instinct. Maybe it was now.

The wind kicked up, carrying snow sideways in white sheets. It was impossible to see more than a few feet, and that worked both ways. Good. Maybe it would mask our tracks, too.

We pressed uphill again, Gavin leaning heavy, my legs burning from cold and fear and everything in between. The storm was turning into our only cover and our biggest threat. But I was not freezing to death in a tree hollow. And I was sure as hell not getting caught after running this far. We disappeared into the white. We were maybe fifty feet higher when I spotted them. Tracks. I froze so fast Gavin nearly pulled me off my feet.

"What?" he breathed, already fumbling for his pistol.

I crouched, pointing downslope to where the snow had settled against a cluster of rocks where the wind hadn't blown it away. Prints. At least four sets. Not ours. Too fresh, too clean. They zigzagged like a loose search pattern. Flanking, is what Gavin called it.

My stomach twisted.

"They're spreading out," I whispered. "They're trying to box us in."

Gavin's jaw flexed. "Smart bastards."

My breath came fast. Not from the climb. From the realization that we were somehow being watched. Calculated against. Hunted like deer. Even in this blizzard.

"Come on." I helped him drop behind an ice-covered boulder, our backs pressed to the cold stone. My fingers trembled as I scanned the tree line. Gavin leaned over, studying the tracks with that sharp, tactical look he got when pain took a back seat to survival.

"They're guiding us," he muttered. "Pushing us toward something."

"What?"

"A kill zone. Or a trap."

Snow whipped into my eyes, but I couldn't blink away the chill crawling down my spine. I reached for Gavin's hand and squeezed once. I didn't even know why. Maybe I needed to remind myself that he was real and with me, that I wasn't alone out here.

He squeezed back.

"We've got to move laterally," I said. "Not up. Not down. Just sideways. Out of their funnel."

"Think you can keep me from falling off a mountain?"

I glanced at him. "Try me."

Sideways turned out to mean hell.

The incline curved around the mountain, all jagged rock and brittle snowpack. One wrong step and we'd be sledding to our deaths or straight into their hands. I edged along first, testing each foothold before letting Gavin follow. His boots crunched behind me, slow and deliberate, but every sound made my heart jump. There was no path. Just blind faith and a cliff wall.

"We're sitting ducks," I muttered. "High ground, no cover. And if they've got thermal imaging—"

"Then we're fried already," Gavin said behind me. "Just keep moving."

My lips were numb. My thighs screamed with every step. But we kept going, scraping along this treacherous shelf like ghosts clinging to the side of the world.

Then I saw it, a flat outcrop. Maybe twenty yards ahead. Barely enough room to stop and reassess.

I nodded toward it. "We'll rest there. If we make it."

"We'll make it," Gavin growled, though his voice was thin with pain.

The wind slammed into us again, nearly knocking me sideways. I braced with a frozen hand against the cliff and blinked away snow. Somewhere in the storm behind us, a crunch echoed louder than the others.

Footsteps. Not ours.

They were getting closer.

Gavin's breathing was ragged now, and I glanced back. His lips were pale. Too pale. No time to panic. No space for fear. Just survive. I reached for him again.

"We've got one move left," I said. "We keep going and find a miracle."

We reached the outcrop, if you could call a slab of snow-slicked rock barely wide enough to crouch on an outcrop, and collapsed behind a boulder jutting up like a broken tooth. I pressed Gavin down beside me, shielding him as best I could from the screaming wind. For a moment, I thought we'd bought ourselves time. Then a voice floated up from below.

"Not far now..."

Russian accent. Smooth. Mocking.

My stomach dropped.

Gavin's hand clamped around my wrist like a vice. I didn't move. Didn't breathe. The wind howled, carrying more than snow this time, bootfalls. Radio static. A man laughing. Louder now. Closer. Footsteps approached from the slope below... and above. We were boxed in.

"They're herding us," I whispered, barely audible over the wind. "Driving us somewhere."

Gavin's jaw tightened. "Toward a choke point."

I scanned the ledge, heart slamming against my ribs. We had no cover. No exit.

Nowhere to run. Then, in the distance, I spotted it. It was barely a break in the cliff face. Could be a crevice. Could be salvation. Or suicide.

My breath fogged in front of me. I glanced down at Gavin, blood on his temple, grit in his teeth, and something inside me steeled.

I leaned in close.

"We're going to have to do something crazy."

He didn't flinch.

"Then let's be crazy," he murmured.

The wind screamed louder, either in a warning or a dare.

And we moved.

The Stand-Off

Gavin Henderson

The cold gnawed at my ribs where the bandage had lost its seal, but I shoved the pain aside. We didn't have time for weakness.

The terrain up ahead was a gift if I was willing to use it right. The path narrowed into a bottleneck, flanked by two massive boulders and a drop so sheer even the wind seemed to hesitate. Snow clung to every surface in powdery drifts, silent but treacherous. A natural choke point. Our one crazy chance.

I grabbed Ava's wrist and crouched behind a wind-bent pine. "We can't outrun them," I whispered. "But we can draw them in. Here." I traced a line in the snow with a finger, showing the plan. "You see this overhang? Loosen it. Wait for my signal."

She didn't blink. Just nodded, calm but alert, already moving toward the ledge with that fluid grace I'd come to trust. God, she was fast. Smarter than almost anyone I've ever run ops with. And she listened. Not out of fear, but because she trusted me.

I did a quick check of my knife, then scanned the path again. Footsteps crunched faintly in the distance. Two, maybe three sets and getting closer. Time was up. I looked back at Ava. She met my gaze, crouched near the ledge, snow-packed branch in hand. Ready.

I gave her the faintest nod. It was not just a plan now. It was a promise. No one got past this ridge alive. Not if it meant losing her.

The first footfall snapped a twig. Loud. Two of them. Mercs. Confident. One was chewing gum like he was walking into a bar fight instead of a tactical kill zone. They didn't know what was coming. They stepped into the choke point. Right where I needed them.

I lifted my hand. Just one motion.

Ava reacted instantly. The branch jerked free, and a cascade of snow and rocks crashed down the embankment. The lead merc stumbled, flailing to stay upright. The second yelled, raising his rifle just as I charged.

I slammed into him, knife drawn. The impact knocked us into the snowbank, blades flashing between us. He was stronger than I expected, but I was faster. At least I was. My shoulder and side screamed in protest as I twisted, driving my shoulder into his gut. He bucked, grabbed for my wrist.

Then Ava was there.

A rock whistled through the air and slammed into the side of his head. He grunted, staggering. She didn't stop. Threw another. This one connected with his arm as I wrenched my knife upward. The merc collapsed with a gurgle.

I spun toward the first one. He was crawling, reaching for a dropped pistol. My boot met his ribs before he could grab it. He went down hard.

Ava grabbed my sleeve, breathless but steady. "You good?"

"Yeah." I breathed through the burn in my side. "Thanks to you."

We just bought ourselves time. Not much. But enough. We regrouped, weapons up. More were surely coming.

I flipped the downed merc onto his back and pinned him with a knee to his sternum. Blood streaked down his temple from Ava's rock.

I stripped him of his gear, checking pockets with practiced speed. Two spare mags. Tactical knife. And tucked against his collarbone—an earpiece, slick with sweat.

I snatched it out and pressed it to my own ear, thumbing the receiver on his lapel mic.

Static.

Then—

"Status report." A voice I'd recognize anywhere. Lev. Calm. Arrogant.

"Echo Team, do you copy? Bring me the nurse. Alive."

Alive.

My stomach twisted.

I glanced over. Ava was crouched low beside the nearest rock outcropping, her face tight with tension. She had heard it. She was the objective. This wasn't cleanup. This was targeted. She met my eyes, and I saw it register. That radio just shattered any illusion we had. They were not out here sweeping up survivors. They were hunting her.

I knelt beside her, still holding the mic. We listened in silence for another few seconds. It was only Lev breathing now. Like he knew we were listening.

Ava swallowed hard. "Why me?"

I didn't have the answer.

But I knew this. We were not running anymore. We were surviving on purpose. And now, I had a damn war to win.

Lev's voice echoed in my head long after the static faded. *"Bring me the nurse. Alive."* Not *any survivors*. Not *retrieve the wreckage*. Just Ava. My hand tightened around the radio before I yanked the batteries out with a sharp twist. I tossed it aside, jaw clenched. This was never a

standard cleanup. It was a targeted extraction. A manhunt. And Ava
was the target.

I turned to her. She was crouched nearby, pulling her hood tighter
against the cold, but her eyes were locked on me, wide, searching. No
need for words.

"They're not after me," I muttered. "They're after you."

Ava nodded slowly, lips parting like she was trying to process, but I
didn't let her spiral.

"It changes nothing," I said, already scanning our surroundings.
Every shadow was a threat now. Every ridge, a sniper's perch. "We still
get out. Together."

"But why?" Her voice was hoarse. "What could I possibly—?"

I didn't let her finish. "It doesn't matter."

Because even if she saw something or heard something back on that
plane, even if that rich Russian bastard thought she was a threat worth
killing for, I didn't care. All that mattered was that someone marked
her. And they were coming. Not for the wreckage. Not for revenge.
For her.

And now it was personal.

I checked the clip in the merc's pistol and shoved it back in my
pocket. Whatever was coming, I would face it head-on. They wanted
Ava? They would have to go through me.

I leaned against a frost-slicked pine, my breath ragged. The adrenaline from the fight was long gone, and now every movement set off a
chorus of pain. My ribs screamed from the last takedown, and my legs
wanted to collapse. I could feel the edge of exhaustion closing in like a
noose.

Ava crouched a few feet away, scanning the tree line with steady
hands and sharp eyes. The wind tossed strands of hair across her face,

but she didn't flinch. She was calm. Focused. She didn't need me to protect her, not like before. That should reassure me. It didn't.

My fingers twitched near my weapon, a reflex. I didn't trust my aim right now. My vision blurred every few seconds, and there was a buzzing behind my ears that hadn't stopped since getting shot. Probably from blood loss. I was slowing down. And if I slowed too much, she died.

My mind drifted, back to men I couldn't save. Brothers who bled out on foreign dirt while I screamed for a medic. Mistakes that never stopped replaying. I'd carried those ghosts for years, buried them under discipline and muscle and cold detachment.

But Ava wasn't a mission. She was not a soldier. She was everything. And if I failed her. If I hesitated or collapsed at the wrong moment, I wouldn't be the one to pay the price. She would.

I exhaled through clenched teeth and straightened, ignoring the spike of pain.

No room for doubt now. No weakness. Time to pull out every last ounce of Marine determination.

Because Ava was watching.

Ava was counting on me.

Ava hadn't spoken in a while, which I noticed immediately. She'd been too quiet since Lev's announcement. She stood near the fallen radio, arms folded tight across her chest, chewing at the inside of her cheek.

Then, just above a whisper: "My address book..."

I looked up from checking my ammo. "What?"

Her eyes lifted to mine, wide now. "My addresses. It was in my jacket. Back on the plane."

My gut twisted. "What about it?"

"My sister's number—her full name—everything. If they recovered it…" She trailed off, visibly shaking. "If they find that, they'll go after her. They'll go after Emma."

For the first time since the crash, I saw it, raw fear. Not for herself. For someone else.

I crossed to her in three steps. "Hey." I took her by the shoulders, firm but gentle. "Look at me."

She did. Barely.

"No reason for them to have found that info. And even if they do, we'll call it in. Sierra Bravo has protocols for this kind of exposure. We'll keep her safe."

"But I—" Her voice broke again, and she pressed a trembling fist to her mouth.

I didn't hesitate. I pulled her into me, one arm around her back, the other shielding her from the wind. "We'll handle it," I murmured into her hair. "They're not touching your sister. I promise."

Ava nodded against my chest, but her breathing still trembled. So did mine.

"We can't stay here," I said. My voice was gruff, not from anger, but urgency. "We've made noise. Those two will be missed. They'll regroup and sweep this ridge."

She nodded, slowly.

I stepped closer, lowering my tone. "We head west, toward the tree line. Use the storm as cover. There's a rock formation on the map. If we can make it there by nightfall, we'll be out of drone range and—"

"I can't let them hurt her, I." Her voice trembled. "I should've found the book. I didn't think—"

"Hey." I stopped her with a look. "We're going to protect her. Sierra Bravo has eyes everywhere. As soon as we get clear, I'll call it in. They'll put your sister under watch. No one's getting near her."

Ava breathed in, shaky, but her spine straightened. I offered my hand. She took it. We turned together, slinging on our packs. I felt the shift like a crack through the ice. This wasn't just survival anymore. It was a mission. A vow. Protect Ava. Keep her alive. Keep her whole. And now... protect what she loved. Because this war just bled into home.

The slope steepened as we climbed, wind clawing at our coats like invisible hands. I led, Ava close behind, boots crunching in the snow. My side burned where the earlier knife caught me, but I gritted through it. My shoulder throbbed. Pain was background noise now.

We crested a ridge, pausing just long enough to scan the horizon. A narrow valley sprawled ahead, rimmed by evergreens. It would be potential shelter if we could reach it before dark.

Static.

Ava jolted beside me, her head snapping up. It was faint, garbled, but unmistakable. A radio signal drifted on the wind. I turned, straining to hear.

"...Green... repeat... Emma Green..."

Ava froze mid-step. The color drained from her face. My heart lurched. The voice continued, clearer now. "Positive ID. Emma Green. Address confirmed. Awaiting orders."

"No," Ava breathed, staggering forward like she could outrun the words.

I grabbed her arm, steadying her. "Don't—don't panic. They're fishing. Maybe bluffing."

Her eyes brimmed. "They know her name, Gavin."

I didn't argue. Didn't lie. Instead, I gently turned her to face me. "Then we make damn sure they never get close. We get out. We warn Sierra Bravo. And we shut them down."

She nodded, lips trembling.

The wind howled around us, but neither of us moved.

And I swore, right then and there, I'd burn the whole damn mountain down with my last breath before I let them touch her sister.

Echoes

Ava Green

My hands wouldn't stop shaking.

Not from the cold, though the snow stung like a thousand needles, but from something deeper. The voice on the radio kept replaying in my head, warping, echoing.

Emma Green.

I choked on a breath. They said her name. My sister's name. The only person left in the world I truly loved, who still called me "little storm" even when she was the one weathering chemo like a champ.

I tried to ground myself, staring at my gloved fingers. They twitched uncontrollably. I pressed them to my lips, to my chest, to the fabric over my thundering heart, but the tremors kept coming.

A memory surfaced like a cruel wave: Emma lying in a hospital bed, her bald head wrapped in a cheerful scarf. "You're the stronger one," she'd said, voice papery, eyes alight. "You'll protect us both."

And now I had led hell right to her.

Guilt sliced through me sharper than any scalpel. My book. I *lost* my damn book when the plane crashed, and they must have found it.

I felt like I might be sick. But then something inside me locked into place. I couldn't afford to fall apart. If I let fear win, Emma didn't get another sunrise. No more spiraling. No more helplessness.

They want me? Fine. But they'd have to go through me to get to her and I would make their lives hell.

"Hey."

Gavin's voice cut through the rising panic like a blade. Low, steady. The kind of tone that belonged to someone who had walked through fire and come out the other side. I didn't look at him right away. I was afraid if I did, the tears fighting their way to the surface would break free. But then his hands were on my shoulders, strong, warm, grounding me like an anchor in a storm. I finally met his eyes.

Steel-gray. Fierce. Unshakable.

"No one," he said, voice rough but sure, "is touching anyone you love. Not now. Not ever."

He was so close I could feel the heat radiating from his body, see the tightness in his jaw, the flush in his cheeks from the cold or maybe anger. Not at me. At them. Whoever thought they could use Emma to get to me. Whoever dared threaten what was his to protect. It was not a platitude. It was a promise. A vow forged in the battlefield of our shared hell.

I blinked hard, and my breath caught. That tether, the one I didn't know I was dangling from, suddenly tightened. I was not falling. He had me.

I nodded, once, sharp. "Okay," I whispered. My voice was frayed, but it held.

He didn't smile, but there was something in his eyes that softened. His hands lingered, thumbs brushing my jacket sleeves, like he was reassuring himself I was still here. And then he let go, turning toward the slope ahead, his shoulders squared.

"We need elevation," Gavin said, scanning the dense tree line ahead.

The wind bit at our cheeks, but his voice was calm, calculating. It was like watching a machine lock into gear, every decision purposeful. I followed his gaze to a jagged ridgeline stretching above the forest, sun just beginning to burn mist from its snowy edge.

"Think someone friendly will see us?" I asked, adjusting the strap of my pack.

He nodded once. "Or we might at least get eyes on Sierra Bravo. If they're in range, they'll spot movement, maybe smoke."

"And if they're not?"

"Then we keep moving until they are." He looked at me, jaw tight. "But we don't hole up. We push."

I squared my shoulders. "Let's push."

Something shifted inside me. The Ava who staggered through snowdrifts hoping to survive was still here but now, she was guided by purpose. I was done playing prey. If Emma had been pulled into this, I owed it to her to fight smart. And I knew Gavin was hanging on by his teeth. I wouldn't let him down.

Gavin gestured ahead. "The terrain narrows near the ridge. We'll be exposed for a stretch—"

"I can handle it," I cut in. And I meant it.

He arched an eyebrow, then smirked faintly. "Didn't say you couldn't."

We started moving, slow but steady. Every crunch of snow underfoot felt louder than it should. The forest around us was eerily still, like it was watching how this drama would play out. But I wasn't afraid of that silence anymore. We were not just running. We were moving toward something. And I was not alone.

The climb got steeper. My thighs burned, and my breath clouded the air in ragged puffs, but I kept going. Each footfall was deliberate. Each step a vow.

The snow was deeper here, powder on top, ice underneath. I planted my boots with care, mindful of the way the crust could betray you, how it gave suddenly, noisily. We were ghosts now or trying to be.

Gavin led, his movements economical despite the hitch in his gait. I watched how he favored his left side, how he tightened his jaw every time he shifted his weight wrong. I said nothing. Neither did he. He had the determination of an unstoppable force now.

Then it was my turn to slip. My foot hit a patch of glare ice and shot sideways. I pitched forward but Gavin's arm snapped back like a reflex, steadying me before my knees hit. His gloved fingers wrapped around my wrist, firm and unshakable.

"Thanks," I whispered.

He nodded once, already scanning the trail ahead.

Minutes later, he stumbled on a root hidden beneath the snow. I caught him under the arm before he went down, bracing with my body until he was steady. He didn't say a word, just gave me a sidelong glance that said everything. Mutual reliance. A silent pact. We were two warriors together. The ridge loomed ahead, still distant, still treacherous, but every step forward felt like a small defiance against the weight pressing down on us.

Then a walkie squawked.

It was faint at first. A garbled crackle. I froze, heart slamming into my ribs.

"...Sweep left... ridge—"

The rest broke apart in static and wind. But I heard enough.

Gavin crouched beside me, his eyes sharp.

Another voice answered in clipped Russian. Then silence again.

"They're not guessing anymore," I murmured. "They're organizing."

Gavin's jaw tightened. "They're triangulating position."

Every rustle of branches now sounded like a footstep. Every creak of the forest felt like breath on the back of my neck.

Gavin gave a signal, two fingers forward, one curled. Move, but stay low. I nodded, and we started again. Slower now. No talking. The wind had picked up, swirling flakes into thin eddies that stung my cheeks. My thoughts flicked to Emma. To the book I lost. To the men chasing us with her name on their tongues. And I walked faster.

By the time we reached the final slope, every breath scraped raw to the bottom of my lungs. The trees thinned, their skeletons etched against a sky just beginning to warm. Dawn was bleeding over the ridgeline, pale gold stretching fingers across the snow.

Gavin raised a hand, calling a halt.

I crouched instinctively, eyes scanning the slope. Nothing moved, but something felt off. Then I realized that the forest had gone even quieter. No birdsong. No branches swaying. Just the hush of snow settling on itself, and the faint rasp of our breaths.

Gavin knelt beside a log, motioning for cover. I nodded and dropped into a low crawl behind a scrubby evergreen. My pulse thundered in my ears, drowning out everything else.

A flicker of movement far below caught my eye. I sucked in a sharp breath. "They're tracking upslope," I murmured.

Gavin didn't flinch, just nodded once.

A walkie hissed again and then a voice broke through, brittle with cold and command: "Tracks lead to the ridge. We've got them pinned."

My stomach lurched. Gavin stiffened beside me. His eyes narrowed, every muscle going still like a coiled spring. That voice wasn't guessing. It was confident. Certain.

"We're being herded," I whispered. My breath plumed in the freezing air. "They're not just chasing us... they're steering us."

Gavin nodded once. "They want high ground to corner us. Better firing angle."

Panic clawed at my throat, but I forced it down. I glanced over my shoulder, scanning the trail we took. Our footprints led like a Hansel and Gretl trail through virgin snow. Too obvious. Too easy.

Gavin was already in motion, dragging branches over the tracks. I did the same, our hands moving fast and quiet. But the damage was done. They knew. They were closing in.

"We have to get off this path," I said, my voice low but urgent. "Change direction. Now."

He studied the terrain. "There's a split in the ridge, twenty yards west. Narrow, but we might be able to double back under tree cover."

Might. Not will. Still, it was better than waiting here to be picked off.

I gripped his arm. "Let's go."

But even as we started moving, the forest felt tighter. The trees, the snow, the silence. It all felt like a trap pulling shut. Like we were two mice scurrying through a glass maze while something bigger watched from above. We moved anyway. Because that was what survivors did. And what choice did we have?

We broke through the last knot of trees just as the sun spilled over the ridge. Pale gold sliced through the pines. It should have felt like hope. It didn't. It felt like we were exposed. The slope beneath us angled sharply down, slick with old ice. Behind us, the forest rustled. Not wind—Not animals—Footsteps.

A voice, amplified by a bullhorn or maybe just sheer arrogance, called out from behind us: "Drop your weapon!"

My heart slammed against my ribs. Gavin pulled me down instinctively, but a shot cracked before we hit the ground.

Bark exploded inches from my head.

I hit the snow hard, ears ringing, vision swimming. Another voice shouted in Russian. Boots thundered behind us, close, too close.

Gavin rolled, shielding me with his body as more figures appeared ahead, emerging from the trees like ghosts in tactical gear, rifles raised.

One... two... five at least.

"We're surrounded," Gavin growled. He didn't sound scared. He sounded ready. Which terrified me more.

There was no Sierra Bravo, no backup, no time.

One of the men stepped forward, weapon steady. "You're done running," he said in accented English. "Hand her over. No one else needs to die."

I didn't even feel the cold anymore. Just heat. Fury, defiance, fear.

Gavin slowly raised his weapon with one hand and reached back for mine with the other.

I grabbed it.

We might be outnumbered, outgunned, and out of options.

But we were not done.

Not yet.

Breaking Point

Gavin Henderson

The first shot cracked through the air just as the morning light hit the snow at our feet.

I dove, hauling Ava down with me behind a jagged slab of granite. We hit the frozen ground hard. My shoulder screamed, but I gritted through it. No time to bleed. The rock barely covered us, cold pressing against my spine as I wrapped my arm across her. She was shaking, but it was not fear. It was focus. Controlled adrenaline. We were both riding it.

I peeked around the edge of the boulder, careful, slow. Movement below. Five... maybe six. Ghosts in snow camo white, spread wide across the slope. One has got a long rifle on a tripod, sniper setup. That was bad. Real bad.

"We're boxed in," I muttered, scanning for options. Nothing but a sheer drop behind us. I glanced back. The ridge fell away in a steep, icy chute. Maybe survivable. If we wanted to break a leg on the way down.

Ava touched my knee. Her eyes were on me, steady and waiting. Trusting. God, that trust burned in my chest.

"They've funneled us," I said. "Trying to pin us here."

She nodded, no panic. Just grit. That was my girl.

Another shot exploded. Closer. Chips of bark and ice sprayed over us. I ducked instinctively, heart slamming against my ribs. They were moving in fast. I could feel it. Heard it in the wind, in the silence between shots. They wanted us cornered. And they were damn close to getting it.

I shifted against the boulder, and pain lanced up my side. Damn it. The wound was bleeding again. Warmth seeped down my ribs beneath the layers, soaking into my shirt. I pressed my palm there, not hard, just enough to feel the truth of it. Not fatal. Not yet. But I was slowing down.

I scanned again. Five mercs, maybe six now. They were advancing in a half-moon, tightening the snare. Flanking wide. No chatter from their radios. Too disciplined. Professionals. Not your average thugs. This wasn't just a hit squad. It was a retrieval team.

I'd been in kill boxes before, Afghanistan, Fallujah, a little border op that went sideways in Venezuela. You learned the patterns. The way they herded you like prey. The way the world got quiet just before they squeezed the trigger. We were in one now.

"We've got no clean exit," I whispered. "They've got elevation and they're moving to cut us off at the tree line."

Ava didn't flinch. But I caught the edge of her profile, jaw tight, eyes scanning with me. She knew. She saw it too.

Another stab of pain radiated from my side. I adjusted, trying not to show how much it was costing me. I couldn't let her see the doubt creeping in. But it was there. Because for the first time since that damn plane dropped from the sky, I didn't know how we got out of this. Not in one piece. Not both of us.

The pressure built behind my eyes, a low throb like a countdown. They were closing in. There was no good cover, no fallback point, and I was bleeding like a stuck pig. My body was not moving fast enough. Not sharp enough. Not enough, period. I started doing the math.

Not the kind you learned in school. The kind you only picked up in warzones: how many seconds it took to draw fire, how long someone might survive in your shadow. Whether a distraction cost one life... or bought another.

If I stepped out, if I gave myself up... Maybe they'd pause. Maybe she could slip away in the confusion. My stomach churned. The thought of her crawling through the snow alone, heart pounding, hunted, made my lungs seize. But it was better than watching her get torn apart because I was too stubborn to let go.

I looked over. Ava was crouched beside me, breathing fast, cheeks raw from wind and fear. Still gripping a branch like she planned to beat a trained merc to death with it. Brave. Fierce. Mine.

And there it was. The moment I knew I'd die for her.

Hell, I thought I already decided that days ago. Somewhere between the crash and that first kiss in the lean-to. But now... now it felt real. Immediate. Heavy in my bones.

I opened my mouth. Started to tell her the plan. The terrible, necessary trade.

But she saw it in my eyes before I spoke. And her reaction was nuclear.

"I could draw them off," I started, voice low, barely above the wind. "If I go loud and fast, you might get a window—"

She was on me before I finished, her hands fisting the front of my jacket like she meant to shake some damn sense into me.

"Don't you f**king dare." Her voice cracked like a whip, raw, shaking. Her eyes were blazing, wild with emotion, but it was not fear. It was rage.

"You think you get to decide that?" she snarled. "That you get to throw yourself away like I won't care?"

"Ava—"

"No." She jabbed a finger into my chest. "You don't get to make that call alone. Not after everything we've been through. Not when I finally—" Her voice caught, and for a second, I saw the heartbreak under the fury. "You don't get to leave me behind."

I swallowed hard. I didn't expect this. I thought she'd be mad, sure, frustrated, maybe. But this was different. This was a woman staring down death and saying screw you, I won't lose you too.

The fight left me in a rush. I leaned my forehead against hers, our breath mingling in the cold. She was trembling, and so was I.

"We survive together," she said again, softer this time. "Or not at all."

And damn it if those weren't the most terrifying, beautiful words I'd ever heard.

The words came before I could stop them.

"You mean too mu—"

I choked them back, biting down hard as if silence could rewind what just slipped. But it was out there now, hanging in the air between us, sharp and raw and undeniable.

Ava went still. Her breath caught, lashes fluttering once before her eyes locked on mine. I saw it, the way her mind parsed every unspoken syllable, how her lips parted just slightly like she might say something, might ask me to finish it. I didn't.

Because if I said it now, if I told her that she had become the only thing that mattered, that I would rather take a bullet than see her suffer—then it was real. Not adrenaline. Not survival instinct. Real. And real meant fragile.

I couldn't protect something I felt this deeply for. Not in this place. Not when I was bleeding, we were surrounded, and seconds from being overrun.

But still, it was there.

Ava didn't press. She just stared at me, eyes searching. And then she did something that broke me more than any sniper could. She reached out and cupped the side of my face, gentle and steady, like she already knew the truth I didn't finish. It took everything I had not to say it again. Because if I did, there was no walking it back. And God help me, I didn't want to.

The world faded around us.

For one heartbeat, the screaming wind, the gunfire, the radio static, all of it dimmed. It was just Ava. Inches away. Her fingers still warm against my face, her breath brushing mine. Eyes locked, silent and fierce. And I knew, if this was the end, I'd die with her name on my lips.

I memorized her like I might never get the chance again. The curve of her cheek, raw from wind and grit. The stubborn set of her jaw. That fire in her eyes, daring the world to try and take her. Take us.

She deserved more than this. A future. Peace. Laughter. Hell, even a messy apartment full of takeout and badly brewed coffee. She deserved the world, not a bullet on a mountain ridge with a man too broken to promise anything but violence.

But she chose to stay. With me. And that meant something. Everything. I gave her a nod. Small. Controlled. She returned it, sharp and sure, like we were reading the same script without ever needing words. And that was when I realized, we were more than survivors now. We were a team. A promise. If we went down, it would be side by side.

But if there was even a sliver of a chance, we would claw our way out. Together.

One more breath. One more look.

Then I shifted my weight, scanned the ridge again, and steeled myself for the chaos I knew was coming. It always came.

The moment shattered.

Gunfire ripped through the air. Closer now, louder. A round punched into the rock above us, splintering shale that rained down like shrapnel. Another burst shredded a tree to our left. Bark exploded. A branch cracked and fell, nearly taking Ava with it.

"Down!" I barked, dragging her closer into the boulder's shadow.

She was fast, but not fast enough. A bullet tore through the sleeve of her coat. She gasped, more shock than pain, and I was already moving, already covering her with my body. No hesitation. Just instinct.

I slammed us both to the frozen ground, curling around her like a shield. My back burned where ice met skin through torn fabric, but I didn't move. Didn't breathe. Every sense was narrowed to her heartbeat thudding under my hand.

This wasn't warning fire.

They were not spooking us.

They were killing us.

The sharp staccato of assault rifles echoed across the slope, methodical, trained. Whoever Lev hired, they weren't amateurs. This was a full push, a sweep-and-clear. My vision tunneled for a second as adrenaline flooded my system, dulling pain, sharpening my thoughts.

I glanced at Ava. Her eyes were wide, lips parted in shock, but she didn't scream. Didn't panic. She clutched my arm like a lifeline and gave the smallest nod. We were still in this.

Barely.

And it was only getting worse.

A radio crackled.

I froze, ears straining past the gunfire, the wind, the hammering of my own pulse.

Then—his voice. Clear. Cold. Distant but unmistakable.

"Push forward. I want the nurse alive. Kill the rest."

I glanced at her. She had heard it too. Her face had gone pale beneath the dirt and blood, but her eyes... her eyes burned. Not with fear. With fury.

"Gavin..." she whispered, voice tight with emotion.

"I know." I reached for her hand. Gripped it. Anchored her. Anchored myself. "We move on my mark."

"Where?" she breathed.

Truth? I didn't know. Every escape route was compromised. We were boxed in on a ridge with a death squad closing in and I was bleeding again.

But I couldn't show that. Not now. Not with that trust in her eyes. I squared my shoulders, felt the ache in my ribs, the tremble in my left leg. I looked her straight in the eye.

"Down the bluff," I lied. "There's a blind spot in the rocks. We can lose them."

She nodded.

God, please let me be right.

I peeked around the edge of the boulder. Movement, ten meters out. We had seconds. I tightened my grip on Ava's hand.

"Ready?" I asked.

She nodded.

"Go!"

Leap of Faith

Ava Green

Gunfire crackled behind us, sharp, relentless, echoing off the stone, holding us captive. I crouched low behind the boulder, heart hammering so loud it drowned out the war around us. We were pinned on a ledge halfway up this frozen cliffside, nowhere to go but over. And I meant that literally.

I risked a glance over the edge, and my stomach lurched. All I saw far below was a writhing, frothing ribbon of whitewater. A river! Jagged rocks lined the banks. It was far, too far. But it was something. Behind us was guaranteed bullets and death.

"There," I shouted, pointing. Gavin followed my gaze, eyes narrowing.

His face said it all. *Are you out of your damn mind?*

"We can't stay," I said, choking on the cold air. "They've boxed us in."

"We jump?" he growled. "That's your plan?"

I nodded, even though I could barely believe it myself. "We either jump and maybe survive... or stay and definitely die."

For a second, I thought he was going to argue. But then I saw the moment it clicked, the flicker of acceptance in his eyes. He swiped a hand across his brow, smearing blood and dirt. "Hell."

"I'll go first," I offered, though I was shaking so hard I couldn't tell if it was from fear or cold.

"No." He grabbed my hand, strong and steady despite everything. "We go together."

A spray of bullets ricocheted nearby, and we flinched as rock splinters rained down. The seconds collapsed into heartbeats. He pulled me closer, forehead to mine, and muttered, "On my count."

One.

Two.

Three.

We ran.

We sprinted like hell was licking at our heels because it was. Snow kicked up at our heels from bullets chasing us. My boots slipped on the icy ground, but Gavin held me upright, our hands locked tight. Every instinct screamed this was insane. Every part of me knew it was the only way.

The edge came too fast. There was no time to second-guess, no time to think about what waited below. Just wind and sky and the deafening roar of the river like it was calling us home.

"Now!" Gavin shouted.

We leapt.

The world fell away. Gravity yanked me into the void, cold air slapping my face so hard it stole the breath from my lungs. My stomach rose into my throat. I was falling, heart screaming louder than my voice. My fingers were still twined in Gavin's. He was with me. We were doing this together. That was the only thing keeping my brain from fracturing completely.

Wind howled past my ears. Snowflakes blurred into streaks. Somewhere in the freefall, I remembered a childhood moment, jumping off a swing set, flying for a second, feeling weightless and invincible. This was nothing like that. This was life or death. Maybe both. Then we hit the water.

It didn't feel like water. It felt like concrete. The shock knocked the air from my chest, ripped my hand from Gavin's, flipped me in the current like a ragdoll. Icy cold invaded every nerve ending, every thought. It was not just freezing. It was obliterating. I nearly gasped except I was underwater. I couldn't breathe. I couldn't see. All I could do was kick, claw, scream into liquid darkness. And hope I was headed up and not down.

The river was a monster. It swallowed me whole, turned me inside out, spat me in a dozen directions at once. My limbs flailed but found no purchase. I didn't know which way to go. Cold clamped down on me like a vise, locking my chest, freezing the scream in my throat.

I surfaced for half a breath, just enough to suck in more water, and then I was under again. The current dragged me sideways, deeper, spinning. Rocks scraped my knees, my shoulder. My body was screaming, burning, but I couldn't focus on any of it. Just one name. One desperate, silent prayer.

Gavin.

I twisted, forcing myself to fight. Kicked. Reached. I broke the surface and coughed hard, gagging on river water, eyes wide and useless against the glare. Everything was blinding white and churning water chaos.

"Gavin!" My voice was raw and drowned, but I screamed it anyway. Nothing.

A wave crashed into me. I went under again. My mind broke at the edges. He had been right there. We jumped together. I felt his hand.

Why wasn't he answering? A sob broke free, half-swallowed by the river. I shoved upward, breaking surface again, blinking furiously. My arms were useless flippers. My chest burned. And then—

A hand. Strong. Solid.

It seized my arm just as I was slipping under again. Rough, callused fingers locked around my wrist. *Gavin.* His grip was iron.

I gasped his name. I didn't even know if it was out loud.

He was coughing, dragging me toward the surface with what strength he had left. His face was pale, his eyes wild and locked on mine. And even though the current still fought to pull us under, that look, relief and desperation all at once, grounded me.

He was alive. We were still together.

Barely.

But together.

The river didn't let go.

It tore at us, relentless and roaring, as if pissed we survived the fall. I tightened my grip on Gavin's arm, wrapping my other hand around his shoulder. His lips were blue, but he was still trying to breathe. That was enough.

"Hang on!" I shouted, though I was not sure he heard me over the water crashing in our ears. He was deadweight one second, then kicking weakly the next. We were both exhausted, lungs heaving, muscles shredded by adrenaline and cold.

I threw my body sideways, trying to steer us toward the right bank, where tree roots and mossy rocks blurred past in a smear of motion. The current spun us like paper dolls. Gavin hit a log with his shoulder and groaned, his grip loosening.

No!

"No, no, no—Gavin!" I wedged myself against him, fighting to keep him afloat. My fingers found his collar, bunched it in my fists. "You're not leaving me now, dammit!"

I kicked hard, harder than I thought I could. Every inch was war. My thighs screamed, my lungs felt shredded from the inside out. But I didn't let go. I would never let go.

We careened around a bend, nearly slammed into a jagged rock shelf. I twisted at the last second, taking the brunt with my hip, pain exploding white. Still alive.

Still holding him.

The world narrowed to three things: the icy sting of water, the pulse under my fingertips, and the weight of Gavin's body clinging stubbornly to mine. And then, up ahead. Rocks. A bend in the river. The current slowed just a little. Enough for a shot.

With the last of my strength, I pulled us toward it.

Please let the river be done.

Please.

The river spat us out like chewed-up debris.

We hit the rocky shallows with a painful thud. My knees scraped jagged stone, and Gavin's body slammed beside me with a groan. I scrambled, dragging us up the bank inch by inch, coughing and sobbing and choking on air that burned worse than the water.

My fingers were numb. I couldn't feel my face. But I *moved*.

I hooked my arm under Gavin's and hauled him higher, away from the current's reach. He didn't help. He was still. Too still.

"No," I whispered, slapping his cheek lightly, then harder. "No, no, no—you're okay. You're *okay.*"

I fumbled at his throat. My fingers shook too much. I couldn't tell—

Then—*there*. A pulse. Weak, but steady.

The sob ripped from my throat without permission. It was ugly and raw and gasping, but I didn't care. I pressed my forehead to his temple, eyes squeezed shut.

"You're not allowed to scare me like that," I breathed. "Not again."

For a second, all I could hear was the water rushing behind us and my own heart thudding too loud in my chest. Then Gavin shifted. Just a twitch but enough. He was conscious.

Almost.

I pulled back and cradled his face with both hands, pushing wet hair from his brow. "You with me?"

His eyelids fluttered. He squinted. "You still yellin' at me?"

Relief broke like sunlight through storm clouds. "Only if you try to die again."

His lips twitched into something that might be a smile. "That's fair."

I rested my forehead against his, this time gently. "We made it," I whispered. "We actually made it."

But as I glanced upstream, the current still raging and our tracks washed away, a sliver of unease slid down my spine.

We were alive.

But we were not out.

We huddled together on the rocks, soaked to the marrow, trembling in tandem as wind sliced through our drenched clothes like razor wire. Every inch of me hurt, my shoulders, my knees, even my scalp, but I pushed it down. Gavin needed me.

I peeled back his jacket. Blood bloomed through the layers, darker now, sluggish. Not gushing, thank God. But he was still bleeding.

I tore off what was left of my overshirt, shaking fingers knotting the sleeves into a crude pressure bandage. Gavin winced as I pressed it down. "Sorry," I murmured, but he shook his head. His eyes were clearer now, less dazed.

"You're... handy in a crisis," he rasped.

I laughed, a ragged, breathless sound that sounded more like a sob. "You almost drowned."

He grinned, crooked and small. "So did you."

I tucked the cloth tighter, working fast before we lost what little body heat we had. "You want a medal or a blanket?"

He reached up, weak but stubborn, and hooked a hand around my wrist. His fingers were freezing, but his grip was steady. "Just you," he murmured.

And there it was, that familiar ache in my chest. The one that had nothing to do with injury or adrenaline. The one that started back in that crumpled aisle when we locked eyes for the first time.

"I'm not going anywhere," I said, quietly fierce. "We survived a crash, a cartel, a goddamn blizzard. You're stuck with me."

"Guess I could do worse," he whispered.

I settled in beside him, draping my arm over his chest. We clung to each other like wreckage in a storm, soaked, battered, alive. It was not romantic. It was not pretty. But it was real. And in this moment, it was enough. I had to figure out what to do about hypothermia.

Then I saw it. Something small moved in the sky.

My breath caught. I lifted my head, squinting against the brightness of the snow-lit sky. There. Just above the tree line. Hovering. A drone. Small, silent, barely visible against the whitewashed backdrop. Its underbelly blinked twice. Red, then blue.

"Gavin," I whispered, jostling his shoulder. "Look up."

His eyelids fluttered open. He blinked sluggishly, then focused where I was pointing. His entire body went taut beneath me.

"That's not Lev's," he said. A pause. "That's one of ours."

My heart stuttered between hope and disbelief. "You're sure?"

"Sierra Bravo uses that model. I trained with it, thermal, optical, encrypted relay. That blinking pattern is a code." His voice was raw but certain. "They're scanning for life."

A wild surge of relief flooded me, but it was immediately chased by something darker. If our people could see us, then so could Lev. If they were tracking Gavin, and now me, it was not a stretch to think Lev still had his own drone in the sky or would see this one.

I bit down on the panic rising in my throat. "We need to signal them."

"It's seen us," Gavin said, gripping my arm. "We're out in the open. If Lev's still scanning frequencies, a direct signal could give our position to more than just Sierra Bravo."

The blinking continued. Red. Blue. Pause. Red.

"What does that mean?" I ask.

"It means they see us."

A breath left me. It was half relief, half dread. I raised my hand slowly, not waving, just lifting it above my head in silent acknowledgment. The drone held its position, steady and quiet, its tiny lens watching us. We didn't move. Not yet. The river behind us, the forest ahead, the sky above full of questions.

Were we saved? Or had the drone just painted a target on our backs?

The drone tilted slightly, a mechanical nod or maybe my mind was just reaching for signs. Gavin shifted beside me eyes narrowed at the sky. His breathing was shallow, skin pale under the bruises, but his instincts were sharp as ever.

"They're probably confirming ID," he muttered. "Thermal scan first. Visual match second."

"How long does that take?" I asked, barely above a whisper, "And do they have our pictures as drowned rats?"

"Hopefully not too long." He said and chuckled.

The silence hung between us, a breath held by the forest itself. No birds. No wind. Just the faint buzz of that hovering eye and the gurgling churn of the river behind us.

I raised my hand again, this time a little higher, fingers splayed. A peace sign? A surrender? I wasn't sure. The drone didn't move.

Gavin coughed, grimacing as he propped himself on one elbow. "If it was Sierra Bravo... we've got a shot. Extraction team. Med evac. Warm food." His voice dipped, almost wistful.

"And if it was not?"

He didn't answer. I guessed he really didn't have to.

The lights blinked once more. Blue... red... pause. Then the drone shifted, banking slightly to the right. It didn't fly off. It didn't descend. It just... watched.

"I don't like this," I whispered.

Gavin's jaw tightened. "Me neither."

Then a new sound crackled into life. A burst of static, faint but present. From the drone? Or from somewhere else?

But the static grew louder.

"We've been found," Gavin said, not to me exactly. More like to himself. As if saying it out loud would make it true. But found by whom? His hand found mine, fingers tight despite the cold.

The drone pivoted, then began to glide away, slow and deliberate. Toward the trees. Where someone waited.

I gripped Gavin's hand tighter.

"We're not alone," I breathed.

And whether that was salvation or doom—we were about to find out.

Rescue Protocol

Gavin Henderson

The sound cut through the wind like a wasp with a mission. Not the usual thrum of trees swaying or river water rushing over rock. No, this buzz was mechanical, tight, fast, unmistakable. I knew that drone. Quad rotors. Sleek undercarriage. Standard recon model from Sierra Bravo's supply line. I'd run ops under their cover before, and this baby was no off-the-shelf toy.

Relief barreled through me, fast and fleeting. I dug into my jacket with numb fingers and yanked out the LED penlight I'd stashed earlier. Three short, two long, three short, classic SOS pulse. A second later, the drone winked back. One, two. Pause. One, two. Recognition pattern. It dipped slightly, shifting toward us like it was bowing to confirm.

Ava was beside me, silent but wide-eyed. "Is that—?"

"Sierra Bravo," I grunted. "One of ours."

The drone's speaker crackled with static, then a clipped voice punched through the wind: "Hold position. Extraction en route."

My lungs finally pulled in a full breath. They'd found us. We were not alone anymore. But I'd been in the field too long to get comfortable. If we could see the drone, so could Lev's team. That signal was hope but it was also like our flare in the dark.

"We're not safe yet," I murmured to Ava. "That drone could be a neon sign pointing at us."

She nodded, already shifting into a crouch beside me, her breath visible in the frigid air. I raised the light one last time to confirm the communication, then clicked it off and tucked it away. The drone hovered like a silent guardian above us. For the first time in days, I let myself feel something dangerously close to hope.

But it was not over yet.

I didn't like being in the open. Never had. It was drilled into my bones. Open ground was exposure, and exposure got you killed. The drone's signal was good news, sure, but it was also a glowing bullseye overhead. If I were the enemy, I'd use it as bait. Track it. Wait for the rescue team to get close. Snipe the evac, wipe the witnesses. Clean.

"Move," I told Ava, low and sharp. I gestured toward a shallow rock overhang about twenty feet to our left. It had probably been carved out by the river at some point. It was just enough cover to break up our silhouette but still within the drone's line of sight. She nodded without hesitation and scrambled beside me, ducking beneath the ledge as I staggered after her.

My whole body screamed with every step, but I forced it to move. I couldn't afford to collapse. Not now. Once under cover, I dropped to one knee and started scanning the tree line. Trees, snow, nothing. But that quiet? Th forest had gone too quiet. It was not natural. No bird calls, no snapping twigs from squirrels. Just the faint mechanical hum above and the soft crunch of Ava shifting behind me.

Something was out there.

I scanned left, steep incline, rocks. Right, more of the same. In front, a narrow funnel where the river bent and disappeared behind a ridge. A kill zone, if I'd ever seen one. I tapped the gun's lip to drain out any water, checked the chamber, one full load. That was it. No grenades, no backup. Just wounded me, a knife, and a goddamn prayer.

I glanced at Ava. She was crouched behind a boulder, calm but alert, every line of her body coiled and ready. Her eyes met mine, and we didn't speak. We didn't need to. We were here. We were seen.

And we were not going down without a fight.

A radio crackled. At first, just static. Then a hiss of Russian, guttural and fast.

"They're at the river! Move now!"

A pause, followed by a burst of curses. Angry. Desperate. Then nothing.

No more guesswork. No more hoping they had lost our trail. They knew where we were. And they were coming.

I turned to Ava. Her face was pale, jaw tight, eyes locked on mine. She didn't ask. She already knew.

"They'll be coming," I said anyway. "Fast."

She nodded once, her shoulders squared. "How long?"

"Minutes, maybe less."

I drew her close, my body automatically shielding hers. "We hold. We fight if we have to."

She didn't flinch. Didn't ask if I was sure. She just grabbed my hand and squeezed. "Together."

That one word landed like a vow. I'd fought beside good men before. Brothers. Marines I'd bleed for. But this, her, it was different. I wasn't just guarding her life. I was guarding the possibility of something after this. And hell if I was letting that get taken. From either of us.

I repositioned behind a boulder, gun ready, pulse steady. The drone hovered above like a silent witness. But the real storm would be coming from the trees. And I'd be ready when it broke.

Snow drifted down in thick, lazy flakes. The scene was too peaceful for the hell we were caught in. I crouched low. I had no rifle. No real firepower. Just a half-loaded sidearm tucked tight against my ribs and a dull ache where adrenaline had stopped masking the pain.

Above, the drone hovered. Its quad rotors sliced the air in rhythm with my heartbeat. That sound used to mean backup. Now, it was a coin toss. Who would get here first?

The silence broke barely audibly. Snow shifting under boots. Behind us.

I adjusted, blocking Ava with my body without drawing attention to the move. My fingers brushed hers, then curled around the gun. She gripped the knife I had given her like she had trained for this. Her chin lifted, eyes sweeping the forest. She was ready, or as ready as anyone could be in a kill box.

There it was. The beat of rotor blades. Not from the drone. The sound was deeper. Thicker. A chopper.

Sierra Bravo.

I didn't celebrate. Not yet. Not when I could still feel movement coming in from the trees. Flanking us. They were not waiting for the air team. They were going to hit us before extraction ever touched down.

I scanned the angles. No good shots. I'd have to draw them out, buy time. Ava's shoulder pressed into mine. Warm. Steady.

Above us, rescue circled.

Behind us... death crept closer.

I did a mental sweep—cataloging what was left, what was usable, what was just dead weight. Half a clip in the pistol. No spare. The river likely swallowed the other. Knife in my boot, blade nicked but sharp. Just instincts and muscle memory.

I glanced at Ava. She was crouched beside me, soaked through, cheeks flushed from cold and adrenaline. She should look wrecked, broken. Instead, she looked fierce. Wild. Alive. There was something in her eyes, like she had made peace with this moment, whatever came. I had seen the same look in soldiers facing insurmountable odds ready to go down swinging.

I was not at peace with any of this.

My fingers twitched. Not from nerves. From calculation. Six rounds. Seven counting the one already chambered. I could make that count. I had to. Ava shifted closer, just enough for her hand to brush against my forearm. Not clinging. Not comforting. Just there. Anchoring us both.

"We've made it this far," she whispered.

Her voice was hoarse but steady.

I met her gaze. "We're not dying now."

It was not bravado. It was a contract. Between us and the mountain. Between me and whatever god kept us breathing this long.

The drone banked overhead, signaling again with its lights. I translated the sequence. Sierra Bravo's code for **"eyes on targets, extraction inbound."**

We were minutes away.

Maybe less.

Snow started falling heavier now, thick and blinding. Maybe nature was trying to erase the scene before it was over. Ava adjusted her grip on the knife. She was ready to fight. Hell, she already had. Every step since that crash had been a battle. And now... it was almost over. Or just beginning. Depended on who got here first.

The air shifted, thicker, vibrating with pressure, just seconds before I heard it.

Rotor wash.

Ava and I both looked up as the treetops shuddered, needles raining down in slow motion. The chopper crested the ridgeline, nose-mounted gun sweeping the tree line like a predator scenting blood. It was Sierra Bravo. I'd know that matte-black paint and SB logo anywhere.

My heart thudded, once, like a battering ram in my chest. We had a prayer.

"We've got eyes," I muttered.

Ava gripped my arm, fingers digging in just enough to say *don't let go now*. I didn't.

The drone banked again, flashing a coded confirmation. The chopper slowed into a hover, downdraft kicking up snow like fog. They were holding steady, waiting for a clear to land signal. But they were too far out for a safe drop. We were still pinned between the open river and the tree line.

I raised one arm, keeping low, flashing the LED from my pen light to land.

The pilot angled the nose down in reply. Good. They saw us.

But they were not descending yet. Which meant one thing.

They didn't think it was safe.

Neither did I.

I scanned the woods again. Shadows moved behind the tree line, fast and wrong. Not the rescue team. Too erratic. Too silent. Mercs. Flanking.

I turned to Ava. "It's gonna get loud," I said, voice clipped.

She nodded. No fear now, just fire.

The blades roared louder, pulsing through my bones. The bird was holding but it wouldn't land in a kill zone. The thermals must have picked up the mercs. I knew the math. If we wanted to get out, we would have to *hold* this ground long enough for them to touch down.

I checked the pistol in my hand one more time.

Seven rounds.

Ava braced beside me with her little knife. Not a real weapon. But I had seen her wield fear like a blade. She was not backing down.

Neither was I.

The cavalry was here.

Now we just had to survive long enough to reach them.

The moment shattered.

Gunfire ripped through the stillness like a goddamn thunderclap, sharp, close, way too close.

"Down!" I roared, dragging Ava flat as bullets chewed through the tree behind us. Bark exploded overhead. I heard her gasp, but she didn't scream. Good. Screaming wasted oxygen.

Across the riverbank, shadows emerged in bursts—three, four, maybe five mercs sprinting out of cover. They'd circled wide and were charging now, rifles raised. One of them dropped to a knee, sights locking on our position.

I fired before he did. Two rounds.

One found a shoulder. He spun backward, screaming.

But there was no time to count bodies.

More muzzle flashes strobed from the tree line. A bullet slammed into the rock behind us, ricocheting into snow. Ava was gripping her knife like it was Excalibur. She didn't flinch, didn't fold. She was watching the flank, just like I taught her.

"Left!" she yelled.

I twisted and squeezed off a shot, clipping another bastard trying to sneak around.

Above us, the chopper circled lower, finally making its descent. Rotor wash kicked up a white storm of snow and debris. The gunner on the door pivoted the mounted weapon and let loose a burst. Thunder followed. One merc went down hard, body tumbling like a rag doll.

But it was still not enough.

They were trying to outpace the bird. Get to us before the landing skids hit dirt.

I counted three more closing in fast. One threw a smoke canister, cheap but effective. The poor visibility dropped to zero in seconds.

"We've got to move!" I shouted.

Ava nodded, eyes sharp. "Which way?"

Anywhere but here.

I aimed and fired at the canister's source. I couldn't see the target, but it bought us seconds. Behind us, the Sierra Bravo chopper swung in lower, skids slicing through haze. I knew where it was landing.

"Now!" I yelled, grabbing Ava's hand.

We ran, no cover, no guarantees, just desperation and the hope that rescue was faster than death.

We were ten yards out when the world erupted again.

Gunfire screamed from behind, wild, desperate bursts from mercenaries who knew they were seconds too late and still tried to make it count. A bullet zipped past my ear with a whisper of death. Another slammed into the snow near Ava's feet. She stumbled but recovered. Didn't slow.

The Sierra Bravo chopper hovered low now, side door wide open. Two operators crouched inside, rifles up, covering us. The side gunner pivoted again and laid down suppressing fire. A roar of rounds chewed into the tree line behind us. The noise was deafening, but it was the best damn sound I'd ever heard.

"Go!" I shoved Ava ahead, shielding her body with mine. My ribs screamed with the effort, my vision graying for a second, but I kept moving. No way in hell I was falling now.

The snow was deep, churned by rotor wash and chaos. I couldn't tell if my legs were moving forward or just flailing, but then hands grabbed Ava. Strong ones. Sierra Bravo. She was yanked into the helicopter like salvation itself just reached down and said not today.

I lurched forward, grabbing the outstretched arm of a rescuer just as something punched into the dirt inches from my boot. I didn't look back. Didn't need to. Ava screamed my name.

And then I was up, hauled into the belly of the chopper as the side door slammed closed. The medic moved to me instantly, hands pressing me down. Voices shouted over the engine. But I didn't hear any of them.

I heard Ava, crouched beside me, hands on my face. "We made it," she said, over and over like a prayer.

But we were not safe yet.

The helicopter veered hard, taking fire as it lifted. Rounds pinged off the frame. Through the small side window, I caught a glimpse of a merc with a radio to his mouth, shouting as we rose.

Whatever he was saying, I knew it was not over. Not yet.

Not until we got out of these mountains. Not until she and Emma were truly safe.

And I swear to God—I would see that through if it killed me.

Extraction Under Fire

Ava Green

The chopper dropped like a noisy hammer from the sky.

Wind and snow exploded around us as its twin rotors churned the air into a screaming white storm. I barely had time to process the blur of motion, blades slicing, guns barking, men in Sierra Bravo gear leaping from the open door with rifles raised.

Gavin shoved me flat as bullets tore through the trees, snapping bark, showering us in splinters.

One of the soldiers yelled over the chaos, "Move! Move! Exfil now!"

I blinked through the snow. It was all happening too fast. The helicopter tilted slightly, side door yawning open like a mouth ready to swallow us whole. Thunder crashed from the tree line as Lev's men returned fire. I flinched as something zipped past my head and hit rock with a sharp ping.

Gavin's arm wrapped around my shoulders. "Go!" he growled, and suddenly we were moving.

My legs stumbled into motion before my brain caught up. We ran, slipping on snow-slicked ground, zigzagging behind spurts of gunfire. I was so blinded by the snow being blown up by the helicopter I wasn't positive I was running in the right direction. The Sierra soldiers formed a moving barrier, precision shots dropping mercs before they could aim. My boots slipped in the churned snow, but Gavin yanked me upright before I fell. The ramp was a blur of steel and shadow ahead. So close. Too far.

A shout behind me. "Nine o'clock—tree line!"

I glanced back.

A mercenary stepped from the woods, rifle raised, eyes locked on mine. Cold, methodical. His finger curled around the trigger.

I froze.

A crack split the air. He jerked, once, twice, and dropped like a puppet with cut strings. A Sierra Bravo sniper, unseen until now, lowered his rifle from a perch inside the helicopter door.

"Go!" Gavin roared.

A hand grabbed my arm, another soldier, pulling me up the ramp by brute force. I twisted just in time to see Gavin stumble, blood trailing behind him in the snow.

"No—" I screamed, reaching but he was already pushing forward, teeth gritted, dragging himself into the bird just as more bullets raked the side.

The metal rattled beneath us. Sparks flew. Someone slammed the side door shut with a mechanical *clang*. We were in. Just barely.

The floor beneath me shuddered as the chopper lifted. I collapsed against Gavin, still gripping his hand, the imprint of that merc's dead eyes burned into my brain.

We made it.

We were not safe.

But we were alive.

The chopper jerked as it clawed into the sky, blades thundering overhead. My ears rung with the chaos, gunfire below, the steady whine of engines being pushed to their max, Gavin's ragged breathing beside me. The bird was rocked with the wind, too loud, too low. I could feel the rotors pounding in my chest.

Then, another sound. Sharp. Electronic.

A voice sliced through, low and venomous.

"Shoot them down. Do not let them escape."

My blood turned to ice. Gavin's jaw tightened.

"We tapped into their frequency." The pilot said.

A pause crackled through the radio line. Then Lev again, colder now:

"Bring me the girl. Kill the rest."

A streak of something flashed past the window, a rocket or grenade, maybe both.

The pilot yelled, "Evasive!" and the entire helicopter tilted.

I grabbed the wall for balance as gravity tried to throw us sideways. The thing must've missed. Barely.

Gavin curled an arm around me, shielding my head as we were jostled like dice in a metal cup. Every bone in my body hummed with tension. Lev's voice still echoed in my ears.

Not a random threat. A command.

I turned to Gavin. His face was stone, but I saw the fear there. Not for himself. For me. He tightened his hold on the rifle one of the soldiers passed him. "If they shoot us down," he muttered, "I'll take as many of them with us as I can."

I wanted to argue. But I couldn't. Not when Lev's voice was still crawling across my skin like a ghost with unfinished business.

We were not out yet.

Not by a long shot.

It was still loud, rotors whomping, radios squawking, soldiers shouting orders, but it was a different kind of chaos. Controlled. Contained. Safe. Or at least... safer.

My knees started shaking the moment the adrenaline ebbed. I collapsed against Gavin, gasping. My lungs ached like I'd been breathing knives. My clothes were soaked, half-frozen, and sticky with blood, his, mine, I couldn't even tell anymore.

We were a heap of tangled limbs and torn gear on the floor. Gavin let out a low grunt, trying to brace himself as I leaned into him.

"Stay with me," I whispered, fingers trembling as I clutched his jacket.

"I'm here." His voice was hoarse, but steady. "We made it."

A medic crouched beside us, already reaching for Gavin's arm. "Gunshot wound—upper arm. Knife wound torso. Bleeding's slowed, but he's pale." I said.

Gavin waved him off with the last bit of bravado he had left. "Save your bandages. She's the one they want."

The medic ignored him, muttering, "Typical Sierra Bravo," and pulled out gauze. I barely noticed. All I could do was hold on to Gavin. My hands fisted into his shirt like he might vanish if I let go.

His breath brushed my ear. "It's over."

I shook my head. "He said he'd find us. And Emma."

His hand came up, cupping the back of my head, tucking me into him like he was trying to make a shield of his own body. "Let him try."

And for just one fragile second, I believed him.

We'd survived the jump into the river. We'd survived the bullets. We were airborne.

But even wrapped in Gavin's arms, I knew—

The war wasn't done.

Not even close.

I didn't realize I was crying until I tasted salt on my lips. At first, I tried to hold it back, tighten everything down, clenched my jaw, and swallowed it whole. But then Gavin shifted, wincing as the medic applied pressure, and his arm curled tighter around me. I heard the thud of his heartbeat beneath my ear.

It was steady. Alive.

And that was what undid me.

The sob broke loose, raw and shaking. I buried my face in his chest and just let it happen. The fear, the guilt, the grief. I couldn't hold it anymore. Not after falling off a cliff. Not after nearly drowning. Not after watching him bleed and still fight for me. He didn't speak. Didn't try to shush me. He just held me tighter.

His warmth seeped into my frozen skin. His hand drifted across my back, slow and grounding, like I was something fragile he was afraid to drop. It was the gentlest I'd ever been held in my life.

I didn't know how long we stayed that way, wrapped in each other, chaos buzzing around us. All I knew was that it was real. The world had narrowed to his arms, his heartbeat, his quiet strength holding me together when everything else fell apart.

"You saved me," I whispered into his chest. "Back there. The river. The ridge. You—"

"We saved each other," he murmured back, lips brushing the top of my head.

His voice broke something else inside me, something soft and secret. A place I didn't realize was still open to hope for a tomorrow.

I tilted my head, just enough to meet his gaze. His eyes were bloodshot, rimmed with exhaustion, but the way he looked at me? It was fire and promise.

And it felt like the first breath after surfacing from the dark.

The medic pressed a thermal blanket into my hands, nodding toward Gavin. I shook it out, my fingers still trembling, and draped it over his shoulders. He was shaking too, though he tried to hide it, ever the strong protector. But when he shifted, he gasped through his teeth.

Blood. Fresh and too red.

"Shit," I muttered, pulling the blanket aside. His shirt was soaked through on one side, darker now than it was minutes ago. "You're bleeding again."

He tried to wave me off, but his hand barely made it halfway before it dropped. "I'm fine."

"You're full of crap," I snapped then caught myself. Gentler, I said, "Let me help."

The medic moved to assist, but I was already kneeling beside him, peeling his shirt back and grabbing gauze. My hands didn't feel like my own. They were too slow, too clumsy, but I pressed down anyway, watching his jaw lock tight against the pain.

"You don't have to—" he started.

"I want to," I cut in, meeting his eyes.

There was blood between us now, mine on his jacket, his on my palms, but it didn't feel grotesque. It felt... intimate. A bond born of fire and snow and things we couldn't name yet.

He exhaled hard, sweat beading on his temple. "We really have to stop meeting like this."

I huffed a breath that might have become a laugh. "You nearly die, I patch you up. It's becoming a theme."

His lips twitched. "Let's try dinner next time."

The medic gave us space, moving to the other side of the chopper. I rewrapped the bandage as best I could, my fingers finally steadying.

"Better?" I whispered.

He nodded. "Better."

And for the first time since we fell from the sky, I almost believed him.

For a few long minutes, it was just wind and altitude.

No bullets. No bark shattering. No ice cracking under boots. Just the thrum of rotor blades and the muffled comms of Sierra Bravo soldiers double-checking gear and securing their coms. Inside the chopper, it was strangely still.

I leaned against Gavin, letting the warmth of his body and the blanket seep into my bones. His breath was slower now, more even. My fingers remained laced in his shirt like an anchor, and I didn't let go. I didn't want to.

The adrenaline was fading, and in its place was something fragile. Raw.

I glanced around. The medic reloaded supplies. The sniper nodded toward us in quiet respect. The pilot called in coordinates, voice calm and clipped.

We made it.

And yet—I couldn't shake the weight in my chest.

I closed my eyes, and I saw Emma. Her bald head wrapped in a scarf, grinning as she stuck her tongue out at her chemo nurse, her middle finger to the cancer, to fear, to giving up. I saw her alive. Not as a memory, but a real, breathing sister who was hopefully safe right now.

I felt Gavin shift beside me. His hand slipped over mine, slow and reassuring. He didn't say anything. He didn't have to. Tears pricked at my eyes, but I blinked them back. Not yet. Not again.

The horizon stretched wide outside the helicopter window, blue-gray clouds over mountains and trees that tried to kill us. But in this moment, I was still here. He was still here. And the storm had passed.

At least, I think it had.

Then the radio flared.

Static first. Then a voice. Calm. Familiar.

And just like that, peace shattered.

The voice that crackled through the Sierra Bravo comms line was unmistakable.

Lev.

Not screaming this time. Not frantic or furious like he was when we slipped from his fingers. No, this was something worse. Controlled. Composed. Coiled like a serpent just before it struck.

"You think you are safe?"

The air in the helicopter went still. Even the medic paused mid-wrap, eyes flicking toward the front where the radio rested.

"You think extraction means you have won?" Lev's accent curled around every word like a blade. "This isn't over. You've taken something from me. And I always get it back. I will find you. I will make you pay."

Gavin.

Me.

Emma.

All of us.

My jaw clenched. I felt Gavin's hand tighten around my own, my knuckles white beneath the blanket. My lips were parted, breath shaky, eyes locked on the front like it was a ticking bomb.

I whispered, "He's not done."

"He can come for us." Gavin said and glanced at me. His eyes met mine tempered now with something harder. Steel. Survival. Fire.

We were alive. But the war was not over.

We were not out. We were not safe. Not yet.

As the helicopter banked toward distant safety, I leaned in closer again.

Because whatever came next, we would face it, together.

Safehouse Fever

Gavin Henderson

I woke to the sound of my own breath.

Slow. Measured. No gunfire in the background. No hum of blades overhead. Just the gentle creak of a wooden ceiling above and the faint whisper of wind sliding over a roof that didn't leak. And I wasn't cold. My side throbbed, sharp and insistent. I shifted, groaning, and something warm brushed against my ribs, steady, sure fingers pressing down gauze.

"You're lucky," Ava said softly.

My eyes snapped open to find her sitting beside the bed, her face half-shadowed in the dim morning light filtering through the window. Her eyes were rimmed with fatigue, but they shone anyway. Her hands moved with calm confidence, taping off the last edge of the bandage like she'd done it a thousand times. Probably had.

"Wasn't feeling lucky," I rasped, voice rough with sleep and dehydration. "Still not sure I am."

She huffed a breath that was almost a laugh, but not quite. "Could've fooled me. You were leaving a blood trail in the snow and still managed to drag us into the damn helicopter."

Her hand lingered a moment on my bare skin, palm flat just above the dressing. Heat radiated from that touch, but she pulled away slowly, deliberately. I missed the contact as soon as it was gone.

"You passed out not long after they lifted off," she said. "I had to sit on you to keep you from getting back up."

I grunted. "Sounds about right."

She gave me a small smile, wry, tired, but real. Her eyes flicked down to the bandage again. "I should've stitched it myself. Medic did okay, but he didn't know you're the type who'll rip it open just to be a stubborn ass."

"Not wrong."

I reached for her hand, stopped just shy. "You okay?"

She nodded, but I saw the flicker in her eyes before she answered. A lie, maybe. Or just too much truth to fit in a single word. Either way, I didn't push. Not yet. But as I settled back into the pillow, chest aching, the full weight of what could've happened slammed into me.

We could've died. Worse. She could've died and I lived. And that thought cut deeper than any bullet.

The safehouse smelled like cedar and old wool. It was a far cry from the steel and smoke of the crash site, but I couldn't stop looking over my shoulder like I expected someone to come bursting through the door.

I swung my legs over the edge of the bed, ignoring the tug of stitches at my side. Ava had already drifted into another room, kitchen, maybe. Her absence left a hollow in the air, like her warmth hadn't quite faded.

I stood slowly. Everything ached. Muscles pulled tight from days of running, lungs scraped raw from cold air and adrenaline. But I needed to move. I needed to know this place was real and safe.

The cabin wasn't large. Two bedrooms, a central living space, a wood-burning stove ticking quietly in the corner. Reinforced windows, sandbags stacked beneath the sill, radio gear tucked beneath a blanket on the table. Sierra Bravo-standard for off-grid safe zones. But none of that made my chest loosen.

What did was the silence. Not the kind that felt like a trap. Not the kind you got before a sniper took the shot. This silence was... gentle. Honest. Outside, the storm that chased us through hell was nothing more than a whisper of snow brushing against the logs of the walls. The sky was a pale wash of gray. Daylight was trying to break through. I did a full perimeter check anyway, slowly—old habits—but everything was locked down tight. The other cabins were occupied with Sierra Bravo personnel who just glanced at me or waved.

When I stepped back inside, I saw her. Ava. Curled on the wide sofa, hair damp, legs tucked under her, a steaming mug cradled in her hands. She was wearing an old Sierra Bravo T-shirt, oversized, threadbare from years of deployment laundry, and nothing else but thick socks and a look I couldn't quite read.

My breath caught.

She looked alive. Not just alive. She looked like someone who'd fought death and won. And the sight of her, small, strong, real, hit me harder than the cold ever had.

She looked up and caught me staring. Her lips parted, but she didn't say anything. She didn't have to.

I crossed the room like I'd been shot again. Because for the first time in forever, there was no chase, no fire, no mission. Just her. And it scared the hell out of me.

The tea was still warm when she pressed a second mug into my hand. I didn't ask how she knew I'd be back so soon. Just wrapped my fingers around the ceramic and eased onto the couch beside her. The heat seeped into my palms. I was not used to things being this quiet, this calm, with no impending mission.

She tucked her legs beneath her again, leaned a little into my side like she was testing the weight of closeness. I stayed still. Didn't flinch. Didn't pull away. Truth was, I didn't want to. Her shoulder brushed mine, and even that small point of contact felt like gravity shifting under my feet.

The only sound in the room was the low pop of the fire and the faint click of her spoon against the rim of her cup. No orders. No radio chatter. No screaming. Stillness. For a guy like me, it was disorienting.

We sat there in silence, breathing the same air. Her head tipped toward me slowly, like she had been thinking about it for a while. When it landed gently on my shoulder, something inside me cracked, not loud, not shattering. Just... quietly giving in. I glanced down at her. Her eyes were closed, lashes resting like shadows on bruised skin. There was still a faint smudge on her cheek, probably a small bruise from some branch during our running. She smelled like soap and cedar smoke and something warmer underneath, something that made my pulse skip.

I shifted my arm just enough to slide it behind her, fingers resting at the base of her spine. She didn't move, didn't tense. Just breathed. Every moment we'd shared until now had been urgent. Life or death. Sprinted. Screamed. But this, this silence was louder than all of it.

I didn't know I needed it until she gave it to me. And now that she was here, resting against me like I was not broken, like I didn't nearly die dragging her across a mountain, there was no part of me that wanted to move. Not anymore.

Her skin was softer than I expected from such an incredibly strong survivor. I brushed a thumb across her cheek, just above the faint bruise forming along her jaw. It was not swollen anymore, just tender. A mottled bloom of purple and yellow that made my gut clench. I didn't say it, but I could still see the moment it happened, her falling, that bastard Lev's boot striking her hard.

"I'm sorry," I murmured. My voice sounded like gravel.

She lifted her face, eyes clear and sharp now. "For what?"

"For not stopping him sooner. For not—" I cut off, jaw tight, hesitant to admit my failure to her eyes. "For not being enough."

Ava reached for my hand before I could pull away. Her fingers threaded through mine, slow and steady, like she was trying to remind me I was real. Like I was not a ghost made of scars and mistakes.

"You saved me," she said, simple and true.

I shook my head. "We barely made it."

"Exactly," she whispered. "But we made it."

She shifted, her body angling toward mine, our legs brushing. Her thumb traced slow circles over my knuckles. I felt like I was unraveling with every pass. Like some teenager fumbling my way through a first date. We'd been getting to this moment for days. Through blood and snow and gunfire. Through every second we weren't sure whether we'd get another. Now it was just us. No mission. No chase. Just her hand in mine. Her lips parted slightly. Her breath, close.

When I kissed her, it was gentle at first, more breath than pressure, just the sigh of a promise. But she leaned in, meeting me halfway, and the second kiss went deeper. Hotter. It stole the air from my lungs and gave something else in return. Something I didn't know I still had. Hope.

Her hands found my shoulders. Mine slid to her hips. We pulled each other closer like we'd been doing it in our dreams, like every second of our lives apart was a mistake we were finally correcting. Every wall I'd built, every rule I'd lived by, started to fall. And I didn't even try to stop it.

She climbed into my lap like she'd always belonged there. No hesitation. No pretense. Just a quiet, certain need. My hands slid up beneath the hem of the shirt she was wearing, palm meeting bare skin. She was warm, soft, alive. Her breath hitched as I skimmed the curve of her spine, and her fingers clutched at my shoulders like she was anchoring herself.

"You sure?" I asked, even though I had no idea what I'd do now if she rejected me.

On the mountain we were driven by desperation, by some need to prove we were alive but here, now, this was real. This could lead somewhere, and I didn't know what to do with that idea. I only knew I needed this woman and more than just physically.

She answered with a kiss that silenced everything else. Deep. Unapologetic. Her teeth scraped my bottom lip before she softened again, like she couldn't decide if she wanted to devour me or dissolve into me. Turned out, I wanted both.

We shifted together, bodies angling until her back met the couch cushions and I was above her. She pulled me down with hands that trembled only slightly, her gaze locked on mine. There was no fear in it, just fire. Trust. That was what undid me.

I kissed her again. Her throat, her collarbone, the hollow beneath her jaw. I followed the shape of her like a man tracing scripture, relearning how to pray at the temple of Ava.

Clothes fell away slowly. Not ripped. Not rushed. Just peeled back with reverence. Every inch of her skin was a truth I wanted to memorize, to honor with gentle touch and kisses.

She arched into me, her sighs barely audible beneath the crackle of the fire. Her hands roamed, unhurried, curious. When she reached the scar on my shoulder, she paused.

"What happened here?" she whispered.

"Doesn't matter... until now," I murmured against her skin.

And it was true. Because with her, everything mattered. Every breath. Every bruise. Every second we'd survived.

We moved together, no hesitation now. No room for anything else. She gasped my name. I buried my face in her neck, groaning as we lost ourselves in the heat, in the rhythm, in the release. It was not about hunger anymore. It was about need. Connection. Safety.

I held her like she was the first good thing I'd ever touched. Maybe she was. And when she broke open beneath me, shaking and clinging and gasping like I was her only lifeline, I followed. Hard. Deep. Completely.

The fire crackled low, but inside me, something else had been lit. And I was not sure it'd ever go out. Or if I wanted it to.

She was quiet afterward. Not asleep. Just... still. Her fingers traced idle patterns across my chest, slow and soft, like she was drawing secrets into my skin. The fire had burned down to glowing embers. Shadows stretched long across the walls, and I didn't move, afraid the spell would break if I so much as breathed too hard.

Ava shifted slightly, her thigh sliding against mine. Her cheek rested on my shoulder, and her exhale was shaky.

"You're cold?" I guessed, reaching for the throw draped over the arm of the couch.

"No," she whispered. "I'm just... here."

She fell silent again. I waited. For her to talk. Tell me what she was thinking, feeling. Not wanting this silence to turn into something permanent but not knowing what to say.

Then, hardly audibly, "I didn't think I'd ever feel safe again."

The words slipped out like a confession. And suddenly, I felt her shake. Just once. A tremor through her whole body, as if the fear was finally letting go of her... and taking something with it.

I tightened my arms around her. Pressed my lips to her forehead, then her temple. She didn't resist. Didn't flinch. Her tears were silent but steady, sliding down to my chest. I let them fall.

"You are now," I murmured, voice low against her hair. "I swear it."

She clutched the blanket tighter around us, burying herself into me like she wanted to disappear into my ribs. I wanted to pull her in so deep the world couldn't touch her anymore. Not Lev. Not the memories. Not the nightmares that were surely buried in there.

I didn't know what made a man worthy of peace. I'd spent years thinking I'd forfeited mine. That I didn't deserve this. But now, with her heartbeat steady against mine, her trust wrapping around me like another kind of warmth... maybe I was wrong. Maybe surviving wasn't just about walking away. Maybe it was about who you walked away with.

The fire was mostly ash now, faint orange threads weaving through the gray. I should get up and feed it, stoke the warmth before it faded. But I didn't move.

Ava was curled against me, her breathing soft and even, her hand resting palm-down on my chest like she had claimed it. Every so often, her thumb shifted, just a small motion, rhythmic, like she was making sure I was still there. I was. Totally. For once, I was not watching the door. Not counting exit points. Not cataloguing the sharp objects within arm's reach. I was just... there.

The wind whispered outside, nudging against the windows like it was testing for cracks. But the glass held. The walls held. And in the small cocoon of this safehouse, so did we. I closed my eyes for a second.

Maybe it was longer. I let myself drift. Not fully asleep, but near it. That quiet place between fight and surrender. When I blinked again, she was watching me.

Her face was softer than I'd ever seen it. The wariness that always sat behind her eyes was gone now, replaced by something warmer. Something open.

She brushed her fingers along my jaw. "Didn't peg you for a cuddler."

"Don't spread it around," I muttered, voice raspy. "I have a reputation to protect."

She grinned, and it hit me like a gut punch. That smile. That softness. I'd go back into the fire just to see it again. We laid there for what felt like forever. Or maybe just a few stolen minutes. Time blurred in the aftershock of survival, in the quiet between the storms. But for the first time since that damn plane dropped from the sky, I let myself believe. That we might actually make it. That we could have more than just blood and bullets between us. That there was still something waiting on the other side of all this.

The knock cut through the stillness like a gunshot.

Three sharp raps at the door, measured, intentional. I was off the couch before my brain finished processing, heart hammering, hand instinctively reaching for the pistol on the end table.

Ava startled, blanket falling away from her bare shoulder. "What—?"

"Stay behind me," I ordered, already moving.

Another knock. Louder this time.

Then a voice through the door. Calm. Familiar.

"It's Mendoza. Open up. It's freezing out here."

I exhaled just enough to keep my hand from trembling. Pulled on pants and crossed to the door. I pulled it open slowly, just wide enough to see the man's face.

Tomás Mendoza, Sierra Bravo's go-to for extraction and follow-through. Steady. Unshakable. He stepped inside with snow clinging to his boots and cold in his eyes.

"What's wrong?" I asked immediately.

He glanced toward Ava, who had pulled the blanket tighter around herself and was standing now, wary. He looked back at me. Grim.

"We just got word from Riley," he said. "Intercepted chatter off one of Lev's secondary frequencies."

My gut turned to ice at the sound of Lev's name.

"Another survivor from the crash," Mendoza said. "They found one."

Ava was already moving toward us. "Who?"

He hesitated. "Not sure. The voice on the radio called them 'a bargaining chip.' They're alive... for now."

Ava's breath caught like she'd been punched.

Mendoza's voice lowered. "Lev's got them."

Silence flooded the room with the force of a tsunami. I felt it the same moment she did. Her body went rigid, her expression shattering. The color drained from her face.

"No," she whispered. "This is my fault."

"Ava—" I reached for her, but she pulled away, already shaking her head.

"If I hadn't left them... If I'd made them come with us—" Her voice broke, splintered. "I knew he'd go after someone else."

I grabbed her hand, gripping it tight. "We don't know who it is yet. We'll find out. We'll get them back. And he may be lying."

But I already knew what was coming. She was going to offer herself. Trade herself, if she had to. Because that was who she was. And I was going to have to stop her. Or help her. God help me. I didn't know which one I'd choose.

Danger Closes In

Ava Green

I t felt like the floor dropped out from under me. One of the other survivors was in Lev's hands.

I didn't know who. Maybe the co-pilot who could barely speak. Maybe that terrified mother with the toddler clinging to her neck. Maybe the old man who kept asking if anyone had seen his wife's wedding ring. Whoever it was, they had been on that plane. With us. With me.

Now they were his bargaining chip. And I knew who he was bargaining for.

The cabin was too warm. The blanket still wrapped around me felt like a weight pressing into my chest. I shoved it aside and paced, barefoot, heart hammering. Each step was too loud on the hardwood floor, too sharp against the quiet that just minutes ago had felt like peace.

My stomach twisted. I knew what Lev did to people. I had seen his cruelty, heard it in every calculated word, every threat curled in a purr. I couldn't stop thinking about what he might be doing now. We had protected Emma but now one of those people. Tied up. Bleeding. Begging. Because of me. Because I had left them behind.

I sank into the chair across the room, elbows on knees, palms pressed to my forehead like I could physically hold the thoughts in. I tried to reason with myself, tried to remember that we hadn't had a choice. That we had warned them. That they had made their decisions. But none of that mattered now.

They were suffering. And I was here. Safe. Warm. Still breathing.

Gavin's sleeping breaths behind me had been steady a moment ago. Then they stopped. A rustle. A creak of the couch as he sat up.

"Ava?" His voice was gravel. Wary.

I didn't answer at first. My throat was tight. I stared at the flames in the stove and tried to breathe past the guilt.

"I need to do something," I said finally, voice barely audible. "I can't just... sit here."

Because someone was still out there. Because it should've been me.

Gavin stood slowly from the couch, blanket slipping from his shoulders. He was shirtless, bandaged, bruised and somehow still managed to look like a wall of iron. His eyes met mine across the room, and I saw it happening in real time: the shift. The protector coming online. The steel slamming into place behind those intense, stormy eyes.

"We'll let Sierra Bravo handle it," he said, tone even but firm.

"No." I shook my head. "That's not enough."

His jaw ticked. "It's not your fault."

"Isn't it?" I snapped, more harshly than I meant to. "I left them. I walked away when they begged me not to. I chose survival and now someone else is paying the price."

"You didn't cause this." He crossed toward me, limping slightly. "Lev did. You made the only call you could. You..."

"And if it were me?" I interrupted, standing. "If Lev had taken me instead? Would you be sitting here, waiting for Sierra Bravo to fix it?"

His silence was loud. Telling.

"Exactly," I whispered.

His brow furrowed. "It's not the same."

"It's *exactly* the same."

The space between us tightened, heavy with everything we hadn't said, everything we had been trying not to feel since we made it out alive. It was more than strategy. It was identity. Morality. The raw ache of knowing people were suffering while we were not.

"This isn't about guilt," Gavin said, voice rough. "It's about surviving long enough to make it mean something."

I stared at him, breath catching. "Then let it mean something now."

He stepped back like I'd struck him.

But I didn't let up. "I won't just survive, Gavin. I'm not built to sit still while someone else bleeds."

He ran a hand through his hair, fingers trembling. "Dammit, Ava..."

The argument wasn't over. It was just getting started. Because this wasn't about tactics or orders. It was about who we were when the smoke cleared.

"You're doing it again," I said, the words slipping out before I could temper them. "Making the call. Deciding what's too dangerous for me."

Gavin froze. Just for a beat. Then he exhaled hard, jaw set like stone.

"I'm trying to keep you alive."

"Yeah?" I folded my arms, my shoulders tight with the hurt inside. "And in the process, you're cutting me out. Like I can't choose for myself."

"You don't get it," he snapped, louder than I'd ever heard him. "This isn't about control. This is about survival. If we go after whoever Lev has, we're walking into another bloodbath."

I stepped forward. "So, we just knowingly let someone die?"

"No," he growled. "We let the people who are trained, equipped, and not dragging fresh wounds across their ribs handle it."

He was shaking now. With rage or fear or both, I couldn't tell. But his eyes weren't cold. They were blazing.

I matched his intensity. "You don't think I know what's at stake? That I haven't been calculating risk since the moment that plane hit the trees? I've held dying people in my arms, Gavin. I know what it costs."

"And I've buried too many of them," he said, voice cracking. "Men. Women. Kids. People I couldn't save. You think I want to add you to that list?"

The air between us snapped taut. My breath caught.

"I can't—" he cut off, swallowed. "I can't lose you. Not after every-thing."

There it was. The fracture.

I saw it in his eyes. The fear that had been burning behind every order, every shield he had tried to put between me and danger. It wasn't just about survival. It was about love. About loss. About the gaping wounds he was still carrying from the people he hadn't been able to protect in the past.

And I had my own. But that didn't make this easier. Because we were both right. And still, we were tearing each other apart. I turned away before I said something I couldn't take back.

My pulse was still racing, my hands curled into fists at my sides, but the fire had burned out of me. What was left was a raw ache sitting square in my chest. Behind me, Gavin didn't move. I heard him exhale. It was a short, frustrated sound and then nothing. The silence stretched long and brittle between us.

I sank onto the edge of the couch, facing the cold stove, my thoughts tangled. My body still ached from the fight, the cold, the crash but it was the emotional exhaustion that threatened to drag me under now. I had never been great at walking away from someone I cared about. And I cared about him. God, I did.

But I couldn't, not now, not ever, look the other way when someone was suffering. That wasn't who I was. It never had been.

Across the room, Gavin's shadow paced once. Then twice. Then it stopped. He was as lost in it as I was, this fracture that felt like it might not heal. Not quickly, anyway.

He was trying to protect me. And I was trying to do what was right. Neither of us was wrong. And yet... here we were.

The weight in my chest built, pressure behind my eyes threatening to spill over. I blinked it back, biting the inside of my cheek. I didn't want to cry again. Not after everything. We sat like that, the two of us, inches apart and miles away. No apology. No resolution. Just the quiet churn of everything left unsaid.

And for the first time since the plane had gone down, I felt cold again.

The knock on the door made me flinch.

Three sharp raps, clipped and urgent. Not Mendoza this time. This was different. Lighter footsteps, faster rhythm.

Gavin was already moving before I could stand. He reached the door, checked the side window, and opened it just wide enough to admit a Sierra Bravo operative. It was one of the comm techs, face flushed from the cold, hair damp from sweat and snow.

"Sir," she said, not even bothering to greet me. "It's happening."

Gavin stiffened. "What is?"

"Chatter just spiked on an encrypted channel Riley's been monitoring. It confirms tactical movement. Four vehicles, armed. ETA under twenty."

My blood turned to ice.

"Coming here?" Gavin asked, even though we both knew the answer.

She nodded. "They've triangulated this location somehow. Could've been a trace on our comms. Doesn't matter now. We're compromised. Cloud cover prevents air exfil. Our transpo is coming but they won't get here before the hostiles."

He didn't look at me, but I saw the muscle in his jaw twitch. "Get Mendoza. Prep a fallback. Tell everyone we're code red."

The tech nodded once and bolted. The door slammed behind her.

My heart thundered, not with fear but with grim clarity. We didn't have time to argue anymore. That conversation was dead. The luxury of our moral debate, the guilt, the fear, the weight of what-ifs, it all vanished like smoke.

Because the fight was already coming.

I rose from the couch slowly. Gavin finally looked at me. His expression was unreadable, carved from stone. But in his eyes, I saw the same thing I felt. Resolve. There was no apology. No blame. Just a shared knowledge. We were in the crosshairs again. And this time, we weren't running.

The second the door closed, Gavin transformed. His posture sharpened. Movements went crisp and clean, like someone had flipped a switch and brought the soldier fully back online. He crossed the room in three strides, snatched the radio from the table, and started barking out clipped orders.

"Perimeter sweep. Confirm a fallback route alpha and bravo. I want eyes on the ridge and the southern approach."

His voice was low, controlled. The kind of calm that only happened when the stakes were life or death. I recognized it from my hours in the ER beside doctors. I moved too. No hesitation. No questions.

I grabbed the med kit off the wall, popped it open, and did a quick scan, antiseptics, gauze, painkillers, stitching thread. I tossed in the field trauma pack and repacked it tight, efficient. My fingers flew through the motions, practiced after years of trauma rotations and ER shifts, but this was different. This was war. Again.

Gavin checked his weapon, reloaded, then started passing spare clips to the others who had joined us. The crew moved like a hive, quiet, focused, deadly. But my eyes kept flicking to him.

We hadn't fixed anything. The argument still lingered in the air between us, brittle and bruised. But none of it mattered right now. We weren't hugging. We weren't kissing. But we were aligned. Our movements synced. He grabbed a duffel of supplies; I shouldered the backup medical pouch. Our gazes met once as we passed in the hallway, tight, brief, burning with everything we didn't have time to say.

You good? Yeah. You?

Just a nod. For now. Because this might be it. And if it was, we'd go down, side by side. Together.

The safehouse transformed in minutes. Furniture was shoved aside. Windows barricaded with tables. The couch, vertical against the door. Ammunition cases cracked open. Sierra Bravo operators slid into position, rifles checked, radios live. The tension in the air hummed like an electric current, the kind you felt before lightning struck.

I moved through it like I had done this before. Because I had.

Not like this, not with guns and enemy convoys inbound but in hospitals, during mass casualty events, natural disasters. The urgency was the same. The difference now was... I knew the people in the line of fire this time. I loved one of them.

I stationed myself by the kitchen counter where the triage supplies were laid out, checking IV bags and stacking gauze pads like they were sandbags. My fingers moved automatically, but my brain was elsewhere.

Gavin.

He was across the room, backlit by firelight and fading sun, issuing orders with steady confidence. One of the team handed him a flak vest, and he shrugged it on with a wince, the wound in his side no doubt throbbing. But he didn't complain.

He never did.

He glanced my way once, just a flicker, but our eyes locked like magnets. I wanted to cross the room. I wanted to grab his face and kiss him like it was our last moment on Earth. But I didn't. And he didn't either. We couldn't afford it. Not now.

So instead, we held that look. That half-second of everything unspoken: *I'm sorry. I'm with you. Don't die.* Then we both turned back to our roles.

And the seconds ticked louder.

One of the Sierra Bravo techs muttered something into her mic. Mendoza checked the back entrance. I tightened the straps on the medical backpack in case I needed to run. Rechecked my scissors. Set my jaw. I didn't know if we were walking out of this. But I'd be damned if I wasn't ready or slowed anyone down.

The lookout's voice rang out from the hallway like a crack of thunder.

"Multiple vehicles inbound. Less than five minutes out!"

Everything stopped. Then, exploded into even faster motion.

Operators moved with practiced urgency, final checks, last orders, weapons raised. Gavin was already at the window, peering through a gap in the blackout curtain. His voice cut across the room, sharp and low: "Shut it down. We're going dark."

The last lights flickered. Once. Twice. Then the whole safehouse plunged into black.

I sucked in a breath as my vision vanished. Total darkness. Just the soft hiss of the stove and the distant rumble of wheels grinding snow in the distance.

"Power's cut," someone said. "External source. They've jammed the grid."

My heart slammed into my ribs.

Gavin stepped away from the window. Even in the dark, I could feel the shift in him. Controlled. Ready.

He turned to me. His silhouette barely outlined by the embers in the stove, his weapon raised. "They're coming."

I nodded. No words. Just instinct. I stepped beside him and slid my hand along the cool steel of the counter until I found the grip of my trauma bag. I slung it over my shoulder with trembling fingers. The last thing I saw before the glow faded entirely was Gavin's eyes meeting mine, quiet, certain.

The walls rattled as distant engines from heavy tracked vehicles drew closer. Wind howled through the cracks like it knew what was coming. The safehouse was no longer safe. And the evil? It had just made its move.

Face to Face

Gavin Henderson

I had seen combat in a dozen countries. I had led teams through ambushes, sieges, burning villages. I had patched bullet holes with duct tape, glued together knife wounds and fought my way through hell with less than we had now. But none of that had mattered like this did.

Because this time, she was here.

The safehouse was a frenzy of motion, operators locking down windows, reinforcing fallback positions, counting ammo with tight whispers and sharper eyes. The air was thick with gun oil and adrenaline. I moved through it like a conductor before the concert, barking orders I barely heard over the roar in my blood.

"North window's a priority. If they breach the back, we funnel to the stairs and hold." I grabbed a vest from the gear bin and turned. Ava was standing there, arms crossed.

"No," she said, already reading my intent.

I raised the vest between us.

She glared. "I'm not wearing that."

"You are," I said flatly. "And you'll keep it on. No arguments."

She started to speak again, but I stepped closer and lowered my voice. "This isn't about trust. It's not control. It's survival."

Her jaw worked, torn between fury and fear. But after a beat, she grabbed the vest and shoved her arms through the holes, muttering under her breath. I helped her fasten the sides, my fingers brushing against her, warm, alive. So damn fragile. I tucked a compact pistol into her waistband.

She scowled. "You planning on carrying me out of here now too?"

"Only if you freeze up."

"I won't," she said, steel in her voice.

"I know."

We stood there, just for a second. The world narrowed to just us. Her hair was damp, cheeks flushed from the heat of the stove. I brushed a loose strand behind her ear. My thumb lingered on her cheek longer than it should have. Her skin was soft under my callused hand, and for one suspended moment, there was nothing but the roar of the wind outside.

If I lost her this night... I couldn't even finish the thought.

The hallway was dim, lit only by a backup lantern flickering near the end. The team was moving into position, calling quiet updates through comms, but I couldn't hear them. Not over the thudding in my chest.

I grabbed Ava's hand and pulled her aside, away from the chaos, just for a second. Her eyes widened, startled but she followed. We stopped beneath the stairwell, where shadows drowned everything but her face. That stubborn, beautiful face. She opened her mouth, probably to tell me I was wasting time. I didn't let her.

"If I don't make it out—"

"Don't." Her voice was sharp, panicked.

I shook my head. I had to say this. Now. While I still could.

"If I don't make it out," I repeated, softer this time, "I need you to know something."

She started to shake her head again, eyes glassy, but I pressed on.

"I'd rather die than lose you."

It wasn't poetic. It wasn't planned. It just broke out of me like water through a cracked dam. Truth rushing through all the holes I had tried to patch.

"I've lost a lot in my life," I whispered. "Family. Brothers. Things I thought I'd never get back. And then you happened. You fought like hell and dragged me with you. And now—" I swallowed hard. "Now I can't imagine a future without you in it."

Ava trembled. Not with fear. With feeling. She stepped in close, cupped my jaw with one hand, grounding me.

"You have me," she whispered. "You hear me? You already have me. But don't you dare die for me."

I closed my eyes as our foreheads touched. For a moment, we just breathed together. Her fingers against my face. My heart thudding in time with hers. Outside, the wind howled. Inside, I was already bracing for the worst. But if I went down, it wouldn't be alone. I could have stayed there all night, but I knew I had a war to fight.

The first shot was distant. Then all hell broke loose.

A staccato burst of gunfire echoed from the tree line, rattling the windows. Red tracer rounds arced across the snow. Shouts rose from the perimeter. Sierra Bravo engaged with surgical precision, but we were outnumbered. At least a dozen shadows moved like ghosts between the trees. Maybe more.

"Front's hot!" Mendoza shouted into comms. "Multiple hostiles. They're trying to box us in."

I sprinted to the front window, ducking low. My vest dug into my wounded ribs as I slid into position behind the barricade. I raised my rifle, used the sight to scan through smoke and snowfall. I spotted two silhouettes flanking the east side.

I breathed out. Squeezed. One dropped.

Ava's voice crackled in my earpiece. "West window's clear. For now."

She wasn't by my side, but I knew where she was, where she had insisted on being. Inside, tending to a comms officer hit by a sniper round. I could still see her in my head, crouched over her with gloved hands, blood staining her sleeves, voice calm even as glass shattered inches away.

Crack. Another sniper round punched through the top right window, carving a trail through the drywall.

"Down!" I barked.

I didn't know who I was yelling at. Maybe her. Maybe myself.

The Bravo team held tight. Training kicked in. Movements were clean, timed, layered. No panic. But the enemy was pushing. Hard. A flash from the tree line signaled some type of launcher. The rocket sailed wide. It slammed into the snowbank behind us with a muffled boom, but it was a warning. They were testing our walls. Pacing like wolves.

Inside, Ava's voice again. "She's stable for now. But if another window goes, I'm going to need help."

Pride and terror wrestled in my chest. She was holding her own. But if they breached...

I reloaded. Eyes back on the trees. Teeth clenched.

Let them come.

The Molotov hit like a scream. Glass shattered and then fire bloomed.

A wall of heat erupted from the side window as flames roared up the curtains and licked across the floorboards. Someone yelled, "Fire!

East side!" and the entire safehouse groaned as smoke curled into every corner.

"Suppressing fire!" Mendoza roared from the back.

I whipped around, choking on smoke as I bolted toward the blaze. One of our guys pulled a fire blanket from the wall, but the flames were already crawling fast. Too fast. They were trying to burn us out.

"Back entrance compromised!" a voice shouted. "Explosion. Minor breach!"

The floor shuddered beneath my boots as another blast rocked the rear wall. Dust rained from the ceiling. Plaster cracked. The entire structure tilted on the edge of collapse.

Ava!

I sprinted through the thickening smoke, coughing, calling her name. "Ava!"

No answer.

Flames kissed the hallway wall as I shouldered past the med station, squinting through the haze. The red glow made everything look apocalyptic, warped shadows, flickering silhouettes.

Then I heard her. "Here, Gavin. I'm okay!"

I spotted her through the smoke, kneeling by the wounded operator, protecting her from falling debris. She was trying to move her, her hair damp with sweat, face streaked with soot.

"You need to go!" I shouted, grabbing her arm.

"I'm not leaving her!"

The ceiling above us groaned like it might come down. The air was thick, choking. I grabbed the downed woman's other side, and together we dragged her clear of the worst of the smoke. Ava was coughing hard now, eyes red, but she didn't stop. Didn't falter. We crashed into the living room just as another explosion rattled the foundation.

"We have to hold!" I barked to what was left of my team.

But this house wasn't going to hold. And we were running out of time. I debated calling a fallback but Lev's guys had us surrounded.

The tide shifted. Fast. Sierra Bravo was pushing back, retaking ground inch by bloody inch. Through the haze of gunfire and smoke, I caught a glimpse of Mendoza clearing the west hallway with brutal efficiency. Two shots, two down. We were still standing.

But then the air changed. Like the pressure dropped. And somehow, I knew, before I even saw him.

Lev.

He stepped through the gaping front doorway like a demon torn from the smoke. No mask. No armor. Just soot-smeared skin, blood on his boots, and a pistol raised with effortless malice. The fire behind him framed him like a god of ruin.

I raised my rifle, but I was too late.

He moved like a striking snake. One hand grabbed Ava. The other pressed a gun to her temple.

She gasped, sharp, ragged, her hands flying up as his arm clamped tight around her throat. Her boots scraped against the floor. Her eyes locked onto mine. Frozen.

"No!" I roared, moving, but stopping at the same time. Because if I didn't, she died.

Everything slowed. Sound dropped out. The world condensed to one sickening image burned into my retinas.

Ava in Lev's grip. Her body trembling. His smile widening.

"I told you." he purred. "I always get what I want."

My rifle was halfway up, but I couldn't get a clean shot.

Sierra Bravo froze behind me, weapons half-raised, every operator waiting on my signal or my mistake.

Ava's mouth moved. I thought she was saying my name.

I took one step forward, gun angled low, vision tunneling.

He was there. And he had her.

"Drop it," Lev growled.

His voice cut through the smoke like a razor.

"Or I paint the walls with her."

Red dots from Sierra laser sights flickered through the haze, jittering on walls, unable to land on a target. No one dared fire. No one even breathed.

Except me.

My finger twitched on the trigger. Just one move. That was all it would take. But there was no shot. Ava's body blocked most of his chest, his arm wrapped tight around her, gun pressed so hard against her temple it left an indentation.

She was terrified. But not broken.

Her eyes were wide, locked on mine, and I saw it. The silent plea. Not for rescue. Not for mercy. For trust.

I shifted my grip, gun still raised but not aimed. My voice dropped low. "You don't want to do this."

Lev's laugh was a soft, cold sound. "Ah, Gavin. Always pretending you're the reasonable one."

His fingers twitched on the pistol. I saw it. Ava did too. Her body flinched.

"Let. Her. Go," I said, every syllable knifing through my clenched jaw. "You're not getting out of here."

"Oh, I'm not here to get out," he said, eyes glowing like coals. "I'm here to make you watch."

My pulse thundered in my ears. I could see the tension in Ava's limbs, the way her fingers flexed near her side. She was looking for a moment. Waiting. Biding time.

Lev pressed the barrel harder against her skin.

"Say goodbye, *protector*," he whispered, and smirked.

My knees felt like concrete. I didn't lower my weapon, but I didn't raise it either.

Because one wrong move, and the woman I loved died right there. And I couldn't, God, I couldn't—

"You think you can take anything from me?" Lev hissed.

His arm tightened around Ava, yanking her back against him like a shield. She gasped, struggling for breath, but didn't scream. Didn't cry. Just locked eyes with me, defiant, even then.

"You don't have a future," he spat. "You think this is your girl now? Your redemption?"

His voice was acid, his grip unshakable. "You think she's going to save you? Make you whole? You're only a weapon, Henderson. Just like me."

"Not like you," I said, voice flat, deadly calm. "Not even close."

He grinned. It wasn't a smile. It was a snarl wrapped in skin.

"He cried out in his sleep, you know," he murmured, nose brushing her temple. "Soft little whimpers like he was begging you to save him."

I stepped forward.

"Don't," he warned, pressing the gun harder into her temple.

Ava let out a strangled noise, half a sob, half a curse.

"You don't want to do this," I said again, quieter now. More focused. "You want power, fine. You want revenge? Take it out on me. But you let her go."

Lev scoffed. "You think I'm here for power? For revenge?"

He leaned his mouth closer to her ear. "I'm here to break you."

His finger tightened on the trigger.

I raised my hands slowly, gun lowering an inch. My heart pounded so loudly I could barely hear myself think. My mind raced through scenarios, outcomes, angles. No clean shot. Not unless she moved. Not unless he slipped.

"You kill her," I said, "you die before she hits the floor."

"I'm dead either way," he said.

His smile faded. His expression hardened into something primal. "But you. If I take her from you, I win. Forever."

Ava's eyes were watering then. Not from fear, from lack of air. She was trying to shift, but he was locked in.

Everything inside me screamed to move. To kill. To save.

But if I did it wrong, I'd lose her. And I couldn't. I wouldn't let him take her from me. But he was sure as hell going to try.

Lev shifted. It was subtle but I saw it. His shoulders tightened. His elbow dropped slightly. His thumb pulled back the hammer on the pistol, slow, deliberate.

Ava flinched. And I died a little.

Everything froze. The smoke. The shouting outside. The Bravo team holding steady in the room. The world went still like it knew the next breath could be the last.

"Don't," I whispered.

Lev smiled. "Say goodbye."

His thumb trembled. Ava's breath hitched.

I stepped forward, just enough to draw his eyes. Just enough to make him second-guess. "You don't have the guts."

"Watch me."

His finger twitched.

Ava gasped.

I moved—

The Showdown

Ava Green

The muzzle of Lev's gun pressed into my temple, cold as ice and twice as cruel. Smoke curled around us, the air heavy with ash and dread. Every breath I took burned, like I was swallowing fire and fear all at once. My pulse slammed in my ears. I didn't dare move. Didn't blink. Didn't breathe too deep.

His arm was like iron around my neck. Too tight to slip free, too loose to pass out. A calculated grip. Control without full restraint. He wanted me conscious. Wanted me terrified. Wanted Gavin to watch my fear.

But I wasn't giving him that.

I forced myself to focus past the panic. Past the shaking in my knees and the sweat slicking the back of my neck. I looked at Gavin.

He was there. Just a few feet away, but it might as well have been a mile. His gun was lowered but his eyes were locked on me. Locked on Lev. Sharp. Furious. Desperate.

Sierra Bravo operatives fanned out around the room like ghosts. Their weapons were trained on Lev, lasers flickering through the smoke like blood-red fireflies. But no one dared shoot. Not with me in the way.

Lev breathed heavily against my ear, almost in sync with the ticking bomb of my heartbeat. His muscles were coiled, trembling with tension and something close to pleasure. He fed on this, on fear. I could almost feel his smirk.

He pressed the gun harder, digging the metal into my skull. I flinched. Not from pain but from the knowledge that he wanted to see me flinch. He wanted to see me break. Not this day, bastard. Not ever.

I kept my eyes on Gavin. He saw me. And I knew, I just knew, he wasn't giving up. He wasn't backing down. And neither was I.

Lev shifted his stance slightly, tightening his grip on my jaw. The gun didn't move, but I felt every ounce of intent behind it.

He leaned in, his voice low and poisonous. "You were supposed to die in that crash."

I didn't answer. I didn't even blink. He took my silence as permission.

"You were just a nurse. A tool. A disposable piece of the puzzle." His breath was hot and foul against my cheek. "But you got in the way. You saw too much. You heard what the Marshal told you, didn't you?"

My stomach lurched but I kept my face blank. I didn't even know what the Marshal had said. Not exactly. But Lev didn't know that. And that scared him.

"I only needed a medic on board," he hissed. "Someone to keep me alive until my people arrived. But then you had to start whispering. Plotting. Running."

He pulled the gun back an inch, just enough to gesture with it, cocking his head toward Gavin.

"And he followed you like a lost dog. You dragged him into this."

He snarled, voice rising, teeth bared. "Do you have any idea what I've lost because of you?"

I met his eyes. "A conscience?"

That earned me a hard jerk of my head to the side. The gun dug in again. But I didn't stop. I couldn't.

"You're not here for power," I said. "You're here because I lived. That's what's eating you."

He growled. "I gave you a mercy, and you spat in my face."

"No," I whispered. "I survived. That's not mercy. That's strength."

His hand trembled. The monologue cracked. I could feel it then, the shift. The unraveling. Lev had come for dominance. But I wasn't his victim. Not anymore.

"Let her go."

Gavin's voice cut through the smoke like a blade, sharp, low, deliberate. He stepped forward, gun still lowered but ready, his whole body coiled like a loaded spring.

Lev chuckled. "Still pretending you have control."

Gavin didn't blink. "You hurt her, and you'll die before your next breath."

That got Lev's attention. The grip around my neck tightened, just a fraction. The gun shifted, then steadied again. I felt the tremor in Lev's muscles, not fear, but uncertainty. Gavin's voice hadn't shaken. That rattled him more than any bullet.

"You came all this way," Gavin continued, calm and cold, "just to lose everything? Your crew's gone. Half your men are dead. You're standing in a house surrounded by operators trained to drop a man between blinks."

"Is that your speech?" Lev sneered. "The brave soldier trying to bluff the big bad wolf?"

"It's not a bluff."

Gavin's tone didn't rise. He didn't posture. That was what made it terrifying. Controlled fury wrapped in the voice of a man who meant every word.

"You've got no exit strategy," Gavin said. "You take the shot, and the next breath you suck will be through a hole in your throat."

Lev snarled but didn't move. His eyes flickered, jaw tight, as if weighing odds he didn't like. For all his madness, he wasn't stupid. I felt it, the shift in focus. Lev's attention pulled toward Gavin, toward the threat he understood. His grip on me softened, just enough. Just enough.

Gavin knew. I could see it in his eyes. He was buying me time. He was giving me a sliver of space. A chance. One that might not come again.

I braced.

Lev's grip shifted, just slightly, as his attention zeroed in on Gavin's voice. That was all I needed.

My hand inched downward, one slow breath at a time. Fingers searching, brushing against the edge of the inner pocket stitched into the waistband of my cargo pants. The scalpel was still there, thin, light, forgotten. A tool no one had noticed in the chaos.

But I hadn't forgotten.

I breathed in through my nose, slow and silent. Counted the seconds. The beats of Lev's pulse thudding through his wrist against my collarbone. I visualized the anatomy, the line of his femur, the crease of his hip. The way his thigh was pressed against mine. And the artery running close beneath the surface.

I shifted my weight imperceptibly.

His arm tightened again. "Don't try anything, sestrichka," he hissed.

Too late.

I found the blade and drew it. The whole thing was barely the length of my palm. But in my hands? It was a surgeon's knife. Now? A weapon.

Gavin kept talking, his voice calm and low. "You think killing her fixes this? You're a memory already, Lev. A ghost with a gun."

Lev snarled, distracted. His grip loosened.

Now!

I twisted. Hard.

In one clean, surgical motion, I plunged the scalpel into the inner meat of Lev's thigh, just above the knee, inside the femoral triangle. Brachial would've worked if I had his arm, but this? This was deeper. Dirtier. Faster. I felt it tear through skin. Muscle. Ripping through the artery.

He howled. His arm spasmed. The gun jerked wide. Blood erupted, hot and fast, soaking his pants in seconds. I wrenched free as he staggered back, clutching his leg and threw myself low. I dove behind an overturned coffee table. Wood splinters scraped my elbows, my knees hit hard, but I didn't care. My ears rang. My heart slammed like a war drum.

Then—gunfire.

The sharp, controlled crack of a Bravo rifle. One shot. Two.

I couldn't see who had fired. It didn't matter.

Time fractured into tiny fragments. Smoke coiling, muzzle flashes sparking like lightning across the room. Lev staggered, half-spun, blood pouring from his thigh like someone had turned on a faucet. He screamed something in Russian, slurring it through clenched teeth. His pistol jerked upward.

"Down!" Gavin bellowed but I didn't know who he yelled at.

Another round cracked through the air.

Lev stumbled back. His shoulder snapped backward like it had been punched by a ghost. He went down hard, crashing into the wall.

His gun spun out of reach, skittered across the floor.

I didn't know where Gavin was until I saw movement out of the smoke. He was charging. Bleeding. Grim. Unstoppable. He reached Lev just as the bastard hit the floor.

Another shot. Close. Too close.

I scrambled behind cover, my hands slicked with sweat, knees knocking into burned floorboards. I forced myself to breathe, to stay low, to track movement.

Was it over? Was he dead?

I pressed a hand to my chest to feel my heartbeat. It was still there. Pounding. Furious. Alive.

Gavin was yelling something. Orders? I couldn't hear him over the ringing in my ears. But one thing was clear: Lev went down. And I was still standing.

Lev hit the floor hard, back first, blood gushing in rhythmic pulses from the gash in his thigh and the fresh hole in his shoulder. The air around him rippled with heat and smoke, like even the house wanted him gone.

His pistol lay a few feet away, glinting in the firelight. Gavin was already there, boot slamming down on the weapon, kicking it toward the wall. He stood over Lev, chest heaving, blood dripping down his side. The look in his eyes was murder held back by a thread.

"It's over," Gavin growled.

Lev blinked up at him, his face smeared with blood and ash, chest rising and falling in ragged gasps. The power was gone. The predator coiled in shadows? Gone. What was left was just a man. Broken. Gasping. Bleeding out on the floor.

Last Breath

Gavin Henderson

The room hummed with aftershocks. Gunpowder clung to the air like smoke from a funeral pyre. Broken glass crunched under boots. Sierra Bravo operatives swarmed the safehouse, weapons raised, shouting calls and confirmations. Fires were being dealt with. One mercenary bolted for the woods and was tackled before he made it to the tree line. Another was cuffed in the hall, bleeding from a leg wound.

But I didn't see them. Didn't hear them. All I saw was her. Ava.

She was crouched near the back wall, bruised and smeared with soot, eyes wide and distant like she hadn't registered we were still here. That we were still breathing.

I moved. Two steps. Maybe three. Then I was on my knees in front of her, hands skimming over her arms, her face, checking for blood, breaks, burns, anything.

"Ava." My voice cracked. "Are you okay? Are you hurt?"

She blinked. Nodded. "I... I'm okay."

Relief flooded through me so hard it nearly knocked me over. I gripped her face, pulled her forehead to mine. We had made it. We—

A flicker of motion behind her. Something shifted in the shadows. Not over. Not yet. A shadow twitched at the edge of my vision. At first, I thought it was just my pulse thundering in my ears, but then, movement. Subtle. Wrong.

Lev.

He should have been dying. He should have been out cold, drowning in his own blood. But the bastard shifted. His body bucked once, then again, stronger. A rattling, animal noise tore from his throat.

I shoved Ava behind me just as he surged upright with a feral howl.

"Move!" I roared, throwing my arm wide to block her.

Lev's hand flashed to his boot. Steel gleamed. A blade. His final trick.

Everything slowed. His eyes were wild, glassy with pain but locked on me like prey. Blood poured down his shoulder. He shouldn't even have been conscious, let alone lunging at me with that goddamn knife.

But rage made monsters into machines. He was on me before I could draw breath. The knife arced for my chest. I twisted. Pain exploded in my side. My wound reopened. Warmth gushed. We hit the ground in a brutal slam of muscle and fury. It wasn't over. This madman wouldn't die until he took one of us with him. We slammed into the floor like a pair of falling stars, no grace, no rules, just pain.

Lev's weight drove the breath from my lungs. His blade flashed again, and this time it dug deep, just under my ribs beside the Kevlar. White-hot agony seared through me. I grunted, twisted, slammed my elbow into his throat. He coughed but didn't stop.

He was relentless.

My hands scrabbled, gripped his wrist, tried to force the knife away. Blood slicked both of us, his and mine, making everything slippery and raw. We tumbled into a table, then crashed against the splintered doorframe. My head smacked wood, hard. For a heartbeat, the world blurred.

He was winning.

Lev snarled like an animal, knee jamming into my thigh, blade rising for another strike. My arm shook under the strain. I braced, shoved, barely kept him from plunging the knife into my throat. This was it. No tactics. No precision. Just violence.

I slammed my forehead into his nose. Something crunched. He howled, pulled back. I seized the opening, drove a fist into his gut, then another to his jaw. He stumbled, but his free hand snagged my collar and flung me back against the wall. The knife followed. It wasn't skill keeping me alive then. It was pure, unfiltered will.

I wouldn't let him take her.

Ava Green

Gavin hit the wall with a sickening thud.

I screamed his name, but it was swallowed by the ringing in my ears. Lev raised the knife again, roaring like some demon from the pit, all blood and smoke and madness. Gavin was barely standing, legs buckling, arm limp, bleeding fast.

I didn't think. I moved.

My fingers curled around the pistol at my waist that Gavin had given me, forgotten in the chaos, but waiting like fate. I raised it, aimed center mass, and pulled the trigger.

The recoil punched up my arms. Lev jerked, staggered, blood blooming across his ribs. But he didn't fall. He turned. Eyes blazing. Rage undiluted. He charged, more monster than man.

I didn't flinch. Not this time.

As he closed the distance, I waited. He was nearly on me. One step. Two. I tightened my finger again and again and again until the gun clicked hollowly in my hand.

His breath caught. His mouth opened in a soundless roar. And then—He fell. Hard. Face first. Motionless. Blood pooled beneath him like a halo.

I was shaking. Breathless. Still holding the empty gun and trembling. But it was done. I thought it was finally done.

Everything froze. The roar of gunfire, the chaos, it all receded into a ghostly quiet. Gavin stared at Lev's body, waiting for it to twitch, breathe, something. But it didn't. It was over. Finally. His knees wobbled, the adrenaline draining like the blood from his wounds. Then I was there, grabbing him, grounding him.

"I've got you," I whispered. He leaned into me, pain and relief colliding.

"You're terrifying," he muttered, voice frayed.

My laugh broke the silence, wet with tears. "Takes one to know one."

Red and blue lights strobed through shattered windows. Sierra Bravo medics flooded the cabin. Gavin swayed, barely upright now. My hands were pressed to his wound, my fingers sticky with his blood.

"Stay with me," I said, voice cracking but firm.

Gavin found my eyes, and the chaos faded again. "You saved me," he murmured.

"Guess we're even." I tried to smile, but my lips trembled. I was holding on, barely.

Gavin's eyes weren't tracking. He tried to speak again, my name, maybe, but the words died in his throat. I tightened my grip.

"I'm right here. Just breathe."

My voice anchored him. He let go, not into fear or oblivion, but into me. My touch, my voice, my presence. He passed out. But I knew it was only because he knew we were safe. Finally.

I caught Gavin as he slumped. "Gavin!" My cry was sharp, panicked.

The medics lowered him onto a stretcher, already working. Blood pressure, vitals, pressure dressings. One medic turned to me.

"Ma'am, you're bleeding."

I blinked, only then noticing the bruises and gashes on my own arms. The exhaustion hit like a wave. A medic steadied me as my knees gave.

"You need treatment too."

I nodded, dazed, but my eyes never left Gavin. As the stretcher was loaded into a waiting SUV, I climbed in beside him, my hand gripping his. We left with flashing lights and flickering hope. We were alive but scarred.

Waking Up

Ava Green

The world returned in bits and pieces. Light first. Soft, diffuse, like it had been filtered through clouds. Then very familiar smells: antiseptic, faint bleach, something sterile. It wasn't smoke. Not blood. Not pine or gunfire.

I blinked against the glow overhead; my lashes crusted with sleep. My muscles ached in strange, invisible places. My right hand felt heavy, pinned under warm blankets. My head throbbed, a dull, persistent ache, like a fading memory I couldn't quite access.

I shifted slightly, then froze as thoughts crashed in.

Where was Gavin?

The question struck like lightning, sharp, electrifying. Panic bloomed. I pushed against the sheets, heart lurching, gaze jerking around the room. Walls. IV pole. Monitor.

And him.

Slumped in a vinyl chair beside my bed, chin tilted back, the beginnings of a beard darkening his jaw, a bruise rising along one cheekbone like a fading storm cloud.

I was able to breathe again.

"Gavin," I whispered.

His eyes snapped open. For a second, he just stared at me, stunned. Then he was moving, leaning forward so fast the chair squeaked. His hand found mine beneath the blanket, fingers warm and trembling.

"You're awake," he breathed. "Jesus, Ava..."

Relief crashed over me in waves. My vision blurred, not from pain, but from the impossible truth of it. He was here. Alive. I wasn't alone. I didn't care about the ache in my skull or the IV taped to my arm. Didn't care about the pain or the bruises. Only that I got to look at him.

"I thought—" I started.

"I know," he said. "Me too."

We sat there for a moment, tethered by touch and silence, while outside the window, the world dared to look normal.

"Gavin," I whispered again, just to hear it. Just to be sure he was real.

He leaned in, eyes glinting with something raw, something broken and stitched back together again. His hand cupped my face like I might disappear. His thumb grazed my cheekbone. It was so gentle I ached.

"You're really here," I murmured.

"You scared the hell out of me," he said, voice cracking under the weight of maybe too many hours without sleep. "They said mild concussion. Exhaustion. You've been out for two days."

My eyes widened. "Two?"

He nodded, brushing hair away from my forehead. "They said you needed rest. But I..." His throat bobbed. "I didn't want you to wake up alone."

Tears stung at the corners of my eyes, but I didn't look away. Didn't blink.

"You stayed?"

"Of course I did."

I reached for his hand under the blankets. Our fingers met, tangled, locked. I ran my thumb over a scab on his knuckle. The feel of it, that tiny bit of evidence of what we had lived through, made my breath catch. We sat like that for a long time, hand in hand, neither speaking, because words felt too flimsy for what we had survived. It wasn't the adrenaline now. Not the panic. It was the beginning of peace. And wholeness.

I blinked up at him, my voice barely a breath. "We're really okay?"

Gavin smiled, eyes soft and sure. "Yeah. You're safe. We made it."

A sob lodged in my chest, part laughter, part disbelief. I pressed my lips to the back of his hand.

"I didn't think I'd get to have this," I admitted.

His gaze held mine. "You do. Every damn second of it."

The relief didn't last.

Not because anything was wrong. There were no alarms, no shouts, no gunfire. Just quiet beeping from a monitor and the slow rhythm of Gavin's breathing beside me. But that was what shook me. For the first time in days, my heart wasn't in survival mode. There was space. Space to think. To feel. To doubt.

I stared at our joined hands, thumb still tracing his. I remembered the cold, the blood, the fire in his eyes when he had protected me. The way he had looked at me like I was the only thing that mattered. Or was that just from the adrenaline?

I swallowed hard, then shifted, breaking the silence. "Do you think..." My voice was hoarse, uncertain. "Do you think it was all just the moment? The danger. The heat of it?"

Gavin's brow furrowed.

"I mean..." I continued, eyes dropping to the blanket, suddenly afraid to look at him. "Now that we're not running for our lives... are you going to wake up and realize it ... us ... wasn't real?"

The question sat between us, naked and sharp. My heart stuttered. I hated myself for asking but I had to know.

"I don't want to be your trauma story," I whispered, almost too low to hear. "Some woman you saved and then moved on from."

The words cracked something open inside me, a fissure of old hurt, memories of being left behind, forgotten. A history of not being enough. I turned my face slightly, not in shame, but defense. Waiting. Expecting the worst. Gavin didn't speak. Not yet. But I felt the air shift, the weight of his stillness. And it scared me more than any bullet ever had. I was simultaneously fighting tears and an urge to throw up from my nerves.

"No."

The word landed like a vow.

I looked up, startled. Gavin's voice was rough but steady, his eyes blazing with conviction.

"It wasn't adrenaline," he said. "It wasn't survival. It wasn't just the heat of the moment."

He leaned forward, close enough that I could feel the warmth of his breath. One of his hands found my wrist, fingers brushing lightly against the pulse point there, steady now, but only because he was there.

"It was everything."

I swallowed hard.

"I thought I lost you," he said, voice catching, "and all I could think about was how I never told you how much you mean to me."

My breath hitched.

"You don't have to—"

"I want to." His grip tightened slightly. "You're not just some story I lived through. You're not something I'll 'get over' now that the bullets have stopped flying."

I didn't realize I was crying until he reached up and wiped a tear from my cheek with the pad of his thumb.

"Say it," I whispered.

"I want you safe," he said, voice low and raw. "Always. With me. No matter what's next."

His eyes shone, not with fear or exhaustion, but with something fierce. Solid. Undeniable. He lifted my hand to his lips and pressed a kiss to my knuckles, reverent and unhurried. I laughed softly through the tears, that nervous, breathless kind of laugh that only came when your heart had been broken open in the best way.

"You have me," I said, voice trembling. "Always."

There was no battle then. No chase. Just that room, that moment. The war was over, but something else, something better, had just begun.

Our fingers stayed linked, his thumb tracing soft circles over the back of my hand like he was memorizing the shape of me. My tears dried, but the warmth in my chest grew, slow and bright and terrifyingly real. I wasn't floating on adrenaline anymore. There was no rush, no gunfire to drown in, no life-or-death reason to grab what I wanted without thinking. And yet, I still wanted him. Wanted this.

"Gavin," I whispered.

He leaned in. The kiss we shared then wasn't frantic or desperate. It was slow, reverent. A meeting of breath and promise. His lips were soft, unhurried, like he wasn't kissing me for survival but because he finally could. And I kissed him back with everything I had left. No walls. No fear. No question. When we parted, I was breathless, not from exertion, but from everything that kiss carried: gratitude, safety, desire, hope.

"I think I love you," I said, then winced, laughing at myself. "God, that sounds ridiculous after all we've been through."

He smiled. A rare, unguarded smile that reached all the way to his eyes that I had been chasing.

"It doesn't sound ridiculous at all."

He leaned his forehead to mine, brushing my nose with his. "You survived a plane crash, faced down a psychopath, and still stitched people up with your bare hands. If that's not love-worthy, I don't know what is."

I laughed again, and this time it was lighter. Effortless. Something settled inside me, an anchor after the storm. The fear, the hunger, the sheer fight of the last few days... it was over. What was left was this: a battered body, a healing heart, and a man who looked at me like I was more than just a survivor. Like I was his future.

A soft knock broke the spell.

Gavin straightened, just as the door swung open and a tall figure stepped inside. Dressed in tactical pants and a black Sierra Bravo jacket, he carried the weight of leadership with quiet ease.

"Hope I'm not interrupting," Dane said with a half-smile. His voice was smooth, low, commanding, but warm. "Just wanted to check on our two toughest survivors."

I blinked, caught between surprise and awe. This was Dane Marshall, the elusive founder of Sierra Bravo Security who I'd only seen in news pictures. Gavin had spoken of him like a ghost in the machine, the kind of man who only showed up when it mattered most.

"Looks like you both made it out mostly intact," Dane said, glancing between us. "Hell of a job."

I shifted up slightly in bed, wincing at the motion. Gavin stood and crossed his arms, jaw ticking slightly.

"You should know," Dane continued, "that everyone on that extraction team is calling you two legends. Especially you, Green. What you did for your patients, and for Gavin—" He paused, nodding. "Not many people could've done that."

I swallowed hard. My cheeks flushed. Gavin squeezed my hand.

Dane turned to him now. "As for you... I meant what I said before. I want you to stay on with Sierra Bravo. But not in the field, unless that's what you want. We've got an opening here in the region. Stable. Flexible."

He let that hang for a moment, then added, "No pressure. Think about it."

But Gavin didn't answer. He looked at me. Just me. And I knew exactly what he was asking. Gavin didn't blink. Didn't glance back at Dane. His eyes were all on me. I met his gaze and saw it, the question he didn't say aloud. The vulnerability tucked behind all that strength.

Is it okay to stay? With you? For real?

I squeezed his hand. Just once. A gentle answer. Then I nodded. Slow. Certain.

"I want that," I murmured. "I want you here."

Gavin exhaled like I had just given him permission to breathe again.

He turned back to Dane. "I'll think about it," he said, voice even. But the faint grin tugging at his mouth gave him away.

Dane nodded once, satisfied. "Good. You've earned a slower pace, Henderson. Both of you have."

He crossed to the door, then hesitated. "Oh, and you'll have a visitor or two later. That nurse from the evac site, Kiley? She's been asking about you. Says she owes you one, Green."

I blinked, startled. "Kiley made it?"

"Scraped up, but alive. You pulled her through. Thought you should know."

Emotion welled in my chest. One more name I didn't have to mourn.

"Thank you," I said softly.

Dane tipped his head and let himself out, closing the door with a soft click.

Silence returned. But it was a different kind of quiet, warm, settled.

Gavin looked back at me, eyes gentler than I'd ever seen. "So... I guess I'll be around. If that's still okay with you."

I smirked. "I was hoping you would be."

The room settled into a hush again, but this one felt different. I nestled deeper into my pillow, my fingers still threaded through Gavin's. The adrenaline had faded. The bruises ached. But the air was calm. Whole. And then, my phone buzzed.

I startled slightly. Gavin's brow lifted. I twisted toward the bedside table and fumbled for the device, blinking at the screen. My heart did a little jump.

Emma.

Relief flooded my veins. I thumbed the green button. "Hey."

There was a beat of static, then my sister's voice, thick with emotion. "Oh my God, you picked up. Are you okay?"

My throat tightened. "I'm okay. I promise. A little banged up, but... breathing."

"You're in the hospital, aren't you?"

I smiled faintly. "Just for observation."

I glanced at Gavin, still sitting beside me, watching quietly. A lazy grin tugged at his lips like he already knew what I was about to say.

Emma's voice echoed, "Are you alone?"

I grinned. "No. He's here. And no, he's not going anywhere."

Gavin's grin widened as I locked eyes with him.

"Well," Emma huffed, "about time."

Laughter bubbled up in my chest, tired but real. It felt like sunrise.

As I hung up, Gavin leaned in and brushed his knuckles against my cheek. "So, what now?"

I tilted my head, thoughtful. "Sleep. Pancakes. Maybe something that doesn't involve bullets."

He chuckled. "I can work with that."

Outside the window, the sky shifted from night to dawn, the first golden streaks touching the sill. I turned toward the light. For the first time in what felt like forever, there was no fear. No chasing. No more running. I had survived. We both had. And maybe, just maybe, we got to begin again.

Coming Home

Gavin Henderson

The scent of grilled ribs and mountain wildflowers filled the air as I leaned against the wooden railing of the Sierra Bravo lodge deck, a cold beer sweating in my hand. The sun dipped behind the peaks, casting long golden streaks over the clearing below. Picnic tables were scattered across the lawn, covered in checkered cloths and paper plates piled high. Kids shrieked as they chased each other near the trees. Music played low from a Bluetooth speaker someone had rigged to the porch post.

I had one arm draped around Ava's waist; her head nestled just beneath my chin. She was laughing at something Emma had said, probably another jab about my being "domesticated," because the woman had just toasted me with a lemonade and said, "You used to look like a stray dog. Now you've got bedhead and matching towels."

I chuckled, rubbing the faint ache beneath my ribs where the scar still puckered skin. "Worth it," I muttered, mostly to myself.

Because it was.

I wasn't wearing body armor. Not scanning the tree line. Not waiting for an extraction team or counting exits. I was standing in the middle of a summer barbecue, Ava warm at my side, safe and glowing under the Colorado sun.

And somehow, it felt more dangerous than any op I had ever run. Because it was real and I had something to lose.

I took a swig of beer and watched Emma snatch a second brownie from the dessert table. Ava rolled her eyes and leaned into me. "Family," she murmured.

I pressed a kiss to her temple and smiled. "Yours or mine?"

She tilted her head up and grinned. "Ours."

My throat went tight. Yeah. Ours. The life I had never thought I'd have and now, the one I'd protect at all costs.

Ava Green

I tilted my face toward the sun, letting it warm my skin. There was laughter all around, kids chasing bubbles, the hiss of meat on the grill, Emma snorting at her own joke while Gavin pretended not to laugh. I couldn't remember the last time life had felt like that. Whole.

Emma's cheeks were flushed with sunlight, her scarf pushed back to reveal the fine peach fuzz of new hair growth. Her latest tests had come back clean. Remission. The word still felt like magic.

I glanced across the lawn where Sierra Bravo's CEO, Dane, was shaking Gavin's hand. Earlier, they had given him a medal, nothing flashy, just a quiet moment where they clapped him on the back and called him a hero. Gavin had looked like he wanted to melt into the floor. I, on the other hand, couldn't stop smiling. I had practically burst with pride.

I reached for Gavin's hand then, grounding myself in the rough warmth of his palm. He squeezed back like he had been waiting for me to do that all day.

I loved that about him, the way he always noticed, even in a crowd.

My own world was shifting, too. The local hospital had offered me a part-time trauma nurse position, starting next month. No chaos, no commute. Just enough structure to keep my hands busy and my heart steady. I was choosing peace.

I looked up at Gavin, who was already looking at me like I was the only one there. I leaned my head on his shoulder, and he hummed contentedly.

For the first time in forever, I wasn't bracing for impact.

There was nothing but this. Sunlight, second chances, and the man who had stood between me and death more times than I could count.

And stayed.

Gavin Henderson

I tried to stay focused on the conversation. Dane was talking about logistics: rotations, contract shifts, something about training up the next crew. I nodded, added the occasional grunt, but my eyes kept drifting.

To her. Ava.

She was across the lawn, radiant in a sundress, her laugh lighting her whole face as Emma pulled her into another hug. I couldn't stop watching her. Like if I blinked too long, I might wake up back in that godforsaken forest, wondering if she had made it.

She had. We had. Lev's claim to have a hostage had been his last lying attempt to coerce Ava into his grasp but he had failed. He was gone. We had survived.

Dane clapped me on the back hard enough to jolt me into the moment. "You sure you don't want to try your hand at management, Henderson? You clean up well."

I snorted, tipping my bottle toward the sky. "My ambition starts and ends with a quiet life and a woman who steals the covers."

"You've got the second part nailed," Dane chuckled, then peeled off toward the food table.

My hand drifted to the scar at my side, fingers brushing the raised ridge through my shirt. A small price to pay. Hell, I'd have done it again in a heartbeat.

Ava glanced my way. Just a look, nothing flashy, but it hit me like a body blow.

You good? I mouthed.

She nodded, smiling like she knew exactly what I was thinking.

That was all it took. I crossed the lawn without another word, boots crunching on gravel and grass. Not because I needed to check on her. But because I could. Because we had made it. And now, I got to walk toward her, not away. Every damn day, if she'd have me.

Ava Green

I barely heard what Emma was saying. Gavin's breath was warm at my neck, his voice a low rasp just for me.

"Let's get out of here. I want you all to myself tonight."

My pulse answered before my lips did, skipping, fluttering, heat blooming low in her my. I tilted my head to meet his eyes. That look. It never failed to undo me, like he was gravity itself, and I couldn't have resisted him if I'd tried.

I murmured, "Thought you'd never ask."

We excused ourselves quietly, slipping between laughing coworkers and the wafting scent of grilled corn and brisket. Gavin's hand found mine, rough, steady, grounding.

As we crossed the edge of the lawn, Emma called out, "Don't do anything I wouldn't do!"

I flashed a grin over my shoulder. "Then we're in trouble."

Laughter trailed behind us, fading with the sunset. We didn't speak much on the drive home. We didn't need to. Gavin's fingers were tangled with mine over the gearshift, his thumb brushing slow circles against my palm.

Outside the truck windows, the mountain range glowed with the last blush of dusk. It was all so achingly normal: soft music on the radio, her sister alive and teasing, Gavin warm beside mw. For the first time in what felt like forever, there was nothing in the back of my mind. Just this. When we pulled up to the house, a rental tucked into a pine-lined ridge, Gavin killed the engine and looked at me.

"Last chance to back out."

I leaned over, brushing my lips against his.

"Not a chance in hell."

Gavin Henderson

We had barely made it inside before I had her pinned to the door, not with force, but with gravity. The kind that had been building between us since that first crash of chaos, only now there was no smoke, no fear, no reason to hold back.

I brushed her hair from her face, fingers grazing her temple like she was something fragile and holy.

"You saved me," I said, my voice rougher than I had meant.

She cupped my cheek. "We saved each other."

The kiss that followed was slow. Deep. A claiming and a surrender all at once. I took my time, like the world wouldn't interrupt us anymore. Like she was my whole world because she was.

Her shirt came off in layers, her laughter, her breath, the soft fabric sliding from her skin. My hands shook a little, not from nerves but from the weight of reverence. I didn't just want her. I knew her.

I kissed down her neck, tasting sun and salt and the faint trace of her perfume.

"You don't have to go slow," she whispered, teasing.

I chuckled against her skin. "I want to."

Because that night wasn't about heat or desperation. It was about memorizing every inch of her without fear of what waited outside. We moved through the room like a slow tide, her hands in my hair, my mouth at her collarbone, every kiss saying I'm here, I'm yours, I'm not going anywhere. When I finally lifted her into my arms and carried her to the bed, I looked down at her, breathing hard.

"You're everything," I murmured.

She smiled, radiant, arms wrapping around my neck. "Then come prove it."

Ava lay back on the bed, hair splayed across the pillow like a halo. I stood over her, chest rising, lips parted, eyes filled with something raw. She reached for me, fingers skimming the hem of my shirt, lifting it slowly. I let her, arms raised, eyes never leaving hers. The fabric peeled away, revealing the planes of muscle and the scars that spoke of battles survived. She traced one with a fingertip, the long pink line along my ribs, the one she had thought would take me from her.

"I love your scars," she whispered.

I caught her hand, kissed her knuckles. "They love you back."

She laughed, then pulled me down to her, skin to skin, mouths finding each other again. That time, there was no rush. Only us.

Ava kissed my throat, then my chest, following the path of my heartbeat with her lips. She undressed me fully with slow, savoring touches, her hands lingering like she was unwrapping something sacred. I groaned, my body arching under her worship.

"You're killing me," he murmured.

"No," she said softly. "I'm loving you."

On the bed, we moved together in quiet synchronicity, a rhythm that was more communion than conquest. Each sigh and gasp felt like a vow.

I want you.

I trust you.

I choose you.

Forever.

I cradled her like she was precious and dangerous all at once. My mouth at her ear, her name falling from my lips like prayer.

Ava let herself go, completely, without walls. When her cry echoed through the room, it wasn't just pleasure. It was freedom. Love crashed through her, fierce and full. She had never felt more alive.

The room was dim and warm, lit only by the golden spill of the bedside lamp. Sheets tangled around our legs, I lay with one arm draped over Ava, the other pillowing my head as I watched her breathe.

She was tucked into my side, hair a wild halo across my chest, lips curved in the faintest smile. One leg was thrown over mine, like she was claiming her territory.

I brushed a thumb along her bare shoulder. "You're dangerous, you know that?"

Ava hummed without opening her eyes. "Mm. That's rich, coming from the guy who fought off a cartel with a knife wound in his side."

I chuckled low in my chest. "I'm not talking about that. I'm talking about this." I lifted her hand, kissing each fingertip. "You. Being this soft. This close. That's the real threat."

She snorted, eyes fluttering open. "You're getting sentimental on me, Henderson."

"I almost died," I said with a shrug. "Twice. Pretty sure that earns me the right to wax poetic."

Ava propped herself on one elbow, smirking. "So... you're saying I inspire poetry?"

"Only the filthy kind," I deadpanned.

She laughed, really laughed, and collapsed back against me, breathless. I closed my eyes and let the sound wrap around me like a blanket.

Just her laughter, our shared heat, and the quiet hum of a world that had finally stopped trying to kill us.

"I want a thousand more nights like this," Ava whispered against my collarbone.

I kissed her hair, inhaling the scent of her. "Then I better stay alive, huh?"

She answered with a gentle kiss to my jaw, and silence settled again, this time not from exhaustion, but contentment. We had earned that stillness. We had fought and bled for it.

Ava Green

Morning spilled in slow and soft, the kind of light that felt like forgiveness.

I stirred first. My body ached in the sweetest way. My skin hummed where Gavin's arm lay heavy across my waist, anchoring me to the new world we had carved together. For a second, I didn't move. I just listened, to the quiet, to the steadiness of his breathing, to the pulse of something warm and golden inside my chest. Gavin murmured my name, sleep-thick and low. His eyes blinked open, and he smiled like he was seeing a miracle.

"I thought I'd wake up and it'd all be a dream," he said.

"Me too," I whispered.

He shifted to face me fully, brushing a strand of hair off my cheek. "So... I was thinking."

I arched a brow. "Always dangerous."

Gavin grinned. "Move in with me."

My breath caught, not from surprise, but from the softness of it. The way he said it like it was the most obvious thing in the world. Like it had always been waiting.

I stared at him, heart full, lips curving slowly. "I thought I already had."

He huffed a laugh, pulling me closer. "You did. I just wanted to make it official."

I kissed him then, long and lingering. No fireworks. No rush. Just a seal.

"Yes," I said against his lips. "Always yes."

Outside the window, a bird sang into the sunrise.

Inside, we held each other close, not because we were afraid, not because we were hiding, but because we finally could. Because survival wasn't the end. It was the beginning.

New Beginnings

Ava Green

I wedged the last throw pillow into the box like it was a final piece of a chaotic puzzle and slapped a strip of packing tape across the top. Gavin watched from the doorway, arms crossed, a lopsided smirk tugging at his lips.

"You own more throw pillows than I've had hot meals," he said, lifting the box marked **Books & Chaos** like it weighed nothing.

I grinned. "They bring vibes, Henderson. Ambience. Softness. You could use some."

He snorted. "I've got you now. That's enough softness for a lifetime."

We moved around my old apartment like we'd done it a hundred times, smoothing down flaps, writing labels, sneaking kisses between tasks. He found my old mug with the snarky slogan, **World's Okayest Nurse,** and raised an eyebrow. I snatched it away, laughing.

"That one's non-negotiable," I warned, and he saluted me in mock surrender.

By the time we stacked the final box by the door, I was breathing like I'd just run a marathon. Not from the effort. From what the moment meant.

"That's it," I whispered.

Gavin slipped behind me, arms wrapping around my waist. "You sure?"

I nodded, leaning back into his chest. "I want this. Us."

He kissed the side of my neck, slow and certain. "Good. Because I was already planning where your coffee mugs were going."

I turned in his arms and kissed him, softly, lingering. The apartment that had once echoed with late-night loneliness now felt like a closed book. Chapter finished. I was ready for what was next.

We stood in the doorway, the weight of the past behind us, the road home ahead. Gavin squeezed my hand. "Let's go."

I smiled. "Let's begin."

Gavin Henderson

Ava planted her hands on her hips and eyed the living room like a battlefield she intended to conquer. Her hair was pulled up in one of those messy buns she swore wasn't intentional, and her shirt had ink marks smudges from labeling boxes. She was radiant. I watched her fluff a pillow with enough force to knock it across the couch.

"You know," I said, dropping the box of cookware onto the kitchen island, "I think you've fluffed that one seven times."

"It still looks lopsided," she muttered.

"Pillow crimes," I said, walking over and plucking it out of her hands. "Serious offense."

She arched a brow. "You gonna arrest me, Officer Henderson?"

I pulled her in, looping my arms around her waist. "You've already been sentenced."

"To what?" she breathed, grinning up at me.

"Life," I murmured, brushing my lips against hers. "With me."

She laughed into the kiss, her hands sliding up my chest. The fire crackled behind us, but the warmth in the room wasn't from that. It was from her. Always her.

My cabin used to be quiet. Empty. A place to sleep, not live. Now it smelled like cinnamon tea and her shampoo. There was music sometimes. Laughter. Dishes in the sink and laundry baskets full of socks that somehow all belonged to her.

I had never thought I'd want that. Not really. But watching Ava hang a crooked photo of us, taken in front of the lodge during the barbecue, I felt something settle deep in my chest. Peace. Maybe even happiness.

She stepped back and admired the frame like it was fine art. "See? Feels more like home already."

I tucked a strand of hair behind her ear and kissed her forehead. "It is home."

Ava Green

The trail was familiar but oh so different. I adjusted the straps of my backpack, the rhythmic crunch of boots on gravel keeping time with my breath. The sky stretched open above, brilliant and cloudless, sunlight dappling through towering pines. Birds chattered somewhere out of sight. The scent of wildflowers teased the air.

Gavin walked beside me, close but quiet, like he didn't want to break the spell.

We had been climbing for half an hour, winding up the same ridgeline where everything had been on the verge of terminal months ago. And yet...the air didn't feel heavy. No ghosts clung to the trees. No shadows lurked behind branches.

We crested the final rise and emerged onto a familiar overlook. A valley sprawled beneath us, serene and endless. The river below looked almost peaceful. I stopped. My chest tightened, not in fear that time, but awe.

"This is it," I whispered. "The place from my nightmares."

Gavin stepped behind me, his warmth anchoring me as his hand found mine. "And now?"

I took a breath, really took it in. The view. The silence. The man beside me. All of it.

"Now it feels like coming home."

He didn't speak, just pressed a kiss to my temple. The wind caught my hair, and for the first time since the crash, I let myself stand still. No running, no survival, no worry. Just...here. Now.

A few feet away, Gavin pulled a folded blanket from his pack and spread it across the grass. I joined him, folding my legs under myself. There was a thermos of tea, a small bundle of snacks. A quiet picnic on sacred ground.

I glanced at him. Scruffy, strong, mine and something inside me clicked into place. This place had taken something from me. But it had also given something back.

It had given me him.

Gavin Henderson

I stretched out on the blanket, one arm tucked under my head, the other casually tossing grapes into my mouth with terrible aim. One bounced off my lip and landed in the grass. "Damn. That one had altitude ambitions."

Ava snorted. "Maybe it was trying to escape your bad jokes."

I grinned lazily, shifting to prop myself up on one elbow so I could watch her. She was reclined across from me, hair wind-tossed, sunglasses perched crookedly on her nose. Sunlight glinted off the thermos between us. A slice of apple sat forgotten on her knee.

I eyed the precision of the fruit slices again. "You really did bring your nurse instincts to snack prep."

She pelted a grape at my chest. "Admit it. You love my apple logistics."

"I do." I popped the grape into my mouth anyway. "Also love the way you could save my ass and then still make lunch. Real power move."

Ava grinned and leaned over to steal one of my cookies. "You're lucky I like you."

I caught her wrist, kissed the inside of it. "I'm lucky, period."

She laughed and shook her head, cheeks flushed. We fell into a comfortable silence, the kind that only came after fire and chaos and survival. There, on that mountain, everything felt distilled. Real. Easy.

"Alright," I said after a moment. "Important question. Dog preferences."

Ava raised an eyebrow. "Excuse me?"

"If we get a dog. I'm thinking retriever. Loyal, trainable, loves the outdoors."

"Hmm. I vote rescue mutt. Maybe a three-legged gremlin with attitude."

I laughed. "You would."

"We could name it Chaos."

"Only if it was your chaos."

She leaned in, brushing her lips against mine. "Always is."

I kissed her back, slow and certain. It wasn't just flirting anymore. It was a future.

Ava Green

Mid-snack, my phone vibrated against the blanket. I frowned, picking it up. Probably a spam call or appointment reminder.

But no. It was a message from the Sierra Bravo medical coordinator I had met last month.

Ava—We've finalized the mobile unit schedule. We'd love for you to lead the outreach team. First run heads into the canyon settlements next month. You in?

My stomach flipped. The opportunity had seemed like a pipe dream at first, my way of giving back without losing myself. I'd tucked it away, telling myself I wasn't ready. But now?

I glanced at Gavin. He was leaning back on his elbows, eyes closed, sun on his face. Peaceful. Unaware of the way my heart raced.

I hesitated. "Hey... I got a message."

He opened one eye. "Good or bad?"

"Good. Maybe. It's from Sierra Bravo. They're setting up a mobile nurse outreach. Remote clinics, underserved areas. They want me to lead."

He straightened, eyebrows rising. "Seriously?"

I nodded. "I didn't think I'd say yes, but..."

He watched me carefully. "You thinking what I'm thinking?"

I bit my lip. "That it's a big deal?"

Gavin smiled faintly. "Yeah. And also that I'd follow you anywhere."

The wind ruffled my hair, and the weight of the choice pressed against my chest but it wasn't fear. Not anymore. It was possibility.

"I don't want to do it alone," I said softly.

"You won't." He shifted closer, pulling my hand into his lap, threading our fingers together. "We've done the impossible already. This?" He squeezed my hand. "This is the easy part."

I exhaled, shoulders loosening. "Okay then. Let's do it."

The text still glowed on the screen, but I had already moved past it, into something bigger. A life. A path. And someone to walk it with.

Gavin Henderson

I studied her face as she tucked her phone away, like she had made peace with a choice that had scared her half to death yesterday. I recognized that shift. It was the same one I'd felt when I had decided to let someone in again. Really in.

"You gave me something I didn't know I needed," I said, brushing a leaf from her hair. "A reason to stay. Or go. As long as I'm with you."

Ava's eyes shimmered, soft and wide. "God, you're such a sap when you're happy."

I grinned. "You're the only one who gets to see it."

She leaned over, swiping her thumb across my cheek like she was trying to memorize the moment. "I like happy Gavin. He smiles more. Bleeds less."

I snorted. "Fair point."

The playfulness faded, replaced by something gentler. Deeper. I cupped her face, my thumb tracing the curve of her cheekbone.

"You make me happy," I said quietly.

It wasn't a grand speech or a flashy promise. It was steady. Certain. Like gravity.

Our kiss was slower that time, more of a promise than a punctuation. Not hungry, not desperate. Just home.

Ava shifted closer, curling into me like she belonged there. Maybe she did. We lay there for a while, our picnic mostly forgotten, the sun warming our skin. I felt her breathing sync with mine, her body soft and sure against my side.

No looming threat. No blood loss. Just a future waiting to be lived.

When she murmured, "I love you," it was barely more than breath, but it still landed like an earthquake in my chest.

"I love you more," I whispered back, because it was true. And because with her, I didn't have to be anything else but myself.

Ava Green

We lay back on the blanket, arms brushing, pine needles whispering overhead like the forest was exhaling with us. The sun filtered through the branches, dappling my face in gold. Somewhere in the distance, birds chirped, and the soft rustle of wind in the trees reminded me of the lullabies my mom used to hum before everything fell apart.

I closed my eyes and just breathed.

No blood. No smoke. No alarms or adrenaline. Just breath. Steady, easy.

Gavin's hand found mine in the silence. He didn't squeeze, didn't say anything. He just held it, present and warm and unwavering.

The last time we had been here, I had been fighting to stay alive. Terrified. Frozen. Lost. Watching a plane burn. Now, that memory felt like something distant. Not gone but softened by what came after.

"I used to think survival was enough," I murmured.

Gavin turned his head toward me. "Yeah?"

I nodded. "I thought if I just made it through the next hour, the next day, that would be enough. But now... I want more. Not just to live but to have a life. One that feels like mine."

He squeezed my hand gently. "You'll have it. Every bit. Whatever you want."

The thing was I believed him. Not just because he'd said it, but because he'd proven it. Over and over, in bruises and bullets, in silence and softness.

My trauma still lingered. It probably always would. But it was no longer the loudest voice in the room. Not there. Not with him.

I tilted my face toward the sky again, eyes wide open then. "You ever wonder why we survived that crash and no one else did?"

Gavin hummed. "Every day."

I smiled. "I think it was so I could find you."

Shared POV

The afternoon ripened around them, warm and rich with pine and possibility. They packed up the picnic slowly, neither in a rush to leave, both knowing the moment was more than just the end of a meal. It was a marker. A memory in the making. Gavin tucked the blanket under one arm and reached for her hand without needing to ask. Ava laced her fingers through his, their hands fitting together like they had always been meant to.

As they descended the mountain trail, the wind shifted, brushing their cheeks like a blessing. Behind them lay everything they had survived: the crash, the fire, the blood-soaked snow. Every shadow they had walked through was fading into memory.

Before them, the path stretched out in soft sunlight, dusted with golden pine needles. The world felt bigger then. Not because it had changed but because they had.

Gavin glanced sideways at her. "You okay?"

Ava nodded. "More than okay."

They didn't speak much on the way down. They didn't need to. Every step forward said it for them. They reached a clearing where the trees parted, revealing the mountain peaks in the distance, bold, jagged, kissed by sunlight. The view was breathtaking. But Gavin's eyes stayed on her.

She caught him staring and lifted an eyebrow. "What?"

He shrugged. "Just...can't believe I get to walk through life with you."

Ava leaned in and kissed him, slow and certain. When she pulled back, she whispered:

"Whatever comes next, we face it together."

And with that, they walked on, two silhouettes framed by the fire-touched sky. Not broken. Not running. Just beginning.

Want to join Jax' Inner Circle?

E very Jax Kane book has a secret code word at the end.

Collect them to unlock sneak peeks, bonus chapters, and early cover reveals.

Your secret code word for *Stuck with my Ex's Brother* is: WHITE-OUT.

Enter it here to add to your collection:

https://forms.gle/JTGzCbssuofe3HTp8

A Few Final Words From Jax

H i, Jax Friend!

I hope you enjoyed reading *Protecting the Grumpy CEO* as much as I enjoyed writing it!

Did you know that reader reviews are largely what determine how books get ranked when someone searches on Amazon?

It is **vitally** important for indie creators, like me, to get reviews from people like you.

So, please consider heading over to Amazon and giving this book an honest sentence or two review. You can just look up the book: *Protecting the Grumpy CEO* by Jax Kane. OR click the link https://amzn.to/4niq33f

And if that's not your thing, I'm just glad you came along.

Follow me on my Amazon author page to get 1st notice about my new releases! Another new Sierra Bravo Security story is coming soon! Here's the address for my author page so you don't miss one: www.amazon.com/author/jaxkane and an easy link https://www.amazon.com/author/jax

Thanks for reading! Readers mean the world to me.

Your friend,

Jax